Mark Wales grew up in Western Australian mining towns and decided early that he wanted to join Australian Special Forces. He embarked on a career that would eventually lead him to Afghanistan. There, as a troop commander in charge of 30 elite soldiers, Mark led combat missions deep behind enemy lines.

Today he is an accomplished corporate speaker, reality TV star, actor, and CEO and founder of a tough luxury fashion label. He appeared in George Miller's Mad Max film *Furiosa*.

In 2021 Mark published his memoir *Survivor*, a national bestseller. *Outrider* is his first novel. He lives in Melbourne and Perth with his wife Samantha Gash and their son.

Also by Mark Wales

Non-fiction
Survivor

OUTRIDER

MARK WALES

MACMILLAN
Pan Macmillan Australia

First published 2024 in Macmillan by Pan Macmillan Australia Pty Ltd
1 Market Street, Sydney, New South Wales, Australia, 2000

A catalogue record for this book is available from the National Library of Australia

Typeset in 11.7/16 pt Sabon by Post Pre-press Group

Printed by IVE

Map on page viii by IRONGAV

The author and the publisher have made every effort to contact copyright holders for material used in this book. Any person or organisation that may have been overlooked should contact the publisher.

For Harry.

And for my dad, Robert.
I'm glad we never experienced this, but if we did,
I would've been in the safest of hands.

I love you both.

'I think it may come to conflict.'

Henry Kissinger on the tensions between the USA and China,
The Wall Street Journal, 25 May 2023

'In the practical art of war, the best thing of all is to
take the enemy's country whole and intact . . .'

Sun Tzu, *The Art of War*

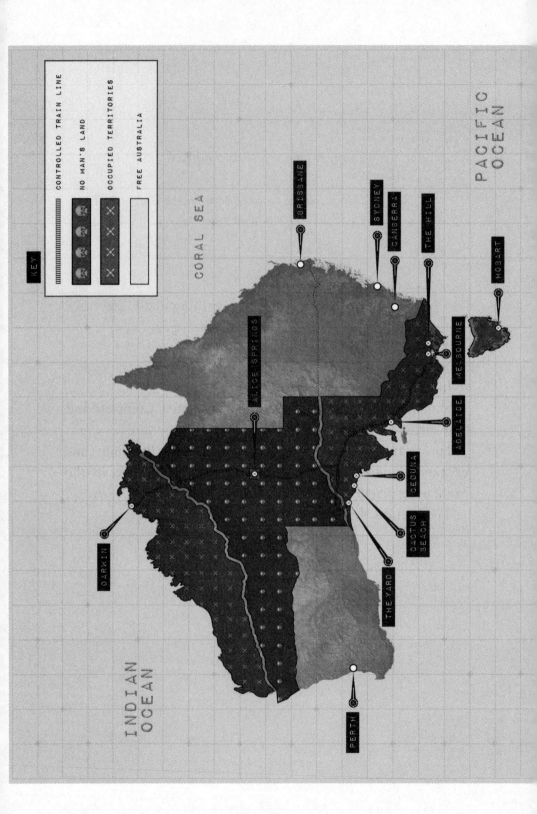

WHEN THE FIRST FOREIGN BOOTS STEPPED ASHORE IN TAIWAN, global war followed swiftly.

In 2029, Australia was invaded.

Shortly after, the state of Victoria capitulated. Complete and total surrender to enemy forces and local collaborators.

For years, a tense peace ensued. Eventually, only one resistance holdout remained. An unassailable fortress in the Dandenong Ranges, 'the Hill' became a refuge for thousands.

Then, in 2034, Jack Dunne reignited the war.

OUTRIDER

PROLOGUE

JACK CAUGHT THE BLACK OUTLINE OF THE DRIVER IN HIS mirror, his hands sweeping across the steering wheel. Jack slipped the stick into fifth gear and slammed the accelerator. The howl of the turbo and the clicking of road stones echoed in Jack's ear as he pushed his truck harder. Behind him was a special kind of hell.

Being caught would mean certain death. Not just for him, but for his son, too. He couldn't let that happen.

The truck rammed its nose up against Jack's bumper and the broad metal grille filled the entire rear view. Jack flicked the red pursuit switch beside the steering wheel, pressed his head back against the seat and felt the pull of the engine as it planted them to their seats. He screamed for Harry to prepare his carbine.

In his side mirror he caught a dirt bike with two riders, within arm's reach of the truck. They had snuck in. The driver wore safety glasses and a filthy kerchief over his mouth, his shin armour made from hammered sheet metal and leather strapping. His passenger, short, childlike, wore a bicycle helmet and held a stumpy shotgun in one arm. He was steadying the barrel for a shot on Jack's side.

1

Jack kept his eyes on the side mirror and drifted the truck towards the bike.

'Fire when you can see their eyes.'

Jack's son, eleven years old, hauled the carbine to his shoulder and flicked off the safety. Two days ago, they'd buried the boy's mother. Now, they were fighting for their own lives.

Jack had only killed seven Australians, and he remembered each face, the colour of their hair, the Victorian Militia Forces badge on their jackets.

His truck hit a straight in the road and Jack slammed his foot onto the pedal, gaining some space. The dirt plume behind him was thick; the pursuit trucks backed off.

He needed clear ground so he could deploy his best asset.

High and left, over the gold wheatfield, Jack spotted his firing position. He pointed at the hill.

'Get the rockets. When we stop, head for that hill. I'll set the mine.' Jack spoke to his son in terse commands, a signal that it was time for Harry to be brave, and follow his training.

Harry slung a rocket launcher over his shoulder and pulled the retaining pin off the cover of the rocket. His helmet sat askance on his small head, and his tongue stuck out the side of his mouth as he wrestled the pin free.

Jack changed down as they entered a sharp bend. Ahead of them was a long slot of a road carved through a ridge.

Good cover.

He slammed on the brakes and before the truck even stopped, Harry was out the door and scampering for the hill. Jack left the engine running and slung his carbine over his shoulder as he ran to the rear. He hauled the 0.50 calibre Barrett sniper rifle off the tray back, his thick arms and six-foot-four mass handling it easily.

Jack paused, listening, and caught the nagging whine of a dirt bike.

He bolted after his son, the sniper rifle hefted over his shoulder.

Running through the wheat stalks, Harry was ahead of him by a kick of a footy. They had done this before, in better times.

Harry laid himself out beside a pile of tree debris. Jack set the rifle down and watched as his son removed the scope covers and called out the range and wind adjustments to the road corner, where the enemy would appear.

Jack knelt beside him with the binoculars.

Weapons out.

Ready to kill their own kind.

The dirt bike rounded the corner.

Jack Dunne shouldered the rifle and clicked the safety off. His sight picture fell across the driver, and he took up the slack on the trigger.

The shots he fired, the nights that followed, would echo across this land for generations.

PART ONE

THE

SPARK

1

JACK PULLED OFF HIS TATTERED BOOTS AT THE RIVER'S EDGE and walked towards his wife's body. She lay in the shallows of the calm river. On a stretcher made from the green shoots of a eucalypt tree, her thin body bound in a white bedsheet. He watched the funeral party fuss over her. Six women, Hillsfolk, washed her ankles, her feet, her body. The eldest woman held one hand to his wife's cheek, the others splashed river water across her torso. They murmured and sang to her as they worked. The sheet clung to her body in the steady rain, and Jack studied her outline. Thin shoulders, her tiny head covered with the white sheet and bound at the neck.

He bit his own cheek and squeezed his fist until his nails dug into his palm, the pain warding off tears. He looked back at his son.

Harry stood alone on the river bank in his filthy black tracksuit, trembling in the rain.

Jack looked back to Gemma.

He was numb. He had known for years that he would outlive his wife, but nothing could have prepared him for this sight. He tore his eyes away from the burial party and studied the towering willow tree further down the bank. Healthy green leaves with bone white bark, its branches shifting in the breeze. The Weeping Willow, the Hillsfolk called it. On the opposite bank of the river, an ironbark tree as thick as Jack was tall lay half submerged, its fresh branches drinking from the river.

Sacha, one of the town's best soldiers and Gemma's mate, stood high on the river bank in her uniform. She blew into a smoking bouquet of bright green eucalyptus leaves and bark. As she blew, the smoke thickened. She lifted the bouquet high above the river and the tendrils drifted across the water and over the funeral party.

Jack had seen how this particular funeral service went too many times before. The ritual was reserved for warriors of the Hill, a unique service created by the Resistance for its bravest.

They lifted Gemma's stretcher to their shoulders with shocking ease and walked her across the river stones and up the bank. Jack pulled his shoes on and walked back to his son, holding him tight to his side. He could feel the boy's shoulders trembling and squeezed him tighter. They trailed the burial party. Warriors were carried to the afterlife by their own gender, a final tribute. Harry wiped his eyes with the sleeve of his filthy black jumper and watched his mother being carried up the river bank to the Five Ways, where the whole town waited.

Jack had been carrying his wife to and from the rotting cane chairs in his yard for months, watching the fading northern light and humming her favourite country music tunes to her. At dusk, jet sorties flew west in tight formations, the propeller units trailing them in formation minutes later, like stubborn younger siblings. Gemma pointed them out with a gnarled hand, gasping at the sight.

A shameful relief had fallen over Jack since she had died. Stoic to the end, she had suffered unspeakable pain. They had stayed behind in Victoria to fight the Occupation when in the West was free land, family and some type of hope. He had put them all, especially Gemma, through hell.

On their last morning together, he had kissed her forehead and she had squeezed his hand with a strength he had not felt in years. The end was coming, and that squeeze was her final instruction to him: *Head west with our son. Live.*

Jack held Harry's hand as they climbed the bank towards the Five Ways junction.

'Chin up now, mate,' he whispered.

They cleared the crest of the gully and saw the entire Hillsfolk gathered at the Five Ways intersection, the broad saddle of land where five roads from the flatlands of Victoria joined. In the old times, horse-drawn lumber carriages would park there. Before the war, it was a watering hole for sports cars and families on vacation. Now, the Hillsfolk cremated their warriors at the top of the saddle.

They jammed the crumbling roads, dressed in worn old uniforms with knee patches sewn on, and ratty parkas patched up with duct tape. Many wore knotted red armbands. An enormous pyre of stacked, dry wood sat at the edge of the lookout where it dropped into the forest valley. The crowd parted to let Sacha and the stretcher bearers through. There were mourners as far as Jack could see, at least a thousand of them, silent and glistening in the soft rain. Heavy mist rolled through the low saddle of the intersection and continued up the face of the hill. A Resistance unit in full battle order whipped their rifles up in salute, and Jack smiled his thanks. Their precision was that of a unit that was more drilled on the battlefield than the parade ground. A man with no neck wearing fox skin over his shoulder and full body armour issued the orders in a booming voice. The other soldiers were gaunt and bearded and black under the eyes from a long campaign – one they all knew would continue for many more years.

A piper kicked off the whine of the bagpipes. In kilt and beret, he slow-marched on the spot as the pipes hit full volume. The old soldiers in the crowd slipped their hands to their sides and stood to attention with full chests. Men and women with rows of medals from old wars and new, people who had not smiled in years, saluted the funeral party as they trod towards the pyre.

The howl of the pipes and sight of the pyre was too much for Jack; the last of his defences fell. As he walked towards the stacked grid of red gum logs, his face contorted. He fought the urge to run away with Gemma's body.

All six bearers lifted her high above their heads and rested her body atop the stack of wood. The pipes stopped, and Sacha circled the pyre and let the smoke drift across the body.

Sacha blew long breaths into her eucalyptus bouquet and it billowed thick grey smoke. The fresh oil of the eucalypt filled the cool air. She summoned Jack with her eyes, and he stepped forward with Harry under his arm.

Sacha put her hand in her pocket and held her closed fist out to Harry. He took the gift she offered; a thin black leather bracelet with a silver disc attached. Letters and numbers were etched into the bracelet.

Harry rubbed his thumb over the silver disc.

Jack reached for the bracelet, and Harry yanked his hand away, clutching it to his chest.

'You can't wear it until we get west,' Jack warned him.

'Dad, quiet.' Harry hissed as he slipped it onto his wrist, avoiding his father's gaze.

Just like his mother, Jack thought.

The padre walked to the centre of the junction. He wore a multicam fascia draped over the nape of his neck that reached down to his shins, a black cross embroidered on each side. He was a bald, thickset man, and his wire spectacles seemed to be held together with electrical tape.

Jack watched him, hands clasped at his front. He pinched the flesh between his thumb and forefinger, anything to keep himself together in front of the boy.

The padre pushed his dirty glasses up his nose and began to read from a tattered notebook in a deep but gentle voice.

'Gemma Leaven Dunne was born 5 June 1995 in Healesville. The youngest of three siblings, she grew up roaming the banks of the Murray River. Her first love was her pet Labrador, Josie, who followed her everywhere.' The crowd chuckled and the priest smiled and looked up from his notes. 'And she continued to roam throughout her life. By her early twenties, she was stationed at the Australian embassy in Kabul, Afghanistan, as a diplomat. During the evacuation of Kabul, she was the last Australian off the ground . . .' The priest paused, gathering himself, and the crowd quietened. 'Evacuating only after she had, alone, executed what became known as "The Airlift": rescuing forty-two orphans . . .' his voice shook slightly, 'including eight babies, in what was the largest evacuation by helicopter ever. That record stood until the evacuation of Taiwan six years later. Gemma, from that point on, avoided commercial flights, maintaining that it was more fun to fly in a helicopter jammed with kids.' The crowd's laughter punctured the air. Jack found himself smiling, knowing the crowd's eyes were upon him. Harry looked at him, his green eyes shining with pride and tears.

The padre closed his book and looked to the crowd.

'Gemma was awarded the Star of Courage for her act of selfless valour in extreme peril.'

Jack lapsed back to numbness. The citation for her award hung in his office, and it read like a comic book.

The priest went on. 'On the tarmac at Kabul Airport, she was stopped by a long-haired soldier resembling the Marlboro Man.' Jack's face flushed red. He rubbed his son's shoulder and looked down at the bitumen. The crowd gave a timid laugh, and once again Jack could feel their eyes upon him.

'After a brief but heated argument about a passenger manifest, she decided she rather liked this quiet but resolute soldier. A couple of years later, their son Harry was born.' The padre studied the crowd. 'Gemma Leaven Dunne left this heavenly Earth on 14 August 2034.'

The padre stopped and bowed his head. Jack cleared his throat and put his hand back on Harry's shoulders. He recited a prayer, from memory.

'Do not mourn me. I am the wind in the grass. The faint breeze across the Hill. I am the call of the bird, and the swirl of the autumn leaves. Do not mourn me, for I am here. An angel took my hand and said it's time to take your place. This is your place and with it, you will show us the way ahead, to peace, and to a free world.'

Harry sniffed, and Jack squeezed his shoulders.

The padre moved to the pyre and held his hand above Gemma's face. The bagpipes started their low groan and Jack felt the ice in his legs as Sacha walked towards him with her smoking torch.

Jack pulled his son closer, and as he did, he caught a low howl climbing the valley from the south. Some of the warriors flinched as the crowd looked skyward. A diamond formation of attack jets ripped over the gathering at treetop height. Jack saw the broad swept wings of an F-35 Joint Strike Fighter, shaped like a notched arrow tip. Three triangular drones boxed the jet at the flanks and rear, no daylight between their wingtips and the nose of the last drone. All four jets banked hard over the Five Ways, and from side on, the aircraft were like thin ellipses of layered metal, the outline of the F-35 pilot visible in the clear bubble of the canopy. A magpie was stencilled on its vertical stabiliser fin, with the initials 'YKMF' beneath it. A tight cone of flame and exhaust distorted the trailing air behind the formation.

The sixty-metre-high ghost gums shimmered under the formation. The jets circled the Hill once, then headed for the airbases hidden underground in the sandy western deserts. The noise faded, and the crowd chattered. F-35s were rare, even this close to the front. But the effect they had on the crowd was immediate: *we are still in the fight.*

Jack smiled and whispered to his son. 'Don't become a pilot.'

Harry squinted at the shimmering trails of hot air left in their wake.

As the bagpipes started again, Sacha blew long breaths into the bouquet, turning it to stoke the ember within. She approached Jack and held the bouquet out to him as, with a final steady blow, the bouquet whumped into flame. Jack stepped forward, placed his palm on his wife's forehead and closed his eyes, and all the sound of the world faded to nothing.

I'll see you again. Soon.

He squeezed once, then took the bouquet and pushed it into the dry bracken underneath his wife. The flames raced up the pyre.

The Resistance fighters shouldered their arms and fired once across the valley. Jack flinched at the roaring guns.

Smoke billowed out from the pyre as the flames reached up towards Gemma.

If there'd been a lower point in his life, Jack could not recall it.

He pulled his son in tight, shielding Harry from the flames. Harry shuddered under his arm, weeping. The heat radiated across their bodies, and as the wood pile crackled and hissed, Jack realised he was crushing his son in his embrace.

Too young for this. For the war.

The thrall and the vice-like grip of combat, its tragedy, the blind terror, he wanted to wrest it from his family line. After two generations of fighting, surely they had earned that privilege. As he watched the shroud burn and peel open, he set his mind on the path ahead, his sole purpose, all that mattered now.

To build a future for his son.

2

THREE VICTORIAN MILITIA FORCES SOLDIERS APPEARED out of the dense fog, standing on the road only thirty metres ahead. Jack stared through the windshield, mouth open, unable to believe his bad luck. The men strolled across the road, an orange strobe from a traffic lamp outlining their silhouette. They had the confident stance of men in charge, their weapon barrels pointing up off their shoulders like antennae.

Two bearded young men in trucker caps, green ponchos and body armour circled the battered station wagon ahead of him. One of them opened the trunk and rummaged through it. The other scanned beneath the car with a rear-view mirror that was attached to a broom pole with duct tape.

Jack's scalp crawled at the sight of the VMF.

Traitors.

But they were lethal, combat hardened and aligned with the Chinese Communist Party.

This was the first checkpoint Jack had seen for many years. He leaned forward and looked up through the windshield. *The drones must have missed it. Bad luck comes in threes. Gemma. Enemy checkpoint. One more to come.*

He had descended into the fog, off the hill, and cornered

his truck onto a back road heading to Ed's place, planning to request a release from duty. The last two other Outriders were killed in a public display at Federation Square, a bullet to the back of the head after being caught collecting a source. Jack was the last of them. Outriders make a pledge not to leave their area of operations until death. Like a gladiator that had fought for his freedom, Jack had enough operations completed that he could request exemption.

Only Ed and Dyson, members of the Defence Council, could sponsor Jack's departure. But it seemed that might have to wait.

A large man in a broad akubra stood at the driver's side door as the two VMF soldiers conducted their search. Rain drummed on the roof of the truck, and the wipers swiped an arc through the muddy glass.

There was nothing on their bodies that would give them away as Resistance fighters. No burner phone number, written on paper and long forgotten in a pocket. No handwritten receipt off the Hill. No loose pistol round with English letters stamped on the percussion cap. None of that. Jack sterilised the car and Harry every time they left the Hill. He had only his wedding band, and a fake yellow ID card.

Jack had stowed a muddy hand auger, a box of rice seeds, a toolbox, a foam esky and a coil of fencing wire in the back. He kept his dark beard thick and unkempt. Although he washed gunpowder residue off his hands with hydrogen peroxide, he also kept black dirt under his nails in case their bodies were checked for incriminating material.

They were now rice farmers from the flatlands.

The truck, however, was a different story.

His truck carried two defensive weapons. One was his spare tyre, mounted on the rear door. It was a rubber shell that housed fifteen kilos of C4 explosives ringed with a resin shell containing thousands of ball bearings in a multi-directional blast setting. It was well concealed with epoxy and plastics camouflage, giving the appearance of a perfectly normal functioning tyre – unless you X-rayed it. The garage door key fob mounted to his dashboard could initiate the device.

The other weapon was a long, thin black trunk. It contained a compound bow and, in the false bottom of the case, a lightweight M4 assault rifle with a seven-inch barrel, a suppressor, a compact red-dot aim point, and thirty armour-piercing rounds in the clip.

The signature weapon of an Outrider.

Jack and Harry were one good search away from a train ticket to the Yard, a concentration city where they churned out Chinese naval ships in the South Australian desert.

A hulking, up-armoured F250 truck was parked sideways across the road. A heavy machine gun with a circular aiming scope was mounted in the rear tray, and a long belt of sawtooth ammunition hung from it. A soldier with a sad-looking umbrella stood by the truck, smoking and watching the roundabout.

Jack spoke without looking at Harry.

'Don't talk. No smiling.'

Harry stared back at him with wide green eyes.

'Don't look at me. Just relax,' Jack muttered, to himself more than Harry.

He scanned his rear-view mirror. Three cars, headlights just visible, blocking his exit. One car was waved through the checkpoint. That left only one more ahead of him in the queue.

Jack put his truck in drive and idled ahead. The soldier in the akubra was as tall and solid as a rugby front rower. He had the upright posture and smooth motions of a man who was certain of his surrounds. His filthy Driza-Bone jacket glistened in the drizzle, and he stared out from above an immense grey beard. The man's coat bulged at the waist as he leant forward to speak to the driver.

The two youths searched the underside of the car with the broom pole. One was well-fed, the other whippet thin. Both had matte black Chinese AK-74s slung over their shoulders. They nodded to the boss man and he waved the car through, then all three turned to Jack's truck.

The man with the akubra motioned with a flick of his head for Jack to proceed.

'Don't look at them,' Jack said to his son.

The boy nodded. His face was pale, his hair like a scarecrow. He was sitting on both his hands.

Jack mentally rehearsed reaching his left hand up to the remote control that was velcroed to the dashboard.

'Dad . . .' Harry said.

'Quiet, mate,' Jack said.

The truck rolled forward, and Jack wound down both windows, despite the rain.

The skinny adolescent orbited the car, filming them with a phone.

The akubra man leaned forward, pinning his fat hand to the car door. He looked strong enough to hold the truck in place if Jack tried to drive off. Even standing side on, his shoulders filled the entire aperture of the window.

Jack recognised the man. It was the infamous Stevie Adams. A murderer and petty criminal, Adams had worked under contract for the People's Liberation Army since they arrived in the country, five years ago. That was the new life here, and it had swept people up like a forest fire. A coup, a small war, and a waiting enemy was all it took to upend life in the Lucky Country. Victoria was the foothold, a new engine room for a voracious war machine.

Jack felt that these men deserved a special place in hell, and it was his duty to put them there. Stevie Adams was known for executing Resistance sources with a pistol shot to the back of the head. To him, this was business.

'Comrade,' said Jack. In one moment he had calculated the tight arc needed to draw his knife blade and plunge it into the man's neck. Jack did not often stand within striking distance of the traitorous Victorian Militia.

'Morning. ID please.' He looked at Harry. 'Hello, young fella.'

'Hello,' said Harry.

Jack heard the false inflection in Harry's voice. It concealed his only emotion: terror.

Adams studied Harry for a long moment.

Jack produced a card from his jacket and handed it to him.

Adams scanned the rear seats of the vehicle without turning his head. The whites of his eyes weren't white at all, they were a pale yellow, with red veins running through them.

He turned the ID card over in his hand.

'Dale Bascal,' he announced. He scanned Jack's face, then looked back at the card. His eyes lit up, and he pointed at the 'V' stamped on the corner of the card.

'Which unit?'

'Infantry. First Battalion. Did my last trip in 2021,' Jack lied.

'Kabul?'

He nodded.

Adams gave a low whistle. 'I was a copper. Did one trip in 2012, mostly dealing with prisoners. Don't really need those skills in this war, do we Dale?' he laughed, revealing teeth like grey chalk. He stared at Jack, tapping the card on his palm. Water dripped from the brim of his akubra. He stopped tapping and leaned into the window frame, just a little.

'Do I know you?' he whispered.

Time stopped. The sound of the rain disappeared.

Jack turned and looked into his eyes. 'Probably. Woulda locked me up when were in Afghanistan.' Jack tried to grin at his own joke, but his heart was thumping.

'What's your name, son?' Adams asked Harry.

'Jamie,' said Harry, without hesitation.

Adams drummed his fingers on the door jamb.

'Hear much from the Resistance?' Adams jutted his chin towards the Hill.

Jack shook his head, feigning nonchalance. 'Been keepin' to themselves. I can hear them training when it's cold, gunshots and what. Sometimes blast.'

Adams stared back. 'Sometimes blast,' he echoed, as though in a trance.

Jack kept both his hands on the steering wheel.

Adams looked across at Harry again, for a long time.

He pointed at the rear of the truck. 'Mind if we take a look? Cut the engine.'

Jack knew it wasn't actually a question.

'Nah, go for it.' He switched the ignition off, cold dread creeping up his legs. 'Lemme open the back door for you.'

Jack put one hand on the top of his door and cracked the door lever. Adams whipped around with a speed that belied his size and a metal baton crashed onto Jack's fingers, his middle finger shattering under the blow. Harry gasped and shrank into his seat. Adams pointed the rod at Jack's face, hovering near his eye. He spoke through his grey teeth.

'You stay right there, Dale. Unless you want to earn a ticket to the Yard.' He turned to the bulky kid. 'Check it.'

Jack stared over the steering wheel and slowed his breathing, light-headed from the molten pain. He rubbed his hand as he watched the kid move to the back of the truck.

The back door creaked open and fresh air flooded the cab. Jack heard clanging and metal scraping as the auger was shifted. The kid opened the toolbox and rummaged.

Dread settled in Jack's stomach as the youth slid the plastic case across the back of the truck.

Two clicks of a latch.

A moment passed. Jack eyed the garage remote on the dashboard.

'Nice!' the large youth called from the back.

'Thanks. It's a Mathews VRX. Have a look,' Jack offered. Harry's wide eyes told him how much of a gamble this was. If he pulled the false bottom up, they were done.

Jack checked the fuel gauge. The needle sat on empty. He peered through the gloom at the road ahead, just able to make out the grey silhouette of a tree in the centre of the round-about. A sedan drove past on the curving road ahead. It was fifty metres away, just dull headlights and an outline.

He shifted his gaze to the rear-view mirror. The chunky kid had the bow upright and was weighing it in his hands. The case closed and the latches snapped shut, then the fat kid appeared at Adams' side, holding the foam esky. They looked startlingly alike; father and son, Jack concluded.

'Whas'sis?' The fat soldier dangled the esky by its rope handle.

'Coffee and jerky. Last of our dry stocks,' said Jack.

Adams gestured with two fingers for the esky. He opened the lid and sniffed at it, then handed it back to the youth, who returned it to the truck.

'Right. Have a good day.'

Rain drummed on the roof of the truck.

Jack started the ignition, barely allowing himself to breathe, and put the truck in drive.

'Cheers, digger,' said Adams.

He reached into the cab and offered his hand to Jack. Jack paused and shook it with his right hand. The man's grip was like a bear trap, and just as cold.

The man released Jack's hand then reached further into the cab, offering his hand to Harry. His thick forearm, clad in brown canvas, hovered in Jack's eyeline.

'Young fella,' he said.

As Harry reached up to shake the man's hand, Adams grabbed his wrist and yanked him out of his seat, towards the window. Harry screamed in fright. Jack tried to prise the man's huge fingers from his son, his spare arm pinning Harry into the seat. Adams pulled Harry's wrist closer and yanked his jumper sleeve back to his elbow, revealing a black bracelet loop, inscribed with the words 'GLD: 14 Aug 2034'. He held Harry's wrist up like a trophy.

'Dunne. I knew it.' Adams grasped for his waist and drew an enormous silver revolver out. 'Get out of –'

Jack had already slipped the gear shaft into first.

In a split second, he'd made a choice that would change the course of the war in Australia.

3

JACK SLAMMED THE ACCELERATOR AND PULLED HIS FOOT OFF the clutch.

The wheels of the truck screamed in the wet. At the same moment he wrenched Adams' fingers back with all his might, forcing his hand up to the roof and freeing Harry. As he did, Jack felt a pop in the man's hand. Adams screamed and released his grip. His large pistol swung into the cab and Jack grabbed the barrel with his hand just as it exploded, the heat and pressure of the blast stunning Jack. The bullet shattered the window beside Harry's head.

A gunfight in a phone booth.

The truck surged ahead, dragging Adams by his feet.

Jack hit the garage remote and an explosive bolt fired with a clap. The spare tyre fell from the back of the truck, bounced once, and flopped to the bitumen.

Jack accelerated and swerved around the tray of the F250. Through his open window he locked eyes with the youth manning the gun, who stood frozen under his umbrella, cigarette dangling from his mouth. Adams now appeared beside the soldier, bellowing, reaching into the tray and hauling out a heavy machine gun, a long belt of ammunition following it.

Jack swerved back onto the road. The wheels squealed as they bit into the road. He looked side on and could just make out the F250 and the flashing road light through the fog.

There was a bark of machine gun fire from the far side, red tracer floating over the roundabout and ripping over the bonnet of his truck.

'Down,' Jack said.

Harry ducked into his seat and held his hands to his ears.

Jack eyed the key fob velcroed to the dash.

He reached for it, pressed the button with his thumb, then tensed his body. The tyre exploded in a silver flash and a horrific, roaring crump. An opaque shimmering blast of compressed air radiated through the fog. As the pressure wave slapped Jack's truck, a spider web fracture burst across the windshield. Debris rained down in a grey haze – person and car, clothing, dirt and tree leaves. Jack's ears whined, and all other sound faded beneath that hum.

Jack was still turning the truck around the roundabout towards the blast zone. He would have seconds before the effects of the blast wore off and they radioed in for assistance.

They made their choice.

It was the refrain Jack used when he knew he would have to destroy everyone in sight.

He slammed to a stop in the middle of the road, and Harry lurched off his seat and into the footwell.

'Don't move!' Jack shouted to him.

He leapt out and ran to the rear of the truck. He hauled the door open. On the road, where the smoke and fog was clearing, he could see no men standing.

He clicked his plastic case open, yanked the compound bow out, and pulled two fabric tabs at the side of the foam base. The whole base lifted from the case, revealing his answer to the VMF.

The M4 sat in its foam cut-out, mottled dark green

camouflage paint across its barrel, body and suppressor. He hauled the weapon up and sprinted across the roundabout with the barrel up.

Jack heard only a dull whine as he crossed the grass towards the men. The air stank of burnt metal and cordite. Leaves were fluttering down across the roundabout. His limbs were humming and he could feel the familiar checked grip of his M4 in his hand. He slowed to a stalking pace and pulled his rifle to his shoulder, scanning for targets. The F250 appeared in the fog. Its panels were riddled with grapeshot holes punched through the flank of the car. Every panel on the truck had been compressed inwards, as though rammed by a bull. The tyres were collapsed and aflame, and the mounted gun was bent at an obtuse angle.

Jack crossed a shallow crater in the bitumen, still hot under his boots.

The skinny youth appeared in the smoke next to the burning technical, metres away, circling like a drunk man. He was armless, a gleaming white humerus protruding from one shoulder, his other shoulder a stump of charred meat. Bright red blood showered onto his flank like a fast-running tap. His face had a series of black puncture marks scored into it.

Jack pushed the safety post of the rifle down with his thumb and raised the weapon, never taking his eyes off the youth. He rested the red dot on the youth's head, then pulled the trigger twice in quick succession.

The teen crumpled to the bitumen.

The fat kid stood in the fog just metres away, wearing only a shredded poncho. His jeans had been blown clean off his legs. His hat was gone and his eyelashes, brows and hair were singed to curly grey bits of powder. He didn't flinch at the shots but merely stood there, uncomprehending. Jack shot him twice. The boy flinched, then folded at the waist with stiff legs.

Jack stepped around to the front of the truck, and there

lay Stevie Adams, waving the stump of one forearm in a circle as though fending off some unseen force. His stomach and beard were on fire. The Driza-Bone was in strips, and his one remaining leg was exposed to the waist.

Jack stalked over and stood beside a pool of bright arterial blood that had drained from his hip. The man's shrunken genitals were also on fire. He stank of burning hair and cordite and he stared to the heavens, choking and swatting at nothing with his remaining hand. His silver pistol lay on the ground beside him. Jack scanned the roundabout, then stepped over to the pistol and scooped it up with one hand. It was heavy. He stood over Adams, cocked the hammer of the pistol, and handed it to the wounded man. Adams took the pistol, but lay it across his chest. He spat a stream of blood from his mouth.

Jack looked into his eyes, watched the man reviewing his life as he lay there, dying. Adams turned his head towards his dead son and moaned.

Jack looked back to the roundabout. His truck was forty metres away, in the fog, engine still idling. Jack was hit by the giddy realisation that he was not wounded, and that he had destroyed all three of the soldiers.

Wait. Three soldiers.

There were four.

He hadn't checked the F250 tray. He swung around and levelled his weapon at the F250, cursing to himself.

Crouching, he stalked to the tray, his weapon up. Black smoke poured off the double truck wheels and flames licked up the side of the car. He peered into the tray, safety off, finger on the trigger.

The cupola gunner was crouched on his side with his legs drawn to his chest. His body armour had a badge of a lemon with a red cross through it, and the words 'No Lemons'. For some reason, Jack fixated on the badge, another of the innocuous details of combat that seemed to stick in his mind.

The skeleton of the umbrella lay in the tray, black strips hanging off it. The young man gasped when he clocked Jack, then held both his palms out. He was covered in spots of black sticky tar, all over his face and hands and hair. Blood pulsed in short beats down one side of his neck and fluid ran from his eyes, making tracks on his grease-smeared face.

He was no older than a teenager.

The crack of a pistol shot echoed behind them.

The youth flinched.

'I didn't see nothin',' he said.

Jack studied the youth. Blood ran from his ear in a stream, pooling in between the metal ridges of the tray.

'You saw my son,' said Jack.

Jack pulled a new magazine from his waist, reloaded the carbine, and returned the magazine to his pocket. Time was returning to normal, his mind slowing.

He wrenched the warm pistol out of Stevie Adams' cold hand and slid it into the back of his jeans belt. He picked up an AK-47 that lay next to the skinny kid, then looked across three points of the roundabout. No movement. The fog was burning off in the morning light. He strode across the grass, back to his truck, and pulled open the passenger door. Harry was still huddled in the footwell, shivering.

He ran his hands over his son, looking for marks.

'Are you okay?'

Harry nodded.

He grabbed Harry's wrist and yanked it up, exposing the matte black bracelet. He pulled it off in one yank and reefed his son up by his chest, bunching his jumper in his fist.

'What did I tell you?'

The bracelet trembled in his grip.

He had used more force than he'd meant to.

He put the bracelet in the centre console and shoved the carbine barrel into the footwell, then climbed into the driver's side, put the vehicle in gear and drove off.

They drove southeast, engine humming. The sun was still a light grey patch in the sky.

Jack gripped the wheel hard with both hands.

I almost got my son killed.

He ground his teeth, his temples pounding.

He was weeping, but did not wipe his eyes.

Jack focused on the empty road as the truck wove along the foot of the hill, passing the odd burnt husk of a car on the side of the road.

Harry sat staring out the window, shifting in his seat from the adrenaline.

Jack put his hand on his thigh. 'Deep breaths. We're alright. You're okay.'

Harry wiped his eyes. 'I'm sorry,' he said.

'It's alright. I didn't mean to scare you,' said Jack. 'It's not your fault.' He placed his hand on Harry's neck and pulled him towards him.

'Whose fault was it?' said Harry.

The boy was weeping now; first the loss of his mother, and then this. It was too much.

'I'm sorry.' Jack couldn't believe it. If you'd told him ten years ago that Aussies would be fighting Aussies . . .

We brought the wars home with us.

Jack looked at his son, taking in the unwashed folds of grime across his neck. His perfect lips. Flushed cheeks. He was beautiful. He deserved better.

West. I have to get us west. To the coast.

There, they could be free of the war, mostly. He could surf again. Harry could get a tan and play in the water.

'You've had it hard. I grew up on the beach. Peacetime. We had it easy.' He thought about the screaming kids he had cuffed as a soldier in another land. *You reap what you sow.*

'What now?' The boy wiped his eyes.

'We can still get west. I'll have to sort things out with Dyson first.' Dyson Carr was the Resistance leader of the Hill. The sort of man you wanted on your side.

'What do we do about the windshield? And my window?' said Harry.

Jack laughed. 'I'll fix it.'

'Are we still gonna see Ed?'

'Nah. Not now,' said Jack. 'We won't be able to stray off the Hill.'

Ed Mason had fought in every campaign since East Timor in the '90s and it showed. He was a sharp wit, and a hell of a mentor. That ancient bastard had never revealed how many pockets of the Resistance he controlled, but Jack had heard that he ran the whole show. Victoria, at least. Maybe Australia. He was looking forward to a whiskey with him.

'Where are we going?'

'The chip shop. Then we gotta get back up the Hill . . .'

'I'm not hungry, Dad.'

Jack laughed. 'Me neither. I have to collect something.'

'Can I come?'

'You'll be in the car.'

Jack reversed his Prado into a park at the strip mall. In the dying light, he held his plastic cigarette lighter up to the sun visor until it vibrated once in his hand, then he walked towards the fish and chip shop. He lit a cigarette as he went, and felt the covert device inside the lighter vibrate twice as he passed through the scratched plastic drapery of the shop door. He tensed as he registered that double bump – it meant a bad meeting, with bad people, and even worse coffee. If there was one thing in this world that could break him, it was weak coffee with burnt milk.

There were two sweaty teenage boys and a stout, bald man behind the counter. Jack ordered fish and chips for two, with extra chicken salt. The owner barked the order.

The chips thrashed and bubbled in the vats as Jack waited. He walked back outside to check on the car, and as he turned back to the shop he looked in through its grimy window. A mounted TV inside showed the foggy checkpoint from a top-down live feed; four bodies were laid out on the road, and a convoy of black trucks had sealed off the area.

The ticker tape read, *Victorian Militia Forces checkpoint attack: 'An act of extreme aggression,' President Carlisle. 'Ceasefire likely to be repealed.'*

Chinese characters followed the English on the ticker tape.

Jack stood under the shop awning and stared at his truck, sitting in the rain, holding that precious cargo: his boy.

4

KAYNE WILSON TUCKED HIS PHONE BACK INTO HIS POCKET AS he scanned the carnage at the roundabout. Twisted bodies glued to the bitumen, a charred truck with a kid's body in the rear. The acrid notes of burnt rubber and high explosive residue in the drizzly morning. *A massacre. You just lost your Hill.*

He pulled his leather gloves off and shook his head, listening to the steady tick of contracting metal. He looked up to the Hill. The long spine of the mountain jutted from the clouds as they swept past it. It was 600 metres tall, and covered in dense eucalyptus trees the whole way up.

It was tiger country.

Kayne was the leader of the Cranbourne Boys, an elite unit of the Victorian Militia Forces, the vanguard of the local collaborator enforcers for their foreign overlords. He had driven down here without an escort as soon as he heard that a checkpoint had been hit. He was disgusted. Seeing his own men dead rattled him every time.

He walked to the burnt technical vehicle and squatted his lean frame down to study the body of Stevie Adams. The burnt corpse before him was a husk of the man he had known. He picked the akubra up off the ground and weighed it in his hands.

30

'Ten years, brother. Damascus. Beirut, smashing government troops. And you get whacked here.' He scanned the roundabout, eyeing the hacksawed metal stumps of the looted streetlights. Only a rusted cylinder base and thick bolts set in the concrete foundation remained.

'Did you authorise this?' his sister asked over his shoulder.

Kayne covered Adams' face with the akubra, then stood and pulled his gloves back on. His sister walked across the roundabout, weapon up. Legs like a cheetah, the muscle flexed through her jeans as she moved. Her jet-black hair was pulled into a tight ponytail, one side shaved in an undercut, revealing a blue scorpion tattooed to her scalp. Jessica was younger than Kayne, but tougher than crocodile hide and with more cunning than a dingo.

She held her fist out to her brother and dropped a handful of brass shell cases into his palm.

Kayne inspected them. The base of each shell was stamped 'ADI F1 23'. He wiped it with his finger.

'Old rounds. Before the Occupation. 5.56 millimetre.'

He looked up and gestured to the truck. 'The blast came first.' Kayne pointed to the pockmarked hull of the smoking truck. 'After that, he popped 'em.' Kayne tapped his boot. 'I dunno, Jess.'

Jess looked at the carnage, then scanned the tree line on the side of the road, her AK-47 in her shoulder.

Jess Wilson left nothing to chance and assumed nothing.

'Well, there's not many folks game enough to tackle a checkpoint solo,' Jess said.

Kayne put one hand in his pocket and stuck his thumb under his rifle sling. He locked eyes with his sister and then pointed at the single star embroidered on her chest rig. The Cranbourne Star.

'You ready to earn that?'

She looked at him and then back to the Lilydale exit, eyes narrowed.

31

'I think I know what's coming,' she said.

'Jess,' said Kayne.

Jess lowered her rifle and looked at him.

'The Principal's coming,' he said.

Her brother always smiled when he delivered bad news. He had done it since they were kids. It annoyed the piss out of her.

She looked down at the bitumen and rubbed her neck.

'I'll handle it,' said Kayne.

She stared back at him and mimicked his deep voice. 'I'll handle it.'

'Let's come up with a plan,' Kayne said.

'This is why I said we need separation from the Chinese. We'll get dragged into a battle we can't handle.'

Kayne pulled his phone out and hissed.

'Shit.'

He raised his eyes to Jess. 'HQ said Principal is wheels down in one minute. He's riding the Dragon.'

Jess walked a circle around the smoking truck. Kayne watched her.

She picked something up from the gutter; it was a yellow card. She turned it over in her hand, then smiled.

'Son of a . . .' She walked to Kayne and handed it to him. 'Dale Bascal.'

Kayne shook his head as he looked at the image on the card. The dark brown hair, slate blue eyes and granite jaw. The only imperfection on his face was a streaking scar that cut across one eyebrow.

'Jack Dunne,' said Kayne, his suspicions confirmed.

Jess shook her head. 'He's dead. They got him a year ago in Docklands. DNA checked out.'

'If that's true, who's this?'

'It can't be.' She studied the card. 'Nah. This is someone else. Similar. Not him. A relative?'

32

Kayne's shoulders were slumped. 'It's him. A hundred per cent.'

'How do you know?' she said.

'The Principal told me. Drones picked up a man, six foot four, plus a child, at a funeral on the Hill yesterday.'

Jess was incredulous. 'What. You told Stevie, right?'

'No. It's compartmented info.'

'So you let Stevie set up here, knowing the last Outrider ever might be kicking around the area?'

'You know how much the Principal wants an Outrider scalp.'

Jess flinched at the very mention. *Outrider.* Rare. Highly trained. All combat experienced, with multiple tours. Extremely high IQs. Their capabilities could turn battles. Storms. Earthquakes. Tactical nukes. Outriders were the most elite troops AUKUS ever created, and they'd been hunted since the Occupation began in 2029.

A low pulsing noise boomed from overhead, like a broken amplifier.

They squinted at the sky.

A matte grey, V-shaped wedge stalked from the clouds into the darkening sky. The jet climbed and banked in front of the low cloud to return. It was barely audible, but Jess could feel the dense frequency pulses of the motor.

'So that's it. We hit him,' said Kayne.

'Yeah.' Jess licked her lips and pulled her ponytail across her shoulder. 'We can get him. But all other operations have to cease.' She was talking to herself. 'We miss him, and we're done.'

The Dragon jet made a single pass over the roundabout and when it completed its turn, its engines had been rotated to the vertical landing position. The pilot nudged the tail of the aircraft around the stripped power poles and trees and touched down adjacent to the roundabout.

Kayne shielded his face from the debris that scattered across the road. As the turbines wound down, the rear ramp dropped to the road.

The Principal ducked his thick frame under the wing of the Dragon jet and walked into full view. Black overalls, sleeves rolled up to his elbows. He was tanned, with big shoulders, like a boxer, his forearms thick and veined. He scanned the battle-field, his face like a stone mask.

He turned to Jess and Kayne, summoning them with his eyes.

Jess had shouldered her weapon. As they walked, she could hear her brother taking deep breaths. She had rarely seen him worried, even as a child.

They stood in front of the Principal, but his eyes were still cast to the mess on the roundabout, the carcass of Stevie Adams.

Another soldier had exited the aircraft and was scanning the road exits, talking into an earpiece in Mandarin.

Kayne's face blanched.

The Principal stood with both hands in his pockets and looked at Kayne. One eye was not quite right, half closed and clouded pale. The Principal regarded him for a moment, then turned to Jess. His good eye flitted across hers like he was speed-reading her mind.

Jess felt her breath catch in her chest.

The Principal turned to the carcass on the kerb a few metres away. The akubra had blown off Adams' face and flies were now rimming his eyelids, drinking fluid.

'Comrades.' His hand went to the black pistol at his side.

Kayne handed over the yellow ID card. The Principal held it up to his good eye, then nodded to himself and handed it back to Kayne.

'Seventy-two hours,' Kayne stuttered. 'We'll bring him in.'

The Principal nodded to himself, then looked at Adams' body. 'What's all this?'

Kayne shifted his weight on his feet.

'We set up a checkpoint. We can't go up the Hill, so we waited here. We heard one of the last Outriders was up there with his son.' Kayne motioned to the immense forest-covered hill, the last bastion of the Resistance.

The Principal looked over the roundabout. 'You set up this close to the Hill, without my permission?'

Kayne swallowed.

The Principal chuckled to himself. 'Your men did well.'

'Yessir. It was my fault. I put them too close to the Hill.'

Kayne's mouth was now completely dry.

The Principal kept his eyes on Stevie Adams. He stood still for a long time.

'We're taking the Hill. I want the Outrider first. Seventy-two hours. His son also.'

'Check. Seventy-two hours.'

The Principal stared up at the forest. 'Lock the Hill down.'

'Yessir,' said Kayne.

The Principal nodded to the deputy and waved his finger in a circle over his head.

The Dragon jet's engines began to spin, and the soldiers swept across the roundabout and stood behind the Principal, facing out. He flexed his gloved hand and rested it on his pistol.

The security man stepped forward. A scar creased the entire length of his face, as though he had been hit with a sabre.

'Sir. Wheels up.'

The Principal stared at the two Australians before him. The security man persisted.

'Sir. We're too close to the Hill. We need to move.'

The Principal turned and strode back to his craft and up the ramp, the security man covering the Lilydale exit. The ramp closed and the jet picked up revs.

Kayne was pale.

Jess bored holes through him with her eyes. 'No big deal. Just an Outrider.'

She looked at Kayne.

'Just the most dangerous troops the army ever fielded. Bit of hand-to-hand training. Target prosecution. Improvised weapons. High-threat driving. Explosives.' Jess was counting off on her gloved fingers. 'Surveillance. Countersurveillance. Smart Weapons with automated kill chains. Tradecraft. Sniping.' She had run out of fingers. 'Close access. Disguises. Sabotage.'

'Let's finish it off. We've got seventy-one and a bit hours.'

Jess looked out at the Hill as they drove off. It was the most dangerous patch of ground in Victoria, and it was Jack Dunne's home.

5

Jack drove along the winding tourist road up Mount Dandenong. He accelerated in slow bursts to preserve diesel. The chips smelt salty and fresh. Hulking eucalypts lined the hill and he turned the corners by rote. He kept his eyes out for the Resistance checkpoint that guarded the Hill. Harry was looking out the window at the bright green ferns, thickets and towering ghost gums.

The road levelled out and in an opening of the forest the old football field emerged. It was converted to a close-quarter battle range. Tyres lined the walls of the field and in the centre stood a three-storey structure of cheap wood and old window frames. A trench range ran along the far side of the oval. A local fighter had parked at the range, he stood beside his young son at the tailgate of his truck, loading up magazines for a shoot.

Jack had stood in that exact same spot. Four years earlier. Getting chewed out by his lovely wife.

Jack tapped on the glass frontage of the holographic scope, his head beside Harry's, peering down the barrel of his rifle. 'See the little red dot, that's where your shot . . .'

'What the hell is this?' Gemma said.

Jack turned around, still holding Harry. 'G'day.'

He was caught. Gemma stared back, trembling, hands on hips.

Jack had told her he was going to Lillydale Lake with Harry but instead he slipped out to the range to have a shot with him. Harry was standing on a timber ammo crate, an M4 on the camping table in front of him.

Gemma was tapping her foot, chin thrust forward. Jack knew that was combat mode for her. She was at her best when she was mad: articulate and forceful, her dark eyes blazed with passion.

She looked attractive all the time, but especially when she was angry. Jack safed his M4 and lay it on the sandbag at the end of the table. Harry turned on the spot, wearing a stained t-shirt with muscly-armed cartoon magpies on it. 'Premiers 2023' emblazoned on its chest. Jack had bought it the year Harry was born. He bought it at the airport on his way home from Ukraine.

Harry's eyes lit up when he saw his mum, he waved to her excitedly, grinning from ear to ear. He had oversized earmuffs on his blonde hair and he looked every bit the dream Jack imagined of a young kid. His own kid.

Jack sighed. 'He's gonna learn at some point. Might as well be me who teaches him.' Jack gestured at the silhouette target 100 metres away. Gemma wrapped her arm around Harry's shoulders and took his earmuffs off.

'He's bloody seven. You don't listen, do you?' Gemma said.

She had dark rings under her eyes, framed by her coal black hair. They were both exhausted. The last two seasons had been a blur. On Z-Day, Taipei was invaded at first light, and CCP boots had secured Taipei by dinnertime. The Americans lost three carrier battle groups in the two days that followed. The entire Royal Australian Navy was sunk in three battles. AUKUS submarines were hunted down and crushed, along with rumours of quantum communication satellites locating them from space. North WA was secured by the CCP for 'self-defence' reasons. Victoria had already collapsed into anarchy. The 'Peacekeeping Force' arrived a year later.

Their world had fallen.

Except for the Hill.

The enemy and their local allies were clever. They were only taking key terrain. That's the only reason there were no Chinese destroyers in Sydney Harbour, and no tanks in Canberra. Yet.

The Hill was the last fortress for the Victorian Resistance.

Over the last six months, Jack and Gemma set their home up with vegetable gardens, chickens and livestock. After putting Harry to bed, in the candlelight they would turn on the solar radio and listen to the ABC to see how much of their country was still free.

Standing at a range on an old footy oval, teaching his seven-year-old how to use an assault rifle, said a lot about this world.

'We should've headed west. When we had the chance,' Gemma muttered, frowning.

'Can't look back,' said Jack. 'They're staying anyway. You don't take north WA, then Victoria, link them with a rail line, for fun. They're not leaving. Not unless they're pushed out,' Jack continued. He nodded to the boy. 'He'll be a part of that, no matter how much we try to avoid it.'

'I know,' Gemma said. 'He's as stubborn as you are.'

Jack tapped the stock of his rifle. 'Skills won't hurt him.'

It was the truth. He looked at his son, hugging Gemma tightly.

Pray he doesn't ever need to use them.

'Pray he doesn't,' said the Resistance fighter through Jack's window.

Jack startled in his seat. He had been on autopilot.

'Doesn't what?' said Jack.

The guard had a broad jaw and beard as wide as his hat.

'I said, "Pray he doesn't see that again." You okay?'

'Yeah,' said Jack.

The guard's carbine was slung across his shoulder with a leather strap, and he stood under a beige parasol. The toes of his boots were taped up.

The armed man waved the other guard over. The man's face was pale. He rubbed the back of his neck with a gloved hand.

'Dunny, how are ya?' said the armed man. 'I heard ya got Stevie Adams.'

'I think it was him. Massive man, big grey beard."

'Yeah, I reckon that's him. VMF will be keen on you. Especially those Cranbourne Boys.'

'I know it,' said Jack. 'Nice brolly.'

The guard twirled the parasol. 'It's great.' He looked down at Jack's finger. 'What happened?'

'Parting gift from Stevie.' He flexed his hand.

The man nodded. He looked through the driver's window to the boy and sniffed the air. 'How are ya, Harry? Ya alright?'

'I'm good thanks,' said Harry.

The armed man waved ahead, and the second man pulled on the concrete bucket hanging on the gate, lifting it clear of the road.

Jack shook his head. He had visions like that before, after combat. Always after fighting.

He had lost his mind once before, after Ukraine. He couldn't afford that now.

Jack scanned his street. Semi-rural homes with bluestone walls carved into the red earth slope of the mountain. Roofs made from corrugated iron, patches of tiling and small squares of black rubber sheet sealing the old homes. Woodsmoke drifted from the top of his bluestone house, and leaves swirled along the pitted tin roof. A kookaburra watched them from a low branch.

Jack drove down the dirt road for another minute, then accelerated up his steep driveway and stopped at the garage door. He fished a new key fob from his pocket and waited for the garage door to crank its way open, then drove in and parked, letting the engine idle a moment. The interior was all bluestone blocks. A heavyweight punching bag and a chin-up bar hung from a beam on the roof. He turned the engine off and they sat in the silence for a moment, then Jack climbed out of the car and reached into the footwell for his carbine.

The boy pushed the garage fob and walked to the driver's side.

'Head up and get washed.' Jack was fishing through the car for expended shells. There was no response. When he turned, Harry was still standing there.

Jack stopped collecting the shells and knelt down with his arms out. 'Come here,' he said.

The boy ran to him. Jack hugged him hard and buried his face in the kid's hair. The boy wrapped his arms around his waist with a strength Jack hadn't felt before.

'Hey, it's okay. It's okay.' Jack felt the suck and rise of his chest. He pushed him back and held his shoulders.

'They'll come up here,' said Harry. His hands were shaking. Jack held them.

'They could,' Jack said. 'But we'll be fine. I promise.'

'You can't promise though,' moaned Harry.

Tears ran down Harry's face. Jack pulled him into his chest. These were hard times. His own childhood had been a dream, but his son was born of war, he knew nothing else.

6

When Harry went inside and Jack knew he was alone, he put his hands to his face and squeezed hard. He reached back into the truck for his zippo lighter and held it against the sun visor until he felt it vibrate, then waited for the double vibration that would tell him the download of the dashcam footage was complete.

When it came, he locked the car and walked to the bluestone wall of the garage. He placed his hand on a sanded patch and a tiny green light flashed once.

There was a click and a faint breeze as Jack pushed on the wall and it rolled aside. Inset lighting under bookshelves glowed to light the space. Grit fell from the tunnel entrance, and he stooped as he walked into the bunker.

The shelves were stacked with paperbacks and red wine bottles with butcher's paper and wax seals. A compound bow and quiver was mounted against the bluestone, and below it hung three matte black assault rifles in ascending length and power. A pistol belt hung beside them, together with hand grenade pouches and a knife with a bone handle. A map of Victoria was mounted on the wall, marked with red diamonds, Post-it notes and pins. There was a tattered picture of his fire team standing in a field of dead sunflowers, a Russian T-90 tank, turretless, billowing flames behind them. Below that, a picture of Jack and Harry up on a surfboard in waist-deep, emerald water. Jack took in the sheer delight on Harry's face under his blue bucket hat, the broad smile on his own. It was a different world and a different time.

Jack stood on a battered Afghan rug and removed his shoes. Beside him, a bedsheet was pulled across the hardware on the desk. He whipped it off, revealing a wide monitor panel mounted on the desk. Jack pressed his palm to the monitor. It measured his finger and bone geometry and his skin temperature, and scanned his iris before it powered up.

Jack waited, rubbing his hands, watching his breath condense.

'Lights. Medium heat.' Strip lights under the desk and above the door bathed the bunker in light. A whirring under the desk produced gas-heated air. Jack placed the zippo lighter atop a plastic mat on the desk, and the images from the truck's dashcam appeared on the monitor. He fast-forwarded to the explosion. The camera had caught it just as he rounded the bend and stopped in front of Stevie Adams' burning body.

He went back to the video. The explosive tyre used shaped C4 plastic explosive and electric detonators. Jimbo had done his job well – the device had levelled the checkpoint. But he had used precious detonators and C4 explosive in the process.

'Stuff doesn't grow on trees,' Jack muttered.

He scanned the remaining video, which showed thermal imagery of a naval ship at the Docklands with a block transformer and a set of metallic prongs, five metres long.

The object looked a lot like a rail gun: a twin set of prongs that, once electrified, could fire a tungsten rod at three kilometres a second and destroy anything in its path. It reminded Jack of an intelligence phone intercept Heads had briefed him on. A Chinese scientist had been heard referencing 'orbital rods' for use against stealth bombers.

Jack shook his head. *Australia: a test range for new tech.*

His phone vibrated, and he glanced down to read the message. A follow-up to the signal he'd received at the fish and chip shop. It said one thing: *RV 2000*. At least that time meant a beer instead of a coffee.

He stood and pulled the door shut. He listened, but could hear no noise from the living area above. He pictured Harry sitting up there, silently processing the enormous last couple of days. When Jack thought about it, he realised he hadn't heard Harry play in a long time. *Now he just sits around and waits for orders.*

Jack shook his head, pushed the thought aside and shouted up the stairs to Harry.

'Grab your things. We have to go to the pub.'

Harry bolted down the stairs.

They'd been summoned to meet with the head of the Resistance on the Hill.

7

JACK ROLLED HIS TRUCK THROUGH THE DIRT CAR PARK WITH the headlights off. The moon was high and full, and the eucalypts threw menacing shadows across the car park. The thrum of a vibrant country bar travelled through the evening, and he could hear the whir of a generator behind the pub.

He parked the truck and walked to the back of the vehicle, then scanned the park.

'Take this.' Jack held up a twenty yuan note for Harry. 'Grab an orange juice and watch the door for me.'

They crossed the car park together. The howls from the bar grew louder as they approached. By the front door, the bottom of a wine barrel was nailed to the wall, with chalk writing declaring *Friday nights – 200 yuan parma and pint!*

Jack pushed the thick timber door open and the bell over the door jingled. His eyes quickly adjusted in the gloom. A single yellow bulb lit the entrance, and two more dangled over the bar. A weapons rack made from carved weatherboard held a collection of assault rifles and hunting rifles that patrons had mounted while they drank. Some of the rifles had small perspex windows on the scope. Reflex sights for close combat. All were loaded and gleaming.

Some of the men in the room turned to watch as Jack entered. The air was thick with woodsmoke and wax and stale beer. Several people murmured at Jack as he passed, and raised a glass or nodded to him.

A lean man wearing a Stihl chainsaw shirt covered in wood shavings stuck his blackened hand out to Jack. Jack took it, recognising the grip of a man who made a living using his hands.

'Donny, I'll see ya again soon no doubt.'

'Sorry about Gemma.' Donny raised a glass to them both.

Harry walked to a bar stool and asked for an orange juice, while Jack ordered a southern parma and a homebrew ale, and some chicken nuggets for Harry, keeping his eyes on the entrance. Then he walked to a booth at the back of the room, facing the door, and slumped into it.

A single candle in a beer bottle lit the battered stringybark tabletop; the filthy Corona bottle was full of salt and rice. Silver steins hung from the roof in rows, and a stuffed fox snarled down at him from atop the bar. Three dozen framed pictures of young men in sharp dress uniforms were dotted with curled Post-it notes filled with love hearts and exaltations from broken-hearted girls insisting they would wait for them forever. A redwood fire crackled, and a row of candles sat along the mantel. The pub smelled of fresh smoke and damp earth.

Jack scanned the crowd. They were all veterans of the Resistance. The spectacled barman reached over and rang the navy bell once, and when the crowd quietened, he raised a whiskey in a clouded glass.

'Gemma,' he called.

The crowd repeated the sentiment and raised their glasses to the mural of young men and women in uniforms. Several of them turned to Jack, and to Harry too. He nodded.

Jack had known these people for over a decade; had watched the marriages and the babies and the fights and the farewells as young men marched in slouch hats to the trains that shipped them out to the Pacific.

His mind replayed the shambles at the roundabout. He kept seeing Stevie Adams' burning body. The boy laying in the tray of the F250. The 'No Lemons' badge. Harry's smooth face staring up at him from the passenger seat. This war was a special kind of hell, and Harry was trapped in it. Jack had wanted more for him. Footy on the weekends, walks to school, a paper round. A future. *Instead, I pray that he'll see twenty.*

The parma and beer landed on the table. Jack leaned forward and breathed it in. Browned, melted cheese. Pub food with handmade cheese and fresh tomato paste was a delicacy up here.

'Evening, Jack,' said the barman as he placed his pint down on a warped coaster.

Jack took a long drink. He hadn't seen a beer in a long time. It was clad in condensation with a perfect head, amber and clear. It was cold, and good.

He checked his watch. 1956.

The door jingled and a thickset man wearing combat trousers and a khaki shirt limped in. His fists were gnarled and scarred. Compression sleeves covered both forearms like fish nets, yellow splotches, plasma stained. He stepped towards the bar and the patrons fell to muttering, parting like bait fish before a shark.

'Black ale,' the man said, reviewing the bar with no regard for the sudden quiet. The barman handed him his ale, while the locals stole looks at the man, and at Jack.

The man picked over to Jack's booth and slid down into the seat, facing Jack with his back to the room. Dyson Carr, the Hill Commander, was hairless, earless, had short stumps for fingers on one hand, a bony thumb and forefinger on the other, which he used to grip his pint like a mud crab. He'd once spent two years recovering in an underground burns unit, but his mind was as sharp as a kukri blade.

He bunched his hands into his crotch and leaned over to smell his pint. 'I love black ale. Chocolate and roasted coffee notes.' He laughed to himself. 'I can't smell a thing, but your scent receptors can be activated by memory, you know. Scent and emotion are . . . inextricably intertwined.'

Jack had been with him when he lost all his senses in the Crimea Incident.

Dyson paused a moment. 'Condolences.' He raised his glass.

Jack didn't move.

'I mean that,' said Dyson.

His dark eyes shone and his face was a stitched lattice of pale skin transplants with suture scars at their edges. The untreated parts of his head were still purple and angry red. Faint wisps of black hair hung in strands from the man's crown, and a thick blue vein ran down his forehead, visible under his rice-paper-like skin. His black eyes had no lids, lending an unnerving intensity to his gaze.

'Look at you, mate. It's been a rough few years, hey?' Dyson said, without a hint of irony. He paused and sipped his beer, and tracks ran down his chin. 'I can't taste this either.' He chuckled, then fixed Jack with his piercing stare.

'You want to tell me what happened today?'

Dyson stole a chip from Jack's plate and chewed it, his eyes never leaving Jack's.

Jack stared back at him, elbows on the table, one hand rubbing his bandaged finger.

There was silence.

Dyson turned and spoke over his shoulder. 'May I please have the room?'

The pub fell silent. Jack saw that the patrons were all looking to Donny to speak. Donny drank his beer, placed it on the bar and stood for a moment. He did not speak. Instead, Donny walked to the gun rack, pulled a black carbine off the wall and walked out the door. The rest of the patrons followed suit, shouldering their weapons as they headed for the door.

Dyson gestured to the barman. 'You can stay. I need a witness for this.' Harry stayed too, watching the remaining men with wary eyes.

Dyson settled into his seat, his weeping eyes still locked onto Jack's. 'They're gonna clear the Hill. They're locking it down now. The ceasefire is repealed.'

Jack felt his gut tighten at the confirmation. He had been trying to come to terms with this all day, but to hear it confirmed hit like an anvil on his chest.

'When?'

'Our guess is seventy-two hours. Plus a night. Probably at dawn.'

'Target strike or full clearance?'

'Probably both.'

'Well, for a clearance they would need a Brigade. Couple of thousand men, minimum. Plus all the supporting artillery. That won't roll out in five minutes.' He considered the task the Chinese faced.

'Jack, I can drive from one end of this hill to the other in ten minutes. You can run to the bottom of it in five, if you're fit. We're talking frontage as wide as a few footy ovals, five or six kilometres long. Plus some mopping up. They'll have the VMF with them. Cranbourne Boys will do all their targeting missions.'

'Well, they can come. It's not exactly tank country though, is it? Or good for direct fires. Look at the overhead cover,' said Jack.

Dyson's dark eyes shone as he sipped his ale. 'All this is in peril. What the hell were you thinking?'

'I was going to see Ed. I need him to release me. I want to take Harry west.'

Dyson clicked his tongue. 'Risky.'

'I know. We got unlucky,' said Jack.

'Jack, they were probably looking for you. You don't have a VMF checkpoint that close to the Hill after a funeral like that for no reason. There was another one at the other end of the Hill, too. They were hunting you.' He drank his beer and leant forward to whisper, 'I'm not concerned about a Brigade plus clearance. I'll deal with that. It's the Principal I'm worried about.'

'What about him?' said Jack, an edge creeping into his voice.

'They're sending him,' said Dyson.

'What?' Jack could feel the colour drain from his face.

Dyson let out a chuckle and sat back, rubbing his stumpy hands together. 'Yessir. They're putting their best onto you. Quite the compliment.'

Jack wasn't laughing. He was staring down at the table. It was well known that the Principal was by far the most competent Special Ops commander in the Chinese army. He loved dirty work. He refused promotions, opting to keep fighting instead. He'd been ordered by the Premier to assume command of the Strike Force in the Anzac theatre. And getting rid of Outriders had been a successful part of his strategy.

Dyson recited his resume.

'He cut his teeth at the border with India twenty years ago. He bashed and drowned about a dozen Sikh officers in the glacial rivers at the Galwan Pass. Ask Heads about it.'

Heads was the intelligence officer for the Resistance.

Dyson was sitting forward in his seat. 'Because of the treaty at the Galwan Pass, the CCP wouldn't allow firearms to be used. So to clear the Indians off their positions, he requested a microwave beam weapon. You know, heats people up, like a TV dinner.'

Jack studied Dyson's mangled eyelids.

'He cooked the Indians in their positions from the other side of the valley. Just piles of cooked flesh dressed in uniform. They took the Pass without firing a single shot. Got an Order of the Double Dragon for it.' Dyson admired his beer.

'Very creative man,' said Jack.

Jack knew this was a serious issue. One of his great gifts was taking terrible news and keeping a mask of indifference. He was using it to its full extent, sitting in front of his old boss.

Dyson sipped again.

'We'll be ready in twelve hours. They could come early. It won't just be a strike to target you or the leadership, they want the whole Hill. They want a CCP flag at the top and a pile of smoking Resisters all around it.'

Dyson turned his glass in his hand.

'They'll bring their best toys up here. VMF troops too. You could have a dozen clones of the Four Horsemen and you still couldn't stop them.'

Jack shook his head. He waved to the bartender for a whiskey.

This is not ideal.

The bartender delivered his drink and Jack drank it in one hit. Harry was looking across from the bar with a frown. His dad was not a whiskey drinker.

There was a spark in Dyson's gaze.

'Task Force Leopard. VMF. The Principal. Everyone's coming.' Dyson chuckled.

'I don't see much snow up here,' Jack said.

'You know he was born in Perth? The Principal?'

Jack raised his eyebrows. 'Really?'

'Yes. Ask Heads. He led a flamethrower unit in Taiwan. Up Mount Yangmin.'

Dyson leaned forward. 'All this –' he gestured at the bar, then leant in, 'we knew we would have to fight for it. You just brought that day forward.'

The enormity of it was hitting Jack. He watched a line of condensation trickle down the side of his empty beer glass.

The Hill was the last holdout in southeast Australia. There was no other truly free land until you hit Perth, or the hard border at New South Wales. South Australia was a no-man's land. The Hill wasn't just a firebase or an operations hub, it was the beacon of the Resistance. It had gained an international reputation as a thorn in the side of China: to lose it would be a huge moral victory for the CCP.

Dyson sipped again and propped his chin on his scarred fist. 'There's one hope.'

Dyson scanned the room and leaned forward.

'The Yanks have offered up an asset,' whispered Dyson.

'Ah. I knew I was here for a reason,' said Jack.

Dyson continued. 'They dispatch a field officer who can coordinate US strategic support. The good stuff. Weather, cruise missiles, maybe more.'

'I know what they can do,' said Jack.

'You're the last Outrider, and under AUKUS, we can only couple such assets with Outrider-badged folks. Guess that means you're it.'

Jack shook his head. It was too big a job to digest in one drink. He waved to the barman, requesting another.

'It'll cost you,' said Jack.

'I know. You want freedom, for you and your boy. Granted. Bring me the asset, you can go. I'll even give you a truck, and the fuel.'

Jack stared at Dyson. His eyes told Jack he meant what he said.

Dyson sipped his beer. 'Ed passed the approval on to me this morning. Come up to HQ. Heads and I will brief you.'

'I would need to be the main effort. All the air support. Four Horsemen too,' said Jack.

'You say yes, they can be on stand-by in a few hours.'

Jack stood. 'Let's go. I want to talk to Heads. And I want the contract in writing. What you just offered.'

Dyson turned to the barman, pointing. 'Did you hear that? Prep the food mate, everyone will need a feed before the assault.'

The barman nodded and slipped out the back door.

As Dyson stood, he added, 'Oh, and you're on their kill list.' Dyson pointed at Harry. 'Him too.' With that, he headed for the door, looking at himself in the mirror as he left.

Jack looked at Harry, still sitting at the bar with his orange juice.

It was official. The Chinese Communist Party was coming for them.

8

THE DRIVER OPENED THE CAR DOOR FOR DYSON AND DYSON climbed in. The barman ran over and rapped on the window, a folded sheet of paper in his hand.

Dyson wound the window down and took the paper.

It was a printout of an email, forwarded by a contact. Dyson watched Jack and Harry get in their car. He watched the car pull out, then went back to the document.

He held a torch to the text and ran his gnarled hand along the lines as he read.

```
        TOP SECRET / SCI / AUKUS
The Whitehouse, Washington, August 2034
US Policy, Programs and Strategy in Victoria,
Australia
OPORD: 14 August 2034
ACTION:
The Chinese Occupation in Australia is now
well into its fifth year. The two principal
elements in our Australia strategy are a
program of covert action to support the
Victorian resistance, and the diplomatic/
```

political strategy to pressure the Chinese
Communist Party to withdraw from Victorian
shores and re-orientate in the broader Pacific
third island chain, including Taiwan and
Japan. This directive establishes the goals and
directives served by this program.

Policy Goals and Major US interests. The
ultimate goal of our policy is the removal
of Chinese forces from Victoria, and the
reunification of Victoria with the Australian
Federal Government. In the mid-term (2034-2039)
the USA will pursue interim objectives that
will bring us closer to achieving our ultimate
goal. Achieving these objectives will be in the
US national interest, regardless of the outcome
of the struggle in Victoria. These interim
objectives are:

a. Demonstrate to the Chinese Government
that its long-term strategy for subjugating
Victoria is not working. If the war in Victoria
grows progressively worse for the CCP, its
confidence in achieving its long-term objectives
in Australia is likely to wane. Achieving this
objective is the best way to build pressure on
the CCP and force a change in policy that will
be favorable to the people of Victoria.

b. Deny Victoria to the Chinese as a base.
Our program will deny Victoria to the Chinese
as a secure base from which they can project
power and influence throughout the region. This
policy will prioritize the degradation of naval
manufacturing capabilities, especially with
relation to the naval 'Yard' based in South
Australia.

c. Deny the subjugation of the Dandenong
Ranges to the Chinese forces. (Main Effort)
The ongoing operations security of this
insurgent enclave continues to embarrass the
CCP and is a *cause célèbre* for the Victorian
insurgency. Maintaining the operational
security of this enclave will provide a
substantial psychological victory at low to
moderately low cost. The aim of this objective
is to either hold the mountain or necessitate
the use of disproportionate force by the CCP
(up to WMD use) to discredit and undermine
the CCP in the Pacific. This has been allocated
Main Effort due to CCP intentions to clear the
mountain stronghold before August 2034.

Support Operations 2034:
+ Operation Outrider: Approved. Asset
has been diverted from primary task to your
mission.
+ Dispatch Joint Interagency Deployment Force
under USS *Admiral McRaven*.
+ Phase 1 – insertion – to be complete no
later than 17 Aug 2034. RV to occur off Cactus
Beach. Initial infiltrate to consist of not more
than one Special Activities Division officer to
support operation c. through end 2035.
+ Support: Through, By and With operations
to be undertaken with Australian Special
Operations (SO) and Rebel Forces (RF) against
the Victorian Militia Forces (VMF). Denial and
degradation operations to be centered on CCP
Task Force Leopard, and denial of the capture
of Mount Dandenong.

+ Logistical support: Smart munitions, drones and exo-skeleton packs will be prioritised for mountain warfare. All other logistics to be sourced locally. Microchip shortage continues.

+ Offensive support: Strategic offensive support will be allocated in the event of the loss of Mt Dandenong operations centre. Send update after retrieval.

+ Reception. Reception and extraction to be undertaken by at least one qualified OUTRIDER.

TOP SECRET / SCI / AUKUS

Dyson folded the paper up and stared out the window. The Yanks were coming. They were actually coming to help this time. Sure, they were only sending one person, but that one person had access to the best support weapons on Earth.

'There's hope,' Dyson said. 'If Jack and his kid don't get skinned out in the desert heading to pick him up.'

He pulled out his phone and texted his intelligence and operations officer. The message contained just one word:

OUTRIDER

9

KYLE PARKER, OR HEADS AS HE WAS FAMOUSLY KNOWN, PUT his phone back in his pocket and looked up at the humming operations shelter.

'Ladies and gents, Outrider is green.' A few hoots and claps echoed around the room.

Kyle pointed to the bank of screens. 'Please bring up all mission feeds in the secure briefing centre. Thermal, infrared drone feeds and all High Activity Zones for VMF and Chinese forces. Focus on the Hill and the border crossing points.' All eyes in the room remained on him.

'Set up the SCIF – Dyson and Jack are coming.'

The analysts ran to the Secure Compartmented Information Facility, a concrete faraday cage with cobalt wire mesh and no windows. This was where you went for a chat away from prying eyes and ears. The SCIF was filled with the lifeblood of any war: information. It was the nerve centre of the Resistance.

Heads opened a tiny black notebook and scanned his hand-written mission notes on the Hill. He knew the battlespace better than any person in Occupied Victoria. His exceptionally large cranium and this miniature notebook held all the data – the track width of a T-100 tank, their turret rotation speed, the call signs of his sources, feeding information back from the operations centres of the PLA. This book was the Holy Grail of Intelligence.

Dyson knew the layout of the friendly forces and had the links to Resistance allies. Jack had all the field skills. Between the three of them, they would figure out the best approach to complete their mission: to collect a strategic asset that could tip the balance if the Hill clearance went ahead.

Jack cleared the booms then screeched up to the main roller door of the ops centre and blasted his horn. The door rattled open and Jack eased the truck into the concrete hangar.

Four lean, tattooed soldiers with matted hair stood near a pot belly fireplace in the corner, weapon parts laid out in rows on a table. One soldier had a tablet hooked up to a robot that looked like a slab of brushed metal with four legs. An enormous brown dog in a leather harness, closer to a werewolf than a pet, lay in front of the fire. The dog raised its head as Jack approached the table, watching him closely.

The soldiers shook Jack's hand and hugged him. The leader of the Four Horsemen, Cole, a swarthy man with a thick neck and a red Hawaiian shirt, offered his condolences. Jack acknowledged them with a nod, then gently thrust Harry forward by the shoulders.

'Thanks. Can this young man hang with you while I get briefed?'

Cole reached for Harry's hand and shook it. 'Damn straight – come here mate, we'll show you our new toys.' The large man threw his arm over Harry's thin shoulders and led him to the robot.

'This is Mrs Rabbit,' said Cole.

Harry beamed and walked up the robot, eyes wide and mouth open.

Jack watched Harry with Cole and smiled. His son already had his hands on the robot and was feeling the seams and controls on the metal case. It was the perfect distraction, after the horror of the roundabout.

The robot arm reached for Harry's hand and he yanked it away. Cole threw his head back and laughed. He was one of those guys who laughed with his whole body, and all his teeth showing. Grinning, Jack turned to go to the SCIF. As he did, Heads appeared behind him. He was dressed in the Resistance officer uniform of filthy blue jeans, Salomon runners and a tan shirt that hugged his broad back.

'You ready?'

They strode down the corridor towards the secure facility, where Heads and Jack placed their encrypted phones in an ammo tin. Heads entered a code on the door.

Heads pulled the dual-lock door open. Two plasma screens lined one wall, each the size of a single bed. Another held a whiteboard with a timeline scrawled on it. The space was dominated by a large table where Dyson sat, a voice recorder next to him.

Jack glanced around the room, beginning to absorb what the next seventy-two hours had in store.

Dyson stood up and walked to the whiteboard. Heads leaned on the desk and announced, for the benefit of the voice recorder, 'Confirm all parties present Hill Commander, Outrider 11 and S2 Intelligence lead for Operation Outrider Mission Briefing. The date is 15 August 2034 and the time is 2105.'

Dyson spoke. 'This is a critical pick-up and delivery of a strategic asset from the CIA. The US has authorised strategic support to aid retention of the Hill. We need to collect the asset to authorise and oversee all uses. I'll specify the authorised effects later, but I received an email tonight from Langley and it is a battle-winning combination of effects. Non-nuclear. That's all I'll say.'

Jack sat up in his seat. He knew Dyson understated effects so it had to be a solid support package. This mission was critical. Everything was at stake. He couldn't fail.

'Your mission: Outrider 11 is to collect the asset at Cactus Beach.'

Jack frowned. 'Why so far west? The Yard is out there.'

Dyson shot him a look that made it clear he had more to say.

'Because he's being launched from the USS *McRaven*. The *McRaven* was off the west coast. She's underway now.'

Heads spoke: 'Are you happy with 2100 in three nights, boss?'

Dyson nodded, and Jack frowned. 'Cactus and back. Seventy-two hours. Have we got that long?'

'Some sources are giving us high confidence that the clearance will come before first light in seventy-two hours time. It could come earlier.'

Jack folded his arms and held his chin.

Dyson watched him and leaned back in his chair.

'Take your boy,' Dyson said. 'They could launch early.'

He had read Jack's mind.

Their bond was that strong.

Your relationship with another man is never the same once you've asked him to kill you. Dyson had asked Jack to kill him after he was burned in Crimea.

'You're right. I think I'll take him,' said Jack. It was a big call. But he would rather Harry with him, no matter what.

'I don't recommend it,' said Heads. 'He could compromise your mission. Leave him here.'

Jack shook his head. 'This'll be the biggest target. He'll be in even more danger staying here.'

'This kid will have seen more action than me,' Dyson said.

They were moving quick. Time was precious.

'I guess air still isn't an option?' Jack asked.

Heads shook his head. 'Not unless you have Gen 6 cloaking, like those jets that flew over the funeral. The corridors are still

61

buttoned up with Chinese Air. They have airborne command and control planes up twenty-four seven. All approaches. Interceptors launch from Melbourne and Adelaide, and the Yard. Approaching by air would be suicide. Plus, the Hill still has anti-air systems all around it.'

'I know. Had to ask. It's a bit of a drive. The real question is, will I have time to catch a wave?' Jack quipped. Cactus Beach was one of the best surf spots in Australia, if you didn't mind dodging the great whites.

Dyson spoke. 'You'll be in and out of that water as quick as you can. We have routes ready to go, and the intel is good.' He motioned to the large screens on the wall.

'Feeds from around the Hill show us some potential breach points. They're all manned. Check these.' He nodded to the first screen, which showed a black and white thermal feed looking down on what appeared to be a vehicle checkpoint. There were eight vehicles on the screen, including a couple of Ram trucks with mounted missile launch tubes. The engine bays glowed white. Crammed in the back of one Ram were about a dozen fighting-age males, and the grey hue of another dozen men could be seen standing around a barrel with a boiling white plume that ran white hot in the display. There were four armoured electric troop carriers – their squat matte profiles made them look like dropships from a science fiction film. They were visible only by the heat ring surrounding the top hatch of the vehicle. Four cannon barrels protruded from the front. Two semi-trailer-sized trucks with stabilising legs were parked a hundred metres away in a clearing. Each one had four telegraph-pole-sized tubes pointing skyward.

Jack swallowed hard. 'Jesus. That's the tourist road.' He had assumed security on the main road leading up to the Hill would be strong since his little run-in with VMF. But this extra support was concerning.

'Correct. This is checkpoint one of eight. The whole Hill is being locked down. That's VMF – not sure which crew.'

'My money's on the Cranbourne Boys,' said Jack.

If you were VMF, ex-special forces, and had combat experience, you joined the Cranbourne Boys. They contracted directly to the Chinese Occupation force and ran their 'peace enforcement'. Overpaid, over-equipped and under-moralised.

'Now, these little gems,' Heads pointed at the missile tubes, 'there's a north and south battery positioned on the tourist road.' He opened his notebook. 'HQ-10B surface to air missile. Mach 6. Payload of eighty kilos. That thing can reach from here to the top end of Tasmania in the time it takes to finish a smoke.'

'They don't want anything coming off or going up this hill,' Heads explained. 'It's completely shut. We'll be driving off.'

Jack winced. 'You said I had the Horsemen. I'll need the best.'

'We'll get you direct support from the Four Horsemen for the exfiltration off the Hill. After that, they'll be positioned in Horsham for air support when you cross into SA.'

'That's not enough,' said Jack.

'I know. We'll also have two teams of Resistance militia in overwatch that will support your breach.'

'Alright.' Jack felt better knowing the professionals would be on his left flank. There was no margin for error. If he was compromised or caught on the exfil . . . it would be execution or forced labour at the Yard.

He looked at his old boss. He could still see Dyson standing at the edge of a trench in blue jeans, torn at the knee, his booming voice summoning a whole squadron across a Ukrainian wheatfield. Under the crumping artillery and tank shells, they had lost their minds, and when they stood ten hours later, they had cleared eight kilometres of Russian trenches with grenades, rifles and bayonets. An entire Russian Brigade Artillery unit lay trampled into the mud of those awful trenches. The president had pinned a Cross of Valour to his barrel chest.

And now here he was, a shell of that man, but even more dangerous.

'The entire campaign could swing on this hinge,' said Dyson. 'Jack, get it done. Our lives depend on it.'

Jack nodded.

Heads continued. 'You'll need to kit the asset out and get him briefed on the road.'

'Do I have a name and description?'

'No. Just a pick-up grid and an RV time.'

'So no air transport, no road transport, no foot movement and no name,' said Jack. 'Nice.'

Dyson stood up. 'Time's short.'

Jack stared at the screens.

'Okay. I'm in,' said Jack.

Heads pulled up a map of Victoria and South Australia, and traced a line from their stronghold to the South Australian coast. 'You breach here,' he pointed at the south edge of the Hill, 'and track the coast. The border post is where we don't have a lot of intel. Normally it's manned with armour. Expect some roving patrols. Drones are likely. We've kitted the car out so you look like a 'roo hunter.

'Cross the border at the most direct route. There's a northern route through Broken Hill, but steer clear of that if you can. There are whole manoeuvre units out there. Once you breach the border, it's 400 kilometres to Cactus Beach. Be in the water by first light.'

'Not much point talking about that if I can't get off the Hill,' said Jack.

'Exactly,' said Heads. 'That's why we have a few teams supporting you. You're the main effort.'

Jack nodded. 'Hell yes, I am.'

Heads went on.

'Mission: Confirmed. Outrider 11 is to secure the asset at Cactus Beach and return him and specialist equipment no later than 2100 18 August 2034, in order to ensure strategic support for the defence of the Hill.'

As Heads repeated the mission, Jack waved him off. 'Got it. Seventy-two hours.' Jack had the feeling of a man who'd been thrown into a fast-moving river. If he survived the exfil, he would have 1600 kilometres of threats ahead, and not much intelligence.

Heads continued the formal briefing.

'Execution: Three-phase task.

'Phase 1: Target southern checkpoint and break out of the Hill. Transit to Cactus, including a breach of the border to South Australia. Avoid Adelaide. I repeat, avoid –'

'I heard you the first time,' Jack cut in.

'Phase 2: Agent RV. When you arrive at Cactus, we will not have eyes – you will need to clear the site yourself. I don't know what equipment they are bringing. We put in a wish list, at the bare minimum they said you'll have the asset. You need to paddle out to the break for the meet. Just wait there, they'll know where you are.'

'So paddle out to Cactus break, alone. In the pre-dawn.' Jack shook his head. He hadn't surfed in years and wasn't even sure he could make the paddle.

'Authentication: Number 8.

'Response: a number that will sum her challenge to 8.'

Jack was shaking his head.

That's old school. Cold war stuff.

'Coordinating instructions: Link up with the Four Horsemen by encrypted short wave. Give them thirty minutes notice before H-Hour.

'Jimbo has fitted your car out. You'll have everything you need to get out and back. Questions?'

'What preparation are you seeing for the Hill clearance?'

Heads consulted his notebook. 'We're hearing at least a complete VMF Brigade with Special Ops advisers, a Chinese Mechanised Brigade as the airmobile reserve. Tanks, at least a Regiment. Don't be surprised if the Principal himself is in the main assault. Sources say he's a fan of the dirty work.'

Jack shook his head. 'Harvard PhD. Hybrid combat. A Western-trained war criminal.'

Dyson stood up from his seat, wincing.

'Jimbo's next. He's got your kit.'

'Better be good,' said Jack.

'It's damn good,' said Dyson. 'You roll with the A-Team.'

10

'FOLLOW ME.' JIMBO, SQUIRE TO THE FOUR HORSEMEN, WAS the Resistance's official quartermaster. He'd tried to give himself the call sign 'Q', but like any self-given nickname, it hadn't stuck. He wore a trucker cap and blue mechanic's overalls. His brown hair had been hacked close to the scalp and he had the rangy limbs of a basketballer. Pens, pencils and a penlight were arranged in a straight row in his chest pocket.

He walked Jack out of the briefing room towards the mechanic's bay. It was all beaten I-beams, the spit of a welder and the sharp smell of burnt metal filings. Jimbo swept aside a frayed welder's curtain with a flourish, like a circus master.

'Here she is.'

A squat black beast of a truck sat raised on a mechanic's ramp.

The sight took Jack's breath away.

A solid beast with a sleek double cab, gunmetal bar work and side steps. A crowbar-thick metal grille. Dark tint. A broad tray at the back. Jimbo had prepped it for a border mission. A kid from the disguise unit swept a dust gun across the bumper, adding a patina to it. Dust and grit caked the wheel guards. At first glance, it would pass for a hunting truck. It was raised a half-foot higher than usual, sitting up on chunky black all-terrain tyres.

She was stunning.

'2024 model. All new parts. We beat her up to look like she's been in the field, but she's a fresh one.' Jimbo eyed the truck, his chin held high.

Jack threw his arm around Jimbo, jolting him.

'Jimbo. You're a gem. I had no idea. Best kept secret on the Hill.'

New cars hadn't been seen since the invasion.

Jimbo exhaled and smiled, blinking hard. The corner of his mouth was twitching. 'This was kicked out the back of a C-17 way up north, in the desert. The Horsemen marked a drop zone and we got enough pallets of technical gear and ammunition to keep us going until the next fighting season.'

Jack raised his eyebrows.

'I've serviced and refuelled everything. You got enough to get to Cactus and back.' He gestured at three jerry cans mounted to the rear. 'For weapons . . .' He pointed to a pistol attached to the driver's side dash. 'Your M4 is stowed here, plus a heap of clips in this bag.' He indicated an old gym bag.

'For the bigger stuff, I got this.' He held up a stumpy, thick-barrelled M-79 grenade launcher.

'This too.' He led Jack to the tray, dropped it level, and slid a long tan pelican case across the rear.

'There she is,' said Jack.

Jimbo clicked the latch on the case then paused for moment, relishing the suspense. Slowly, he opened it, watching Jack's face.

'Good. I like.' Jack nodded.

In the case was a broken-down 0.50 calibre Barrett sniper rifle. The barrel was as long as a man's arm and the muzzle brake as big as a fist. Stowed in the foam was a set of binoculars with a large button on one optic tube.

Jimbo pulled out a large bullet magazine.

'Semi-armour piercing high-explosive rounds. You got two of these mags.' He held up a third magazine with a white squiggly arrow painted on the base. 'These are the guided rounds.'

He ran his finger across the edge of the inch-thick tray, then pulled the rear down. 'Oh, and check this out. Emergency only. I built a single 1.4-metre-wide cutting charge into the tailgate. Switch is on the dash, and there's a back-up here.' He held up a green watch strap with a perspex cover concealing two buttons.

'This is a Bluetooth switch. You can arm and fire the charge from the seat or remotely, from fifty metres. When you fire it, the cutting charge will form a molten copper blade moving at about five thousand metres a second.' He made a chopping motion with his arm.

'So don't stand behind the dropped tray.'

Jack pointed at a large basalt rock that sat in the rear passenger seat. It was the size of a bowling ball.

'And this is to fire from my catapult?'

'Negative.' Jimbo rapped it once with his knuckles.

'This is an AGI-MPM,' he said, mimicking an American accent. 'Artificial General Intelligence, Multi-Purpose Mine.' He handed it to Jack with great care.

Jimbo ran his finger over the top.

'There are seven one-kilogram shaped charges with adjustable explosive yields and a short burst rocket motor. There is an anti-material or anti-personnel blast setting. This device can track, target and destroy up to four heavy armour units, or a platoon-sized group of dismounts. It has sentry mode, too. Lethal range is one hundred metres for anti-personnel. Fifty metres for armour.'

'Heavy,' said Jack.

'Talk to it. Tell it what you want; the AGI will interpret and act. You can add target parameters, too. Tell it what you don't want to hit.'

'No way.'

'Exquisite. Completely banned under Geneva. Use this and you're a war criminal.'

'Again?' Jack said.

Jack felt like he'd been standing still while the rest of the Resistance had raced forward to the next milestone. Weaponry this serious was completely new to him. The enormity of the job was starting to hit. Jimbo held up a single-arm Bluetooth earpiece. Jack took it and turned it in his hand.

'Arm it by speaking your initials, and then authorising activation. De-activate it by asking it to. You can talk to it from up to 500 metres away.'

'Friendly fire?'

'It has all our cars uploaded. It knows what you and Harry look like. It's not gonna hurt you.'

Jack was stunned. 'This is next level.'

'I did the course a year ago. This is just the start.'

'That's 007, right there,' said Jack.

Jimbo beamed at him, unabashed. Jack knew the compliment would fuel him for a week.

Jimbo leaned into the rear cab of the car and fished out a bullet that was as long as a pen and as wide as a fat cigar. The bronze bullet nose was capped with black glass.

'Guided 0.50 calibre rounds,' said Jimbo.

Jack took the round off him and weighed it in his hand.

'I've seen these,' said Jack.

'EXACTO rounds. Extreme Accuracy Guided Ordnance. DARPA built. You only have ten.' Jimbo held up a small set of binoculars. 'Use these for –'

'Spotting. Got it. I did a simulation with my boy. I spotted, Harry shot.'

Jimbo nodded approvingly. 'For comms I have an RF antenna built into the spare tyre on the roof. Your night-vision gear is wired up to your helmet. It's on your front seat. Thermals with augmented reality. All your battle tracking and nav data will pop up. There's a compact drone in there for recon, too.

'I packed three days worth of coffee, jerky for two. And I threw in a jar of Ed's cherry moonshine.'

Jack let out a low whistle.

'There's a swag in the back. Also, take this.' Jimbo fished out a matte black leather jacket from the front seat, the left shoulder padded for recoil. 'It's a Pathfinder. All kangaroo leather, but it has bonded graphene cells in the chest, back and arms. It'll protect you up to 9mm and frag.' He ran his fingers across the leather panel on the back of the jacket.

'There's a graphene antenna wired into this, as a locating beacon. It has an impact activated tourniquet inside each sleeve.' He ran his finger around the upper arm. 'It can double as a flotation cell if you're in water. It's printed to your dimensions – and it's sharp, obviously. Dress it up or down – take it for a night out at the Ceduna pub.'

Jack took the jacket and slipped it on. He rolled his shoulders and held the lapels. 'Jesus . . .'

It fitted perfectly across the shoulders. The neck was lined with black kangaroo fur, and the whole thing smelled of cut leather. It was all matte black and sleek and gorgeous.

Jimbo smiled. 'Comms: You'll have an encrypted Starlink terminal; it's running 500 megabits a second so you'll get all the drone feeds as you go.' He pointed at a large tablet with a cracked screen on the dash. 'Solar powered for everything, run the panels off the roof.'

'You missed something. Mission critical.'

'What?' Jimbo blinked at him.

'Where do I mount my seven-footer?'

'A surfboard? You're not serious,' said Jimbo.

'Deadly. You want me to paddle out at Cactus, I want my board. It's collecting dust in the locker room.' Jack pointed in the direction of the Q-store, and Jimbo obediently jogged off.

'Get me a three-two wetsuit, too,' Jack shouted after him, smirking. 'And throw some wax in!'

Jimbo returned a moment later and threw a block of wax to Jack. It was shaped like a puck, and smelled of coconut. The smell took him right back to the last time he was in the water.

11

JACK FELT THE RUSH OF THE INDIAN OCEAN AGAINST HIS BODY and pulled his infant son in close to his chest. Harry's body was warm and his legs wriggled and kicked in the surf. Jack turned him to face the small waves and he shouted in anticipation of the next set. He laid Harry on the front end of the Malibu and turned it, ready to catch the next wave. Harry wriggled with anticipation. Jack pushed off the sea floor and paddled for a broken wave.

Harry squealed with delight as the board picked up speed and trimmed in the whitewater. Jack popped up to his knees, scooped Harry up under the arms and stood him on the board. Harry tilted his head back to see from under his bucket hat and he squealed and jumped and screamed to Gemma, who was waving from the shoreline with a camera.

To Jack, this was heaven. No deployments or bills. No pain in his legs. No worrying about tomorrow. Just waves, the sun, the salt water and his family.

He ran up the beach with Harry in one arm, surfboard in the other. Gemma wrapped Harry in a towel, while Jack dried off and surveyed the beach. Teens in bikinis. Beach volleyball. A paddle ski contest. An official in speedos, a long-sleeved top and a clipboard, shouting at kids. A family eating bacon and egg rolls.

He turned west, towards Rottnest Island. The sun was rising behind him and it lit the armada parked off the coast. An American Carrier Battlegroup sat in the water, an island of metal and steel shimmering in the early light. The USS *Abraham Lincoln* was the anchor of the group, and the corvettes and destroyers orbited the hundred thousand tonnes of US metal. Grey helicopters were shuttling officers to and from the coast. The submarines, as long as a football field, lurked somewhere deep in the void of the Indian Ocean, listening.

Gemma held her hand to her face.

'Do you think it's gonna happen?'

'Yeah. They'll cross the Strait,' said Jack. 'We just have to hope it doesn't get out of control.'

Gemma plucked Harry up and sat him on her hip.

'I'm scared,' she said.

Jack had met her during the evacuation of Kabul. She had flown out of the field on the stub wing of a Blackhawk.

Fear was not something Gemma Dunne had time for.

They stood watching the carrier fleet.

'I am too,' he said.

Jack heard the deep snarl of a dog beside him and turned to see where it was.

12

'ZEUS! HEEL!' SNAPPED THE STOCKY DOG HANDLER.

Jack snapped out of his thoughts and back to the cold hangar, where the werewolf-like dog he'd seen earlier was being put through its paces.

Harry stood beside Horse, the muscular dog handler. His attack dog, Zeus, was in a training drill and had chomped down on a team member's forearm.

'Horse, get him off!' said the woman, rolling her eyes. It was Sacha, Gemma's mate, who had passed Jack the smoking bouquet at the funeral that morning.

She had a thick bite sleeve on her arm and, holding it level with the ground, she had lifted the Belgian Shepherd clear of the deck. It wriggled and thrashed for purchase on the sleeve.

The dog weighed as much as Harry, yet she held it level to her side, smiling under the strain and growling back at the dog.

'Release!' yelled the handler.

The dog released its bite, dropped to the floor and walked to the handler, circling his legs and sitting on Harry's foot. The handler reached into his belt pouch and offered the dog a treat.

Harry reached out to pat the dog's head as it chewed.

Horse put his gloved hand on Harry's arm.

'Steady. He's not a pet. He's one of our pack and I'm his alpha. Only I can pat him.' His voice was gentle, unexpected for such an imposing figure. He scruffed Harry's hair reassuringly, then clipped an elastic bungee cord onto the leather harness around Zeus's neck and chest.

Zeus was one hell of a dog.

Black fur, teeth like a T-Rex, inquiring eyes and a total absence of fear.

Jack watched them both, lost in thought. Harry had the wide eyes and half-smile of a child lost in wonderland. Lost was the gentle reservation he displayed around most adults.

Dyson slapped his shoulder, jolting him.

'Look at these hitters.' Dyson leaned against the car, folded his scarred arms and watched.

'Everyone wants to be a Horseman. The best we got. The queue has been moving fast, last couple of years.' Dyson flicked his chin towards Harry and the pair. 'Would you be keen on him joining the crew?'

'No. I would not.' The thought made Jack's stomach tighten. Harry was all he had.

'You know about these two, right?' said Dyson.

'I heard bits,' said Jack.

'The handler is Horse. You know Sacha. They each did a tour in South China.'

Jack nodded. He had heard about the Aussie SAS missions in South China. Inserting through jungle to hit air defence networks. The four-man strike and recon patrols were widely considered suicide jobs.

Dyson pointed his charred index finger at the handler. 'Horse's last dog, Prometheus, was wounded, shot three times on a target. Horse copped a round through his jaw. Blew most of his teeth out. Had to do field dental surgery on his own face.'

'Jesus,' said Jack, screwing his face up.

'While the team covered him, he strapped his dog up and carried him for two days and two nights. Sixty kilometres of jungle. Enemy patrols. Drones and tracking dogs chased 'em, bombed 'em the whole way.'

'No shit.' Jack was incredulous. He had heard something about Horse surviving a lost patrol, but not this detail.

Dyson nodded. 'Only two people made it back from that mission alive. You're looking at both of them.'

Harry was standing between the pair. They acted more like fun summer camp leaders, not elite soldiers.

Dyson shook his head. 'Prometheus was dead by the time they got him to the sub. Horse lay with him in the med bay for days before he snapped out of it.'

Jack shook his head at the bravery of these people.

'Not sure you ever recover from something like that,' said Dyson.

Jack looked at Dyson's melted head.

You're right about that.

Dyson nodded at Zeus.

'Zeus was created by IVF. Same lineage. They're inseparable.'

Sacha had pulled the sleeve off and was showing it to Harry. She had beautiful coal black hair, and a Māori sleeve tattoo of green scales and swirls and bone fishhooks encircling her lean arm. She was as lithe and panther-like as the dog.

Jack and Dyson leaned against the truck and watched her talking to Harry. She was kneeling in front of him and smiling, but Jack couldn't hear what she was saying. Although she had been Gemma's friend, Jack was realising how little he knew of her past.

Dyson nodded at her.

'Sacha worked in the AUKUS spy teams. A Russian scientist developed an AI guided nuke and was trying to sell the plans to Iran. Those nukes could sink the UK into the ocean.'

'She was surveillance?' asked Jack.

'No. She did the wet work. They tracked the scientist for days, booked a hotel room next door. Sacha coded his lock, hid in the bathroom. When he returned from dinner, he walked right into the bathroom. She tasered him, then choked him out.'

Jack eyed her. Those hands had done some nasty work, in a rough war. Now one was entwined with his son's.

'She was in the Olympics. 2028. Jiu Jitsu.'

Jack shook his head, and Dyson chuckled as he walked off.

Jack approached the trio.

Horse and Sacha each shook his hand with a smile and a nod.

'This little man is a bit of a weapon,' said Sacha as she rubbed Harry's cheeks. 'Most of the fighters won't go near Zeus. Not this fella.'

Harry blushed and looked at his shoes.

'He's no knuckle-dragger like his old man.' Jack tucked Harry under his arms.

A tall, thin operator appeared from behind the welding curtain. He approached them, tablet slung over his shoulder. The robot Cole had introduced Harry to earlier, Mrs Rabbit, trailed behind him. A black glass aperture on the edge of Mrs Rabbit's back scanned the room, and the robot glided noiselessly, stopping beside the skinny man.

'You heard about these recovery robots, Jack?' said Sacha.

Jack shook his head.

'I'll show you. Let's load Harry up.'

Harry looked at Jack for approval.

'Lie down there, Harry. Act like you're wounded.' Sacha pointed at a spot on the concrete near the roaring pot belly fire.

Harry got into position and lay on the ground. He grabbed his shin and started moaning.

Sacha smiled, and spoke to the robot: 'Recover. Priority one. Litter casualty.'

Mrs Rabbit turned, galloped to Harry and collapsed to the deck beside him. A translucent graphene sheet the size of a towel extended from the side of the crouched robot. The sheet covered Harry's shoulders and hips in full. Then it tensioned and rolled Harry over in one swoop, scooping him onto the robot's back. Harry squealed with delight.

The robot dropped its hips to guide Harry's feet to the ground. He stood up and walked around the robot, his hand never left it.

'Do they think like us?' Harry asked Jack.

The robot spoke before he could respond.

'I'll help you. I cannot allow you to be harmed.' The robot's voice was soft and feminine and direct.

Not unlike Gemma.

Harry knelt and put both arms around the robot. He held it a moment longer than Jack expected.

'Come with me,' said Jack. 'I want to talk to you.'

13

JACK WALKED TO THE CAR WITH HARRY. THE BOY TURNED TO face his father, looking anxious. Jack tugged his hoodie back off his head, gazing at him, trying to read his mood. His son stared back at him with bright green eyes; Gemma's eyes. His blond hair was matted and his face dirty. Harry broke the stare and buried himself in his dad's arms. They held each other for a moment, then Jack pushed his son back, holding his shoulders firm.

'You can stay if you want,' he said.

Harry shook his head. 'No. I want to go with you. They might come early.'

I know.

Jack held his hands up to his temples and shut his eyes for a moment. He had trained Harry for this kind of mission, but he'd hoped he would never need to use it.

Jack showed Harry the car and its secrets. He didn't tell Harry the whole plan – Harry would discover the mission as they went. For now, they just had to focus on getting off the Hill.

'Let's go over the plan.'

'Okay,' said Harry, his eyes focusing.

'Pre-departure?'

'Oil weapons. Test fire. Lasers on. Sights on low. NVGs on. Radio check. Eat. Drink one litre. Evacuate the bowel.'

Jack nodded. 'Action on contact?'

'Prep your M4, crack one rocket launcher open and stand-by. You shoot, I operate the wheel.'

'Good. Car down?'

'Move to overwatch. Take laser binoculars. You have the fifty calibre. You spot, I shoot.'

'You know why?'

'No.'

'The bullets we have are guided. That's all I'll say.'

'Oh!' said Harry. 'Like the ones from the simulator?'

'Yeah. We have ten of them.'

'Okay,' said Harry.

'Casualty?'

'Secure casualty. If immobile, leave in secure area with grab bag. Activate beacon. Proceed on foot.' Harry paused. 'You know I won't leave you though.'

'You'll do exactly as I say. If it comes to that.'

Harry bowed his head. 'I hope not, Dad.'

The list of nightmare scenarios continued.

'Checkpoint?'

Harry pointed at the rear of the truck. 'The back tray. Get them to the back of the car. Don't stand behind it.'

'What if there's no hope?'

'There's always hope. There's always a way,' said Harry.

'That's the truth,' said Jack.

Jack pulled him in close. Nothing was certain in this world, but at least they would be together. The boy was all he had left. They were going to live together. Or they would die together.

They walked back inside the hangar.

The steady chords of AC/DC's 'Hell's Bells' played from a floor speaker. Two chase utes were fully loaded, the Horsemen standing at the bonnet of their car, huddled over a map. Their vehicle had a mud-splattered flank, and the car bore a bumper sticker that read: 'No airbags. We die like real men.'

Horse and Sacha prepped Zeus and Mrs Rabbit while their teammate, Beetle the Sniper, walked around their vehicle, triple-checking everything.

Their team leader, Cole, appeared, approaching Jack with a warm smile. The pair hugged.

'G'day, Cole,' said Jack. 'Thanks for taking care of Harry.'

'Always got your back, mate,' said Cole, grinning. Half Maltese, he had the kind of exotic Mediterranean skin that made him look twenty-five even though he was closer to forty. He was a top commander and had done tours in Ukraine and South China. The real deal.

'I'm glad to have you guys on this one,' Jack said. 'We'll need the help.'

Cole slapped Jack's chest. 'We're always looking for work, mate.' He turned to his three soldiers. They were dressed in full combat gear, chest rigs, helmets and carbines. He raised his voice over the music. 'So we advance to contact. Drones hit what they can. We clean up the rest. You punch through the gap we create. No dramas?'

'That's the plan, mate. We'll hold until we see you hit a good portion of them,' said Jack.

'I love it, brah.' He turned and circled his finger in the air. 'Start up. Rolling in five!' The Four Horsemen mounted their utes, driver in the front, gunner in the turret.

Dyson emerged from the planning room, adjusting slowly to the light as he descended the stairs one at a time. A young soldier ran to help him, but Dyson fended him away. As he walked towards Jack and Harry, the attendant soldier produced a thin cigar and held up a zippo for him.

He nodded to Jack. 'Godspeed.'

Dyson turned to Harry. 'You know your old man was the best shot on the Outrider course? Bad bastard,' said Dyson.

He inhaled the cigar and blew smoke sideways across the room. 'That was ten years back. He's still decent, though.' Dyson gripped Harry's shoulder with his clawed hand.

A bell rang across the room and the Horsemen shouted in near unison, holding a single finger up.

'One minute!'

The lights cut out. Harry and Jack climbed into their seats and Jack hit the ignition button. The diesel turbo engine brought the whole room to life. Jack feathered the accelerator and felt the engine rock in its housing. Under night vision, the fire threw shadows across the room. Jack looked in the rear-view mirror at the HiLuxes behind him. Two gunners with their arms draped over their weapons. The silhouette of a dog's head sticking out the side window of one car.

The door chain rattled and Jack flexed his hands on the wheel. His hand still ached, but he felt good, alert. The door rose, smooth in its mount, moonlit bitumen beyond it. Jack put the car in drive without looking down and studied the road. The VMF checkpoint was at the bottom of the Hill. They had no idea what was coming. He felt a sense of elation. He had done all he could. It was time.

The radio crackled to life. 'Outrider 11, Sledgehammer now go, go, go.'

The Horsemen's vehicles launched ahead, gunners squatting down to clear the overhead door frame.

Jack planted his foot and the truck lurched forward, onto the bitumen. He pulled out into the dark and sped down the tourist road under the moonlight, the two chase cars running fast ahead of him.

Behind him, four humming drones with their payloads laboured out the door in close formation. They rose above the treetops, on a course for the VMF checkpoint on the Mount Dandenong Tourist Road.

14

JACK FELT THE HUM AND THRALL OF THE ENGINE AS HE SKATED through the corners, accelerating into them. He was seven minutes from the base of the hill where the four-car checkpoint and the SAM site was set up.

'Alpha count,' he said to Harry.

'Three per car, twelve in total. No change.' Harry had his finger to the cracked iPad screen, counting the white-hot figures as the numbers were read.

Jack could see the green haze of the infrared lights thrown from the Horsemen's assault cars. Jack flicked his high beams three times then slowed to the left lane as the technical sped on towards the target. Sacha was standing upright with her feet planted double wide, Mag 58 machine gun pointed down the road. A flag fluttered off the side of the car, bearing the black and yellow of the Resistance.

As he sped past a battered tourist sign that read 'Mount Dandenong Tourist Road', Jack unclipped the radio fist mike and waited for the first control line.

'Two minutes to contact,' came the call from Cole.

Jack could see the lead chase car down the hill, a few hundred metres away. It was lighting the trees ahead of him.

Jack didn't take his eyes off the assault cars. Harry was locked onto the drone feed, watching Jimbo's view as he swept the drones to the target.

Both Horsemen cars erupted into gunfire, Sacha firing a thirty-round belt from her car, Beetle belting a dozen grenades off the back of his. The trees in the foreground erupted, shattering in plumes of yellow, red and black smoke.

The Horsemen were earning their keep.

Jack guided his car to the right side of the road. Looking downhill, he had a clear view of the checkpoint. It was a melee. Three armoured cars were already spewing gouts of flame from their ammo lockers high into the night sky. The flames lit up an advancing group of two dozen Hill fighters. They were sweeping down the terrain.

Jack was struck by a realisation.

We're the ruse. That's the assault force. Dyson, you clever bastard.

The real attack was the savages before him, his Hillsfolk fighters. Their dark silhouettes swept across the checkpoint, too close to be countered with heavy weapons.

Machetes, axes and tomahawks swung and shone in the moonlight. A burning enemy soldier tumbled from the back of a truck, bathed in yellow flame. He sprinted downhill, fleeing the fighters, but two men chased him down. As he collapsed beside the bitumen road, they used the full force of their weapons on the man's burning body.

Jack's stomach was up in his throat.

They had achieved the element of surprise, but he had to move fast. He put the car in drive.

'We'll punch through,' Jack said to Harry. 'Don't look.'

Harry kept his eyes on the tablet.

Jack flicked the night vision tubes up on his helmet as they approached the burning camp. The smell of charred metal and acid cordite settled in the cool air.

The Resistance fighters were mopping up the camp; the contact had lasted all of two minutes. A tall, lean man dressed in denim and flannel was hacking at another hapless enemy driver. He reached under a burning armoured carrier and dragged out another man, kicking and flailing. He pinned the man on his back, moving steadily as though dealing with a farm animal. He did not swing the axe high when he struck. When the man's elbows dropped, he struck again and again and again, until he had sheared through the man's shoulder into his chest cavity. He threw the body to the dirt and walked into the flame-lit night looking for another target.

The two Horsemen cars were positioned on the main road, leaving a gap for Jack to drive through. Sacha was retrieving ammo cans and reloading belts onto her machine gun. She waved them past. 'Keep going – don't look, Harry,' she said.

Jack didn't acknowledge them, he just guided the truck through the carnival.

He jockeyed around the chase car and was greeted by more carnage on the other side of the road. The top half of an enemy soldier had been blown clear of his tank; a Resistance fighter with a wheelbarrow was cutting the chest rig equipment off the body with a pair of secateurs. The wheelbarrow bristled with rifles and helmets and body armour, and a length of ammunition belt swung off one side.

Jack drove past a truck and then stopped as a Resistance soldier appeared out of the darkness, dragging an enemy soldier by his chest straps across the road. He paused in the car's headlights and turned to Jack, his compact tomahawk in his other hand. It was Donny, the arborist, dragging a stocky man in a neat CCP uniform. The soldier was bleeding from a gash that spanned his whole forehead.

Donny jutted his head through the passenger window. Harry shrank into his seat.

'See this?' Donny pointed at the chest plate. It was neat and clean. 'And this?' He pulled the prisoner's body up with ease and splayed the bloody fingers with the point of his tomahawk. 'I've seen piano players with rougher hands than that. I'll bet you this fella is ranking commissar. Isn't that right, fella?' He addressed the soldier, then stood and faced the car, an axe murder in the spotlights. 'Safe travels. Keep moving.'

'Cheers, brother. For the Hill,' said Jack.

'The Hill,' Donny repeated. He turned and swung his axe at the man on the ground; as he pulled away, Jack heard a muffled snap, like a thick branch being severed. Jack swallowed down the bile in his throat.

Jack wound the window up and grabbed Harry's arm. 'Look at me,' he said.

Harry looked to Jack, shoulders rising and falling, near hyperventilating.

'Breathe. Look at the feed and give me a body count.' It was one thing witnessing a bombing on a tablet screen. But seeing people killed at this range could rewire your mind, and Jack wanted to protect him from it. At least until he no longer could.

Jack looked into the rear-view mirror and saw Donny shifting his feet and changing angles as he hit the man.

Two militiamen were filming him with their phones.

Jack's stomach lurched. He had seen how war changed men. Some couldn't resist the animal instincts it unleashed in even the best of men.

'We're through,' he told his son.

'Really?' said Harry, his gaze locked on the screen.

'Yes. First hurdle.'

They drove out in the darkness, the burning hulks receding in the mirrors. The chase cars stayed put.

If there was any doubt before about the ceasefire, tonight's actions should clear it up.

The Resistance just declared war.

PART TWO

THE
ROAD

15

JACK ACCELERATED INTO THE BLACK NIGHT. THE BONE-coloured moon loomed on the horizon. The air thinned and their ears equalised as they descended the remaining slope of the hill. The road was a pockmarked, cratered mess, covered with long branches and dead leaves. A tiny wallaby skipped off the road into the scrub. They drove under night vision through the outer suburb of Bayswater, an old industrial zone that serviced Melbourne. It had been stripped bare since the Occupation.

Streetlight covers hung from their hinges, their bulbs long since removed by agile looters. A pack of rake-thin and scabby dogs lingered on the road shoulder, sniffing the air. Car hulks littered the four-lane road, some lifted onto double-stacked bricks, tyres gone, windshields taken, doors removed.

'Wouldn't want to live here, Dad,' said Harry.

'Mate, I used to drive this road a few times a day. Do you remember it?'

Harry looked at him.

'Gymnastics. I remember coming to the gym here in my red shirt.'

'Yeah. You were bloody young. Along here there was a Woolies and a Macca's. The old Bunnings.' Jack pointed to a skeleton of a warehouse, corrugated iron stripped from its walls and roof, piles of rotting mulch in the car park. 'That was a Bunnings. You could buy anything there. Millions of parts. All gone. They lifted the metal for the ship yards.' Jack shook his head; people could get a fistful of yuan coins for a truckload of metal scrap. The payment barely offset the calories needed to loot the metal.

'It would take me twenty minutes to get down this road, thanks to all the traffic.'

'Traffic?'

'Cars. All four lanes full of them, as far as you could see.'

'That many? That's a hundred. At least.'

'There were millions of cars in Melbourne. Some families had two.'

'Two cars?'

'Yeah. Most of the metal is at the Yard. The people too. Building ships, tanks. Everything.'

Harry was quiet for a long time.

'What happened to Dyson?' he finally asked.

Jack pretended not to hear.

'What happened to Dyson?' Harry said again, louder.

Jack took a breath.

'He got burnt. In Ukraine.'

'How?'

'We were in some trenches and there was a big bomb. We got hit.'

'But you didn't get burnt.'

Jack scratched at his stubble.

I should have.

He could see Dyson's skeleton within his silhouette, black skull and scapula and fine finger bones inside a blood-red body, burnt against a rising sun. Streams of white projectiles ascending from a billowing mushroom cloud. Smoke rising from Dyson's uniform. The slap of the shockwave. The roasted smell of burnt hair. Dyson's chest was marked with the hatching of his check shirt, flash-burnt into his skin. He could replay it in his mind, in high definition.

The smell of his burned fingers as he held Jack's shoulder, stumbling through the trenches. He stumbled to his knees and pointed to his own head, reaching for the barrel of Jack's M4. Jack yanked it from his hand and dragged him to his feet. Dyson stumbling, dragging the stubs of his fingers along the earth wall, one eye melted shut. Square jaw clamped down against a pain few men have known and even fewer have survived.

'No, I didn't get burnt,' Jack said. He survived, but part of him died in that trench. It was a secret his whole troop had witnessed and never spoken of again.

A woman wearing strips of dark rags shepherded a toddler off the road. The infant stood clutching a headless doll, staring at the car. The mother shielded her brow as though it were high noon, even though it was pitch dark.

'Scavengers.'

They sat in silence as they cleared the industrial sector and moved to the open freeway. Jack looked for the Southern Cross, still low in the sky, and followed the point of the cross down to the left of the vehicle. They were heading west.

'The border is dangerous. There are patrols around there. Bikes and buggies and trucks. They capture people.'

'Why?' Harry said.

'For trade.'

Harry nodded. He knew the stakes.

'We're not going to get caught. I promise,' said Jack. He meant it. He felt the bulge on his left side, where he had two olive Mk1 grenades attached to his belt. One for the boy, one for him.

The roads opened up into the sweeping grasslands that joined western Victoria to South Australia. The moon sat high now. They stopped on an open plain to refuel with a single jerry can. Harry slid under the car and ran his hand over the inside walls of each wheel to feel for bulges or tears.

Jack looked to the east and could see ridges and trees on the horizon.

They skirted the edge of Ballarat, once a proud goldmining community, now a derelict hulk of a town. Stripped of metal down to wire stubs, even on the cyclone fences. All the panels and roof guides on the gold rush era homes were gone, and small trees grew out of the rusted gutters like sentries in the dawn.

Harry slept for a long time, curled up in his black hoodie with his head tilted back, snoring. Jack ran his hand through the boy's hair, just as he had when he was younger. Back then, he would drive him to Croydon pool for a day of fun. McDonald's on the way home. A time of abundance. Fuel, power, metal. No scrimping. No fear. He would sit Harry beside him as he held meetings with aerospace companies and trained them in fast decision-making. It was easy money. It didn't mean as much to him as his work in the Special Forces, but at least he was doing something good. In the afternoon he could kick the footy with Harry and walk the trails. Gemma would come home early and they'd ride their bikes together. Short days as a government worker. She was a diplomat, but worked on intelligence; he knew this from the nuggets of information she shared. She stewed on ideas, and the threads in her mind and mouth rarely separated. Sometimes they were bizarre ideas – he knew she was working on unusual things.

'If you had a microwave weapon, how would you use it?'

Jack thought about it.

'I would drive around and heat people's coffees for them.'

'You would do that, you people-pleaser. What if you were nasty?'

Harry was in the back seat, playing with his T-rex. Gemma's dark hair framed her face. She had exquisite skin, bright green eyes.

'You mean a standard electro-magnetic radiation weapon, but using microwave frequencies?'

'Yes.'

'Probably for targeting. Especially high-value targets. Think about it. You don't need a clear line of sight to hit someone. You just need to know the room or area they're in, and you could cook that area. Through walls. It's directional, right?'

Gemma nodded.

'Yes. Weird effects. Like voices in people's minds.'

'Really?'

'There's been some cases. Odd stuff. Pulsing noise. Barotrauma. Vertigo. The tech goes back to the Cold War.'

'Be careful.'

She nodded, and they rode in silence for a while.

'I'll be away until Saturday.'

'Where to?'

'None of your biz, soldier.' She stared out the window. 'Eight hours north. Alliance building. Important when you barely have a military left.'

He drove down the hill, leaning against the roll of the car as they cornered the hairpins. Harry chatted away to himself in the back.

The sun caught her thick hair, glistening off the glossy black strands. He put his hand on her thigh and she put hers on top of his.

An hour later, she stepped into a cab.

One week later, Jack was driven by a government car onto the apron at Essendon airport. He jumped out of the car before it stopped, and ran up the ramp of the cavernous C-17 military cargo plane. Two medics were stood over a mobile intensive care bed, unhooking the oxygen lines off the patient.

Jack ran to the bed and gripped the hand of his wife.

Gemma.

Strapped to the gurney in an induced coma, breathing tube down her throat, eyes taped shut and blood leaking in viscous streams from both ears.

16

THE RADIO OPERATOR COWERED AS HE WATCHED KAYNE absorb the radio message. Kayne slammed the encrypted comms handset onto its mount. The desk bounced, sending pens and a coffee cup flying onto the lino floor. The radio operator flinched.

Jess turned from her operations map, hands on hips. Kayne closed his eyes and rubbed the back of his neck.

'Twelve KIA. Four tanks. Two trucks. All gone. The Brigade commissar has been found.'

'Okay. Let's get him debriefed,' said Jess.

'They found half of him, Jess.'

'Oh,' she said. 'They don't commit forces like that for no reason. Maybe a feint. PR coup? Reinforcement from the west?'

Kayne rubbed his temples. 'Outrider exfil?'

Jess bit her lip. 'Well, he got Stevie Adams. Now a commissar. What would you do?' she said.

Kayne slammed both his hands on the table. 'I would run. So we find him. We run a targeting operation on Dunne when he spikes on our networks.'

Jess watched him.

He wiped his mouth, walked over to the battle map pinned to the corkboard – a 1980s tourist map of Australia with a cartoon koala reminding people to pick up their rubbish. Kayne traced his finger along the vertical border between Victoria and South Australia, then traced a line south through the Sandy Desert to the 100-metre-high limestone cliffs of the Great Australian Bight, down to the Southern Ocean and the freight train waves that pounded those cliffs.

He tapped his finger along the vertical border area. Jess knew he was thinking hard when he did that.

'If that was an Outrider exfil, what land options would they have? Not many. Maybe the train line from the Pilbara, but unlikely. Too much coverage,' he said.

He tapped his finger at the Nullarbor Crossing.

A stretch of desert along the cliffs of the Southern Ocean that connected west with east.

'Here. This was used as a meeting point for Resistance supply runs when the invasion began. Truck, air and boats shifted supplies from the West.'

Kayne slammed his hand on the border.

'Dunne. He's a Perth boy. Betcha he's headed West. Or someone from the West is comin' for him.'

Kayne slapped his hand down on the radio operator's shoulder. The man buckled and his headphones slid off.

'Drones up. Activate the spotter network. Cover the border to South Australia, at the Broken Hill and Ceduna entry points.' The man was nodding as he rose from his seat.

'Get the team leaders in here. Now,' Kayne said.

The operator scuttled from the room.

Kayne whipped a steel flask from his pocket, unscrewed the lid and took a long drink.

Jess stared at her brother. His bloodshot eyes danced across the map. He turned to her, nodding to himself.

'I want Jack Dunne's head in a burlap sack.'

Jess turned and headed for her quarters to pack. She could sense she was becoming the passenger on this ride.

And Jess Wilson was no passenger.

OUTRIDER

17

JUST BEFORE MIDNIGHT, THE HORSEMEN RADIOED A FAREWELL to Jack on the outskirts of Melbourne, then went radio silent as they diverted north towards Horsham.

Jack drove long into the night, and by the early dawn he and Harry were parked on a ridge over the broad wheatfield pan that straddled the South Australian border. Harry was still asleep. Leaving him to rest, Jack set up a gas burner in the dirt beside the truck and heated some water.

As the gas burner hissed away, he studied the long wedge of the Milky Way overhead. The grass sparkled with frost.

He walked to the back of the truck and pulled the release handle on the tailgate. It clicked open smoothly and lowered itself on hydraulic arms.

Jack ran his hand along the edge of the tray. It was smooth. No seams or burrs. He rapped his knuckles on the underside and felt only a low drum. He tried the whole length of the door.

All solid, no cavities.

He ran his fingers across the perspex-covered wristwatch.

Pray we don't need it.

He woke Harry up as the water boiled, then made his coffee and poured it into a thermos. They sat in the warmth of the cab and ate old ration muesli bars. Harry mixed up milk powder in a plastic bowl and fed Jack cold oats from a spoon.

'Are they still good?' Harry asked.

Jack laughed. 'Yes, they're great. Eat up.'

But Harry set the bowl aside.

'Eat,' said Jack.

'I'm not hungry.' Harry was slumped in his seat.

Jack was about to repeat himself, then saw Harry looking down at his hands.

He misses her.

He put his coffee aside and slipped his arm around his son. In his haste to get off the Hill, he hadn't checked in with his boy.

'I miss Mum.'

'Me too,' Harry whispered. 'Dad, please tell me what happened. Someone hurt her, didn't they?'

Jack took a breath.

'I'll explain everything once we get through this. Whatever happens, we're together.'

'Don't leave me, Dad.'

He pulled Harry close.

'I'm not going anywhere, I promise.'

'We're fifty kilometres from the border. For the next two or three hours we have to watch for patrols. And drones.'

'What do they look like?'

'Patrols are like us, but their cars are decked out for road combat. They have bikes, too. And they have lookouts on the roads, in the daylight.'

'They'll want the car, right?'

'They'll want everything. Car, us, all the gear.'

'They can't have it,' said Harry. 'Are they friends with the Chinese?'

'Some are. Others are purely territorial, and feral. They eat what they kill.'

Literally, Jack thought but didn't say. He had a mate who ran the border. He'd found a camp with a bone pile near a wide burn pit. A hundred bodies at least, all ages and sizes.

'They'll try to stop the car without banging it up too much. But if they think it's an Outrider, they'll destroy us. So we might have only one chance to hit them.'

Jack thought of the AI mine, concealed on the floor of the back seat. They could also call the Four Horsemen for air support. So, maybe two chances.

As the sun rose behind them, they descended the plains of the crossing point and the grassed expanses where old wheat-fields once lay. A rusted harvester sat expired in a field, its windows and doors and plough stripped. The fence posts were rotten, and a family of crows sat on the coiled wires, waiting for roadkill.

In the distance, through the shimmering glare, Jack spotted a figure on the road. He stopped the truck and got out, grabbed his binoculars and glassed the figure a mile ahead. It was a skinny man and a goat, heading west. The goat was pulling a small cart, and the man tapped its hindquarter with a stick to keep it moving.

Jack looked across the plains. There were no other roads, just open fields.

'What is it?' said Harry.

'Looks like a scavenger. Skin trader, maybe.'

He scanned the low grass near the man for lumps, movement, a flash of metal. Nothing.

Jack got back in the car and drove on.

'We'll pass, but if he's suspect, I'll search him for comms gear.'

'Is he a bad one?'

'Probably not. But he might be able to reach the ones who are.'

Jack covered the mile in good time, and steered wide of the man as he passed.

The man raised his hand in a wave.

Jack eyed him through the window. A tooth or two buried in a grey beard. Filthy dreadlocked hair tied in a green kerchief. Feet and legs wrapped in leather strips. Old shorts and a ragged flannelette shirt, chalky with road dirt.

Jack travelled another thirty metres then slammed on his brakes. Harry stared at his father.

'Get in my side,' he told Harry as he stepped out of the car and moved the seat forward.

The man had stopped walking and stepped away from his goat, holding his hands out to the sides. Jack kept his eyes on the man as he spoke.

'Keep the car in gear. If anything happens, drive two kilometres. Take the carbine and head out into the grass and build a hide. Make a fishhook turn and watch your tracks. I'll find you.'

'Okay,' said Harry.

Jack slammed the door shut and drew his pistol in one movement. As he strode towards the man, he scanned the low grass. The old man had stooped, his arms still held wide.

Jack flicked the safety off his pistol.

He stopped five metres from the old man, regarding him. Flies drank from each corner of his eyes. Blackheads bunched across his cheekbones and his red nose. His knees bulged out from his thin legs. A huge wart on his forehead, grey hair protruding from its crown. A leather bladder of water with a metal screw cap hung from his side.

He was a road trader. This man was no fighter, and Jack saw no shrewdness in his eyes.

The old man gestured to the cart.

Not turning away from the old man, Jack walked to the cart, which was just the flat bed of an old wheelbarrow resting on two cracked and patched-up mountain bike wheels. A pile of skins sat in a tight bundle atop it. Blue and green blow-flies swarmed over the pile, and Jack was assailed by the choking stench of the skins. A decent-sized kangaroo skin could buy you half a pound of flour these days. The enemy had whittled the population down, seeking their tough hide for uniform textiles.

Jack pulled the skins up, one at a time, in search of a handset or a walkie-talkie.

Weapons, he could manage.

Comms, he could not.

Comms brought patrols. Drones. He ran his hands into the wallaby pouches and over the goat skins. A sheet of white maggots pattered off one of the skins onto a roo hide, writhing in protest under the sunlight. Jack held up the flesh side of a kangaroo skin.

'Not dried?'

The man shook his head.

Jack flopped the skin back onto the pile and gestured down the road.

'Anyone ahead?'

The man shook his head. His matted grey hair ruffled in the wind.

As Jack walked back to the car, the old man didn't move, standing rigid with his hands gripped together at his groin.

Jack shoved his hand into the dash and produced a gold coin.

'What did he say?' said Harry.

'All good,' said Jack.

He strode back to the man and extended his hand, the thick gold coin wedged between his fingers. Jack felt the man's cracked, bony skin as they shook. He held one finger up to his lips.

The man nodded in agreeance, and when Jack released his hand the man looked at his keep and back at Jack again, then back at his keep, which he held in two hands as though it was

104

too heavy to carry. His lips parted in a smile, his two teeth protruding awkwardly from his gums.

He grunted at Jack, then stooped, trying to kneel, and reached for Jack's hand, but Jack was already walking back to the car. He looked back at the man in the driver's side mirror. Harry put the car into park and shuffled to the passenger side as Jack slid back into his seat.

'What'd he say, Dad?'

Jack didn't answer. Something wasn't right.

He adjusted the rear-view mirror and watched the man whack the goat to get it moving again.

Jack exhaled. He checked the road ahead, put the car in drive and pulled off the shoulder onto the bitumen, taking a final look at the man as he receded in the mirror.

The old man was reaching under the wheelbarrow.

Jack looked again.

He was upright now, tapping his stick at the goat's behind.

Jack slammed on the brakes and Harry lurched forward in his seat.

'What is it?'

Jack watched the man, now a hundred metres away.

He swung the truck around and drove back towards the man.

'You leave something?' Harry said.

Still not answering, Jack skidded to a stop in front of the man and was out of the car before it had come to a stop, his carving knife in his hand. He scanned the sky in all directions.

Nothing.

'Harry, run a drone check,' he called back.

Jack raised the carving knife and held it to the man's face. 'Did you call us in?'

The old man's eyes were wide and he held both his hands up, cowering.

Keeping his gaze on the old man, Jack grabbed the stack

of skins by the far corner and peeled them off the cart. They flopped to the bitumen. Maggots writhed over the wooden boards of the cart, and Jack ran his hand over the surface. One of the boards had a semi-circle finger notch carved into the end. He shoved his index finger into it and yanked the false board clear, revealing a recess beneath. In the recess was a shining new two-way radio the size of a compact mobile phone. All black, with a Huawei logo.

Jack felt the colour drain from his face.

The old man stared back at him.

Jack held the phone to his face.

'Authenticate.'

The old man leaned forward and spoke into the phone in a clear, calm voice. 'Authenticate: Bravo Seven Niner.'

Jack held the phone up to the man so he could watch both at the same time, and clicked through the messages.

He cocked his head to one side and exhaled. 'You . . .'

The man did not flee.

Jack swung the carving knife hard into the man's side. The blade sunk between the man's ribs and with one pull, Jack severed the man's heart.

He collapsed in a pile of rags beside his wheelbarrow, an awful hissing noise escaping his body.

The goat started, and trotted off, dragging the now empty cart behind it.

Jack ran back to the car, sheathing the knife as he went. His blood thundered in his ears.

He held the phone out to Harry, realising too late that the trader's blood was all over his hands.

'Burn it,' he said, snatching his hand back as soon as Harry took the phone.

Harry flinched slightly, but said nothing. He leapt from the car and ran to the side of the road, where he doused the phone with a diesel fuel caddy and set it alight.

Jack had his binoculars out, scanning the sky. Nothing. Blue expanse.

Harry threw the jerry in the back as the phone was incinerated.

'Was he a spotter?'

'Yes.' Jack passed the binos to Harry.

Harry scanned the northern ridgelines.

You're in a spot now.

They climbed into the car and Jack slammed it into gear and hit the accelerator.

'I knew it when I seen him walking. He was scared,' Harry said.

Jack didn't answer, he was gunning the car towards the tree line on the far side of the scrub pan, kilometres away.

Towards the rising sun, a long ochre plume of dust rose from the earth, heading towards the main road.

A raiding party.

Jack pointed. 'Helmet on. They're coming.'

18

'OVER THERE.' HARRY WAS POINTING OUT THE WINDOW TO where he'd spotted some high ground – a low mound of dirt in the dry grasslands.

He knew high ground was defendable.

'It's not high, but it's okay,' Jack agreed.

The dust plume of the pursuers was billowing higher and thicker off their right flank, the dawn light catching the bloom of red dust. There had to be at least three or four trucks. Maybe some bikes.

Harry put his helmet on and pulled his M4 from the wheel well as Jack gunned the truck towards the tree line, moving so fast that the car aerial was bent almost backwards and the car seemed to float across the bitumen. The diesel motor was howling in top gear.

'When we stop, get two rockets. Go to the high ground. Don't wait for me.'

Harry pulled the sling of one rocket launcher over his shoulder, then took a second green tube and placed it in his lap. He tugged at the cover pin but it wouldn't budge.

'Dad.'

'Push the latch down and pull the safety bail forward.'

Harry yanked the cover pin out, bashing his knuckles on the rear of the tube as he did. He slid the tube covers off the rocket, extended the tube a half-length and checked that the safety tab sat home.

Blood flowed from Harry's grazed knuckles.

Jack reached into the side door and pulled the sling of the binos over his head without taking his eyes off the road.

'Get my earpiece from the centre console,' he said.

Harry retrieved a Bluetooth earpiece with a microphone bar and wedged it into Jack's left ear.

Jack knew there was no support available, but still he sent a contact report to Resistance HQ on the Hill.

'Outrider 11. Troops in contact. Stand-by.'

'Outrider 11, copy, troops in contact. We have your location. Nil support available. Advise once complete,' came the garbled radio call.

'Copy,' said Jack 'Switch to local network.' The earpiece beeped twice. Through the local network, he could speak to his weapon systems.

Jack was now parallel with the low hill, less than a kilometre off his flank. He decelerated and looked for an off-road exit or service road.

'I see two bikes. Trucks, too.' Harry reported.

'How many?' There was an edge to Jack's voice.

'Three.'

Five vehicles, plus their passengers. These were not ratios that favoured Jack, unless he could hit them from a flank.

As the vehicle slowed, Jack saw a break in the flat ground across a grass field that led to a copse of trees.

'Start counting and tell me when they turn off the road.'

Jack pulled the wheel left and guided the car through the field.

Harry counted aloud. 'One potato, two potato, three potato.'

Dead grass whipped the bumper. Jack sat high in his seat, looking for tree stumps and boulders that could rip the differential off the truck. He checked his speed and pulled the wheel down to the left, accelerating hard through the turn. Harry had one arm on the side handle, bracing himself.

'. . . eight potato, nine potato . . .'

The car was lurching and bouncing over ramps and bumps. Jack accelerated, pushing the truck to 150 kms, and stole a glance towards the low hill. A burn pile of dead bracken and branches sat at the top. He was circling the base of the mound; he needed to put it between him and his pursuers.

As he turned, he noticed a narrow tree line with a gap in it.

'Fifteen . . . Dad, they turned. I can see the bikes. Trucks are behind them.'

About thirty metres a second, for fifteen seconds. 450 metres.

Between the banksia scrub there was a flash of a pale gravel track in the low ground.

'Road!' Harry saw it first. It was a road alright, an exit route with concealment. Maybe even cover from fire.

Jack changed course and swung the car towards the track. As he approached the tree line, he dropped his speed by half and navigated through the tall banksias.

'Careful,' said Harry.

Jack was swinging the wheel left and right to dodge the tree trunks, each as thick as a man's leg. One banksia stood between them and the road; there was no way around it. Jack slowed to a near halt, then ran the roo bar into the tree and accelerated. The engine groaned and shook as banksia cones battered the roof. The truck lurched forward, and Jack reversed a touch. The tree crashed over the track, a root ball of earth and red rock appearing at its base. Jack accelerated forward, but clipped the root ball with his wheel. There was a crunch under the driver's side, then grinding and squealing. Jack's heart leapt. The steering wheel was pulling right.

'The CV joint.' Jack's mouth was dry.

He accelerated, but the axle sounded like there was a handful of scrap metal in the wheel joint.

'Get ready,' he told Harry.

Jack ground the car down the gravel. It was an old service track, narrow and long overgrown. Thick tree branches hung low over the road, battering the windshield.

As he pushed the car harder, the smell of burning metal filled the cab, coming from the dashboard, where three warning lights beeped.

Jack slowed and rounded the last corner.

Ahead was a low cut-out in the earth, a channel as high as a man on each side and wide and long enough to hold a small convoy. Jack rolled into the cut-out valley and climbed out of the car. The dust plume had just cleared the trees. Jack pointed at the dead tree pile at the top of the hill. It was close. You could run there in half a minute.

'They're on the road. Go!'

Jack cocked his ear and held his breath, listening to the howl of the bikes through the scrub. Harry stood, laden with gear, M4 and rocket launcher slung, rocket cradled in his arms like a baby. His helmet was askance and oversized. He looked like an overburdened school kid.

Jack pointed. 'Go! Stay low.'

Harry turned and ran, M4 bouncing on his butt, rocket tube in each arm.

Jack turned to the car. He slung his M4, then put his hand to his earpiece and squeezed the arm again. It beeped. He reached into the back of the car and hauled up the AI mine, a shard of fake basalt the size of a large bowling ball. As he strode ahead of the car holding it in both arms, he spoke into his earpiece.

'Authorise: Jack Dunne, Outrider 11.'

'Access authorised. How can I help?' a female voice came through his earpiece.

'Pursuing force. Vehicles. Possible drone. Send vector.'

'Target heading 130 degrees. Speed sixty kilometres an hour. Fourteen seconds to merge plot. No drone detected. You want some firing solutions?'

Jack placed the mine in a low gutter, then grabbed a dead branch and placed it in front.

'Target all personnel in pursuit package.'

'Copy, targeting all personnel. Lethal or non-lethal?'

'Lethal.'

'Copy. Lethal.'

Jack looked back, gauging the distance between the mine and the car. The mine was fifteen metres away, and it was darker in colour than the road, but it looked passable. The bikes were loud now, accelerating down the straights and quieter in the thickets. He turned and saw Harry at the base of the hill, moving low and fast.

He ran to the back of the car.

Jack pulled the trailer tray down, hauled out a long pelican case and unclipped it.

'Advise targeting parameters,' said the voice.

'None.'

Jack opened the case. Inside was the disassembled 0.50 calibre rifle, with a multicam spray job. He lifted out the lower receiver and extended the bipod legs. He placed it across the tray, pulled the bolt back, and inserted the heavy barrel into place and locked in the retaining pins. The rifle was enormous, as long as Harry was tall. Jack pulled a thick suppressor tube out and slid it in his back jeans pocket. He lifted out a large magazine. Long brass rounds sat in the clip; the top bullet had three white bands on it and a black nose.

Jack spoke and scanned the trail as he worked the weapon.

'Actually, one parameter: enemy less than twelve years old. Exclude.'

'Copy.'

He inserted the magazine and yanked the cocking lever, inserting a round in the chamber. His hand was still covered in dark blood.

'Initiate on my order.'

'Copy.'

He ran a mental check. *Binoculars. Fifty cal. Check.*

Jack moved to the front of the car and pulled his jarrah tomahawk from the door well, shoving the handle in the back of his belt as he ran towards Harry. His son was now on the side of the low hill; he could see him in the grass, his helmet bobbing as he ran. Jack sprinted to catch him.

His feet sailed through the grass and he felt light. The early sun lit the golden stems, and for a second it was hide and seek in the lupin fields in Western Australia. Tickling Harry.

I can't protect him anymore. This is life or death.

Jack looked left as he ran across the thick grass, legs jelly from the adrenaline. The top of a truck could be seen in the distance. Chrome bar work. Spotlights. A man stood on the tray with a long rifle.

Jack stooped low with the rifle cradled in his arms and trotted uphill towards the dead tree pile.

Harry had circled the pile and Jack saw him kneel and hold his arm up to him.

'Down,' Jack said.

Their own track ran in a circular pattern from the road around the back of the hill. Locked into following the tracks of their car, the assault party would be moving with their flanks in full view of the hill.

Jack was labouring hard in the morning air. The rifle was heavy.

'Vehicle types?' he asked the AI.

'Two KTM 250 motorcycles. Three F250 trucks.'

Jack had propped at a low mound with basalt boulders leading up from the ground. Kneeling, he stood the rifle vertical on its butt, then pulled the suppressor from his pants and locked it into place. He opened the bipod legs, long perforated sheets of metal.

'Get the binos ready.'

Harry already had the bino up, checking the raiding party.

Jack laid the rifle down and checked the scope field of view.

'I see 'em, Dad. Bikes,' Harry hissed.

'Swap. Get the lead one in your sights.'

Jack rolled to the side and took the binoculars off Harry. Harry crawled over and hefted the stock of the Barrett rifle, groaning under the weight as he pulled the stock into his shoulder. Jack lay next to him, propped on his elbows as he scanned. Harry struggled to sit the butt in his shoulder, but eventually found a firing position.

Jack peered over the dead grass and glassed the road.

There.

They were flitting down the service road, long trail bikes, long-range fuel tanks. Leather saddlebags. A tall pillion seat, a small adult behind the driver, gripping the side seat. The driver wore jeans torn through the knees, work boots with the steel caps showing. Bandana dark red from dust. Small swimming goggles on his eyes. Leather knife sheaths.

Their trucks would be right behind them.

Jack was sure they would anticipate his ambush. They would see them. But the lead biker pointed at Jack's truck.

They took the bait.

The truck was now their focus.

The bikes were moving too fast for Harry to hit them with standard rounds. But Jack had put the guided rounds in the weapon.

He trained the black crosshair of the binoculars on the lead rider as he weaved down the service road. Jack pushed a recessed button on the side of the binos. *Range 0240m* appeared in red digits. The text blinked once and then locked in place.

'Lead bike, stand-by.'

Harry keyed the safety, put the lead biker in the scope view.

'Lead bike, I have.'

'Fire.'

Harry squeezed the trigger.

The weapon chugged and through the binos Jack saw the distortion of the air, the spiral swirl of haze as the round arced towards the bikes. The trajectory was way off. The round was headed to miss the bike by many lengths. Jack winced and kept the crosshair on the rider. The round swung hard to the left as it hit the top of its arc, as though pulled by a magnet. A burst of sparks flew off the bike and then the driver was gone.

The passenger, still clinging to the seat, was alone on the bike. It swerved, bucking the pillion rider off, his limbs at full extension as he barrelled head over foot into the scrub.

'Damn,' Jack muttered, impressed.

Harry was silent.

Jack switched to the second bike. It was closing on the covered draw where Jack's car had stopped, the AI mine lurking on the roadside.

A compact man and his pillion braked hard, bike skidding on the gravel. They had seen the bike ahead crash and were scanning the scrub for the riders. Jack clicked the binos on the centre of the driver's back.

'Bike two.'

'Bike two, I have.'

The first truck appeared on the road. It was a battered F250 with monster truck wheels and a flat tray bed with no sides. There were shark teeth hand-painted on the doors. The man standing in the tray pointed his hunting rifle towards Jack's car.

Jack canted the binos on the passenger side door. A thick, tattooed arm rested on the side of the window. He pointed the crosshair on the passenger door and hit the key. *0245m.*

'Switch. Truck one, side door.'

'Truck one, side door.'

'Fire.'

The rifle bucked in Harry's shoulder when he squeezed the trigger.

The bullet arced towards the door and was still climbing when it struck true. A hole punched through the side door and the arm flicked like a whip and disappeared. There was a yellow flash inside the cab, then the truck accelerated, the hunter at the top cowering from the branches. The car drove into the banksia trees at full pace; the rear tray bucked, throwing the shooter clear over the cab.

The truck sat with its wheels spinning in the gravel, a dead man on the accelerator.

'Good hit,' said Jack. The smell of cordite settled across their position.

The second bike sped forward, the ambush now evident.

'Bike two?'

'No.'

Jack knew they were headed into what they assumed was the safety of cover, where his truck was parked.

Two more modified trucks screamed ahead, past the commotion. Bare matte steel chassis. Stripped back. The drivers wore leather helmets and kerchiefs over their mouths, like demented bikers. Roofless, doorless cars. Rusted olive fuel jerrys tied to the rear tray. Each truck had a mounted heavy machine gun and a gunner on the tray.

The trucks and the bike went into the draw and out of view. The stuck vehicle was no longer accelerating and Jack could hear shouting from the draw.

His microphone came to life. The basalt rock of death was speaking in her soft Sydney North Shore accent.

'All targets in range. Fire on your command.'

Jack put the binos down. 'Clear hot.'

'Copy. Firing now.'

A series of low crumps came from the scrub, and the banksias shimmered in the blast. A flock of white cockatoos lifted from the banksias above a pall of black smoke. Jack raised the binos again and scanned. Everything was still. Jack had tried to count the number of blasts.

'How many?' said Jack.

'I counted four,' said Harry, scanning from his scope.

'I got three.'

There was a beep in his headset, then the polite female voice again.

'Battle damage assessment: Stand-by.'

'What'd it say, Dad?'

'It's looking.'

They waited.

Black smoke still billowed up from the draw. A brown wedge-tailed eagle circled above, watching the grass.

'Eight KIA. One WIA, critical, barotrauma, rapid pulse and arterial bleed, left leg. Casualty unarmed. Three antipersonnel rounds remain.'

'Maintain overwatch,' said Jack.

A small black tube with a propeller climbed into the air and hovered fifty metres overhead.

'Air and ground approaches are clear.'

'Let's go,' said Jack.

They started down the hill.

Through black smoke, they approached the nearest vehicle, Jack saw only the torso of a bearded man beside the truck, a triangular puncture mark on his naked stomach. Jack retrieved the man's rifle and gave it to Harry, then quartered the vehicle door with his M4 up. The door had a puncture the size of a coin. The lower half of a man's arm lay in the dirt beside the car, a blue leopard tattoo on the thick wrist. Another detail scorched into Jack's mind.

He stepped forward and cleared the interior. It was an

abattoir. Brain matter and bone and hair were slathered through the cab and smeared across the dash and the windshield. A pale white dish of a skull top lay in the passenger side footwell.

'Don't look. It's a mess,' Jack said to Harry.

Harry lowered his pistol and turned to the next truck, white-faced.

With his pistol raised and Jack covering with his M4, they stalked down towards the draw.

They checked the rest of the vehicles. The firing tubes of the mine had jumped to face height and detonated in front of the cars. Their pursuers' goggles had triangular fragmentation marks in them, necks and chests collapsed.

'That's eight. Where's the wounded?'

His radio beeped. 'Wounded is fifteen metres north. Off your right shoulder.'

Jack knelt with his M4 to his shoulder and looked into the scrub, spying a pair of knees in black jeans. He stalked over. Laying in the dirt was a child, barely a teenager. Twelve or thirteen. Jack remembered the parameters he'd told the machine, and felt the weight of his choice in his gut.

Dirt tracks were raked across his face, but he had smooth skin and blonde hair. Both arms shattered. He was kicking at the earth and whipping his head from side to side, his jeans wet with red blood at his stomach.

The driver lay a few metres away in the barren soil. His right leg was missing entirely from the groin.

Jack passed his M4 to Harry, who then turned and covered the road back from the west. Jack fished a field dressing and a tourniquet out of his jacket sleeve.

He locked the tourniquet around the kid's destroyed femur and cranked it hard. The child groaned.

Jack pulled the kid's jeans open at the wound and saw the fist-sized hole in his quadricep, white sinew and lean muscle. He packed a field dressing into the hole, then wrapped the last part around his leg. The kid moaned, but his eyes stayed shut. When Jack was done, he wiped his hands on his pants, then grabbed a water bladder from the dead man and tipped some in the kid's mouth. He coughed and swallowed.

'What's your name?'

The kid opened his eyes. 'Billy.'

'Billy. Good man.'

The child watched him.

'Dad.'

'Is that your dad?' Jack pointed at the dead man with no leg. The kid didn't look over.

'He was driving.'

Jack looked back at the child. He thought for a moment and then shook his head once.

The kid was still, then he nodded.

Jack rubbed the back of his mouth with his hand, then looked the boy in the eye.

'I can bring him over.'

The boy nodded.

Jack walked to the dead man and hooked his arms under him. He was thin and light, and already a grey waxy colour. Jack dragged him over. The boy buried his head in his father's armpit. He didn't make a sound.

The only noise was the breeze in the trees and the boy still scrubbing his feet in the dirt. Tracks of blood ran from the boy's ears.

Jack knelt at the boy's side and wiped the blood away with his fingers, swatting flies off the kid's face. He put his hand on the boy's chest.

Harry was kneeling with his back to the boy, covering the road. Jack watched the child, watched his breath slowing.

The kid took a long, rattling gasp and then lay dead still. Jack looked at the two bodies, lying together in a tangled mess. He bunched his hands into fists and stood there for a

119

minute. The banksias swayed in the breeze. The eagle called above them.

Jack cut the knife off the dead man's leg, then cut the strap of the man's water bladder. He carried them to his truck and threw them in the tray.

Harry was still covering down the road. Jack turned to call to him but choked as he did. He stumbled and turned back to his truck, grasping the side with both hands and trying to breathe. His vision was a grey tunnel. Harry appeared by his side and pulled his dad towards the car door. He was talking, but Jack could only hear his heartbeat.

'Dad. We have to go. Let's go.'

19

'We'll stop here.'

Harry was driving, perched forward on the seat and peering over the wheel. The sun was high overhead. Jack was in the passenger seat. He couldn't remember what had happened after the ambush. Harry had stopped under a thick gum tree. The morning air was thin and hot and dry, and the horizon glimmered.

'Dad, I need to change the CV.'

Jack stared at him, confused.

'The axle joint, it's broken.'

Then he remembered. The trees, the ambush. The dead kid.

'I'll do it.'

Jack climbed out of the car and went to the rear, rubbing his face. He reached into the tray and pulled out a hi-lift jack. Although he couldn't remember taking it from the ambush site, he'd somehow known it was in the back of the car.

Lying in the tray beside it was the basalt rock of death.

Jack didn't remember picking up the AI mine either, but he must have. Or maybe Harry did. It still had some ammunition left, but Jack wasn't sure he could stomach using it again.

He was losing his edge, the callous shell that had protected him through so much carnage. It was breaking down, right when he, and Harry, needed it most.

Jack moved the mine from the tray to the back seat of the HiLux, out of sight. Out of mind. He sat the jack under the roo bar and wrenched the car high off the ground, then took to the wheel with a pneumatic drill.

Harry was already at the edge of the tree line, scanning the sky and the roads with the binos.

Jack lay the wheel down on a tarp, then pulled the whole metal ball of the CV out of the axle like a kebab skewer. He carried it behind a fallen log and covered it with debris, then guided the spare CV into the axle and bolted it back in. He wheeled the tyre over and heaved it up onto the mounting bolts, then used the tyre iron to lock the wheel nuts in place.

The mechanical work soothed him; he thought of nothing but the job at hand. He lowered the car off the jack, then cleaned his hands with a rag. As he did, he watched Harry, standing beneath the gum tree, scanning the fields. There was a swelling pride in his chest.

He just saved us.

Jack pondered the situation. His emotional reserves were near gone. He had seen it in Ukraine; men fainting in the trenches from stress and fear and despair. He had to keep it together.

He checked his watch. It was 9.20 am. They just lost two hours in that hellhole; it felt like two minutes.

A day ago he'd been shooting up the roundabout.

Twelve hours ago he was on the Hill, getting briefed.

Sixty hours left before the attack.

Just hold on. A bit longer.

They drove down the dirt road and tested the steering. It felt solid. Harry pulled out a bottle of water and some ration pack biscuits. With an old ration spoon, he opened a yellow tin of fruit and tipped it into Jack's mouth as he drove towards the setting sun.

'Better?'

'Yeah. Better.'

'You were gone for a bit.' Harry scraped the last bit of fruit onto the spoon and fed it to him.

'I know. Sorry.'

'I hope there's not more of them,' Harry said.

'The mines were rough. And I should've done the shooting,' Jack conceded.

'No. I like shooting.'

Jack knew what he meant.

'I kind of feel happy. I mean, not happy . . .' said Harry.

'Relieved?'

'Yeah. Relief.'

Jack looked out the window at the crows circling the edge of the wheatfield.

'Shooting our own kind.' Jack shook his head as he looked across the saltbush plains.

'They're not our kind, Dad,' said Harry.

'Yeah, true,' Jack agreed.

They drove on in silence.

Jack could see the Bight and the vast Southern Ocean off to the left, and nothing but flat road and sun and no shadows ahead. Barren red land. Orange sky. Sapphire ocean.

On the horizon, four jets, pairs, zipped over the desert towards the ocean, their shadows flitting across the Nullarbor Plain. Even from kilometres away, it was clear they were huge. They cleared the limestone cliffs, then turned and dove towards the ocean.

Jack immediately pulled over and reversed the car into a bunch of tea-trees. Working quickly, they unrolled a thermal tarp over the car, then waited. The jets popped up from the ocean and made a single pass along the highway. They flew low, shrieking across the Bight. Jack grabbed the binoculars and locked onto a jet. Matte black, a red hammer painted on the tail. He noted the honeycomb angles and sawtooth patterns of the fuselage. They were still tracking along the Bight. Probably sightseeing.

'Fighter bombers. If they had been tracking us, they would've dropped something on us already.'

Harry considered this. 'We've been lucky, Dad. That's twice now.' He looked at Jack. 'This is like a camping trip. In Hell.'

Jack laughed.

It was the first time he had laughed in weeks.

'I reckon,' he said.

They rolled up the tarp and drove on.

'We should be at Ceduna before dinnertime. From Ceduna it's one hundred kilometres to Cactus Beach. You rest; you can take over in a few hours.'

Ceduna was a throwback to the old world. Wide roads and angle parking, a colonial-era pub on the corner in the town centre, lit by a single streetlight. A pair of dogs lay on the road. There was a post office and a chip shop and a hardware store and a mechanic in tattered overalls.

Two long-haul trucks with raw lumber stacks on their trailer rattled along the crumbling street. They were followed by a prospector ute with a rooftop tent and sealed barrels of ore samples on the tray back.

Jack parked beside the other trucks on the road. Their car did not stand out; it was filthy and the gear was stowed – except for the surfboard.

'I'm gonna check for dry supplies. Stay put.'

As Jack walked into the general store, the bell over the door tinkled. The shelves were spartan. Some homemade fishing gear, hooks and nylon and old rods. Hand-poured sinkers. Cling-wrapped noodle cups. Sacks of rice and flour and salt. Old jerry cans. Some rope.

Jack picked up the dusty cup of noodles and checked the use-by date: 30 July 2027. A lifetime ago. He collected a bundle of strapping yarn and a sealed bottle of water and paid in crumpled yuan notes at the counter. The old man looked out over Jack's shoulder at the ute.

'Heading for a wave?'

Jack sensed something. He kept his eyes on the yuan bills.

'Yeah mate. Gonna take the little man to catch a wave.'

'Oh. Keep him away from that eastern front, mate.'

'You know it,' Jack lied.

'Where you drive in from?'

'Mildura. Surf's a bit better here though.'

The old man had oversized ears, red splotches on his nose. *Probably from moonshine.* He put the money into the till as he spoke.

'Local bloke saw an eighteen-footer offshore. Great white.'

'Whoa,' said Jack.

The old man glanced out the window again, his face darkening.

'Shit. Another development team.'

Jack caught sight of an armoured truck circling the roundabout. It pulled up on the verge and a team of soldiers climbed out.

'These bastards come every other week. Rationing. I'm done with it.' He shook his head.

At least on the Hill they had stock and grain and fertile land to grow their own food. Out here, it was all swept up by the Occupation.

The soldiers' weapons were slung and they wore blue hats, helmets clipped to their gear. A woman wearing a blue polo shirt climbed out of the cab.

Jack felt a curious hatred as he watched.

The soldiers stood in pairs at the roundabout, and a sedan slowed as it approached the team. The enemy soldiers spoke through the car window with stooped heads, deep nods. One soldier handed rice-paper candy to a kid on a bike. Their blue hats were a nod to the old UN peacekeeper hats, an imitation so close it was either insulting or funny.

Jack stepped out of the shop and stared at the soldiers. One had made her way to his vehicle and was rapping on Harry's window.

Jack strode towards the car, supplies in his arms. The Chinese Peacekeeper looked up at him. She was fit and attractive. Immaculate desert camouflage pants. A blue polo shirt with captain stars on the sleeve. The words 'Best Future Development Team' were emblazoned on her chest.

'Ma'am.'

She smiled at Jack. She was young – she could be a graduate student.

'Good evening, sir,' she said in fluent English.

Jack stared back at her silently.

'We want to help your community. What can we assist with in this village?'

Jack pointed down the road. 'More streetlights. My car's been broken into twice this year.'

She produced a notebook, holding it at face height, and wrote furiously, a frown on her face.

'More supplies. Dry stocks. Fuel and food. Medicine. There's no antibiotics. You took them all.'

'Our brave soldiers do need them. But thank you,' she said. 'We will do what we can. We still need to . . .'

'Ration, I know,' Jack finished for her.

He looked at Harry in the passenger seat.

'Thank you,' said Jack.

The woman opened her mouth and raised her hand, but

before she could say anything more, Jack climbed into the driver's seat and threw the noodles on Harry's lap.

'Laugh as we drive off.'

They forced a laugh as they reversed out of the car park.

As they drove into the roundabout, the pair of soldiers at the centre waved at them.

Jack raised two fingers off his steering wheel in an outback salute.

'Where did they come from?' asked Jack.

'From the north. She was tryna' look into the car,' muttered Harry.

'I know.'

Wolves in sheep's clothing.

Two enemy soldiers left the corner store with full duffel bags over their shoulders and packets of noodles in their arms.

As they cornered the pub, Jack caught sight of a two-storey wall to his right. The tallest building in Ceduna. The rest were still being rebuilt from the early bomb strikes of the '29 Invasion. The sun hit the wall, casting its glow over the painting upon it. It was a sweeping, hand-painted mural that covered the entire wall. It depicted a sprawling battlefield.

'Look. Look at that!' said Harry. 'I heard about that painting. Look at it.'

The painting depicted a pale horse with a cloaked man upon it, faceless, skeletal hands resting on the pommel. In the foreground, two armies clashed across a burning mountain, soldiers with rifles, dying men with arrows in their chest. Dogs with their heads buried in the guts of the wounded. Battle tanks with red sickles on them, crushed soldiers under the tracks. A dozen bombers in the sky, red sickles on their tails, releasing a trail of bombs. Axes and spears and broad shields made from quilted and riveted metal panelling. In the centre of the mural an angel in clean robes, thick metallic struts as forearms, rose above the fray. Its immense wings arched high, touching at their tips, as it hauled a Resistance soldier up to the heavens. The soldier was a boy, bare-chested but with boots and fatigue pants. The boy's arms hung limp at his sides, pale. The angel's skeletal metal hand rested across his heart, the other on his naked stomach.

On the edge of the mural, a woman in white robes sat with the troops atop a white horse. She had a long ponytail and two wings on her back, one broken, a fine-pointed bone protruding from it. A carbine rested in her lap. She poured forth a clay bowl into the air.

Jack slowed the car and Harry stared, open-mouthed, as they passed. Jack wiped the sweat from his hands onto his shirt.

'I heard about that painting too. Never thought I'd see it.'

'Is that what happened overseas?'

'No. It's the Battle of Wilson's Prom.'

'Really? Is that what you saw?'

'No. It was nothing like that.'

It was worse.

Jack had barely escaped. They'd been shelled to pieces in the scrub. Life, death, angels and demons, all on one battlefield.

20

JESS STEPPED UP TO THE FIRING RANGE MOUND NEXT TO THE rest of the Cranbourne Boys. Shooters were firing in groups, checking their rifle zeros out to 300 metres. A few shooters nearby pulled reload drills in pairs. She unslung her AK-47 and squatted down on one knee, then flipped the safety off and rested the red dot on the centre of the man-sized target 300 metres away.

She squeezed off five rounds, put her rifle down and checked the zero with binoculars. The cluster of rounds had all struck centre of target.

She didn't need to check her zero. It was more of a ritual. If Jack Dunne was tagged in the next forty-eight hours, they would swoop.

Failing a strike on Jack Dunne would make them cannon fodder for a clearance on the Hill. Jess didn't want that.

A hand slapped down on her shoulder.

'Stand up,' said Kayne.

She stood up on the mound and slipped her shooting glasses onto her head.

'Good news: it's Dunne. Bad news: our intercept team is dead. Pursuit cars, bikes. The spotter had his heart cut out.'

Jess stared back down the range. 'We're losing control.'

Kayne stood, arms folded, watching her. 'A second team arrived too late. They found blast injuries linked to an AGI mine.'

Jess shook her head. 'At least we know it's him. Principal will be happy with you.'

Kayne leaned into her ear. 'He wants to see us. In the diner.'

Jess turned to him. He stank of whiskey.

'No more chances. We'll have to do him ourselves,' she said.

Jess replaced the magazine on her rifle and stormed off the mound.

21

THE CAR HUMMED ACROSS THE FINAL SECTIONS OF THE South Australian coast, and in the distance Jack could see the peninsula that housed their destination. They should get there with enough time to have a cup of tea before bed. Early the next morning, a new visitor would be with them.

They drove into the setting sun.

'You ever been here?' said Harry.

'Yeah. I drove your mum across here before you were born. Back to Perth.'

'Really?' Harry perked up.

'We stopped and surfed at all the bays, camped on the beach. Not a car in sight. Nothing but stars and dingoes.'

Harry was silent for a while.

'What happened to Mum?'

Jack had always told his son she'd been hurt in a work accident. But Harry already suspected it had been by design, and that his father knew more about it.

His son wasn't seven anymore. He had grown up fast in this world. Jack took a long breath.

'Havana Syndrome,' he said.

A weight lifted off his chest.

131

Harry considered this. 'Habana what?'

'Likely Chinese or Russian intelligence. They had weapons that could make people sick. Through walls. They called it Havana Syndrome.'

'How?'

'Microwaves. They used microwaves to make people sick. Like a death ray almost.'

Jack could still see the black and white MRI film in his hand, her symmetrical brain tissue riven with white blotches like a Rorschach. You didn't need to be a John Hopkins graduate to know it was bad. She had the brain of a heavyweight boxer. They had held hands and wept in front of the doctor.

Her death was slow, agonising and unfair.

They had told Harry she'd been injured at work. He was too young to know that his mother was an elite human intelligence officer who had been struck down while recruiting intelligence sources. It was murder in slow motion; she took four years to die. It wasn't long before Jack found himself wishing they'd cut her neck in a dark alley. It would have spared her so much pain.

'Yeah. Someone got her.'

Harry stared out the window a long time. Jack heard him sniffing. He put his hand on his son's leg. 'You have to remember, she was a warrior. Very good at her job. She got a medal for it.'

Harry nodded.

'She couldn't kick a footy, but you should have seen her use a rifle.'

Harry smiled and rubbed his eyes. 'And she saved kids.'

'That's right. She rescued forty-two of them in Kabul.'

'How'd she save so many?'

'Kids are pretty small.'

Harry stared out the window, wiping his eyes. Jack reached across and rubbed his bony neck.

'We have to stick together. She knew what was coming down the pike. And here it is.'

'I'll fight. Like you.'

'Oh, Harry. You've done plenty already,' said Jack. 'It's not a life you want.'

Truth was, Jack had lost his nerve.

He had to help save the Hill. This asset might be their only chance. If he did that, he'd earn their freedom.

As night fell, they drove into the limestone ridges over Cactus Beach.

Jack was exhausted. It was their second night on the road and it had been a tough day. As they drove into Cactus Beach it was pitch black, save for the streak of the Milky Way thrown across the black canvas of the night. They parked the car in a limestone bay and set up a double swag. Jack put a kettle on to boil and Harry sat on the tailgate wrapped in a blanket, looking out over the water as his dad set up for the night.

Jack pulled his surfboard off the rack. The first fin he screwed in was pointing backwards. He was so tired he felt like he was half dreaming. He screwed three fins in, then checked the leg rope for wear. Then he slid the board back into its pouch and mounted it to the roof rack. Everything save for the swag was tied down in case they needed to leave in a hurry.

They sat together and pulled the blanket up over them both, and they drank tea and chewed on some jerky as they faced the rolling ocean, taking in the crash of the waves and the salt in the air. *Time to tell Harry.*

'I'll be out before first light. We're gonna have a visitor with us for the ride home.'

'No way. We're taking them back to the Hill?'

'Yes. They can bring some good weapons, the Yanks.'

'Alright,' said Harry. He cupped his tea with both hands and whispered into it. 'Dad?'

'Yeah.'

'What would you do if you knew who killed Mum?'

'I don't know.'
'Would you kill them?'
Jack thought for a minute.
'Yes.'

22

THE BOOMING REPORTS OF THE WAVES PICKED UP IN THE dawn. Jack woke once, but the steady drum of the waves slipped him back into sleep. The sound of the waves merged with the crumping explosions of a grad rocket salvo and Jack was crouching in a trench. He could smell the wet, rich soil of Ukraine. A dozen Abrams tanks churned into a tree line that intersected Crimea's yellow wheat plains. The low whir of the turbine motors could be heard from the trench line Jack occupied with Dyson. Dyson stood with Jack, long-haired with broad, thick shoulders. A handful of grim-faced fighters filed past with their rocket launchers and machine guns over their shoulders.

Jack turned and followed Dyson down the Russian trench into their makeshift command dugout. Dyson put both arms on the trench walls and hoisted himself over a dead Russian who had been stomped into the mud, whose body armour and badges had already been looted. Artillery screeched overhead, heading 600 metres into Russian territory.

The command post was the size of a large phone booth with thick pine logs for overhead cover. Four Ukrainians stood there passing around cigarettes and lighting them for each other.

The stink of the place. Dyson wore rugged jeans and a checked flannel shirt with the sleeves cut at his huge biceps. His body armour was streamlined and clean, and his helmet was in his gloved hand.

'We just blasted a 120-metre-wide hole in the minefield. First units are rolling off the line of departure, and will make the first trench line in fifteen minutes.

'Pack your swimmers. We'll be bathing in the Black Sea by sundown.'

The soldiers grinned to each other.

'We'll move soon. Expect a counterattack at the first line.'

Dyson and Jack were part of a fully covert and deniable deployment of AUKUS Special Ops soldiers, sent to lead the Ukrainian counteroffensive. It was heavy lifting. No diplomatic cover, no NATO support, and no hope if they were caught. Orphans at war.

Neither Jack nor Dyson had slept in the last forty-eight hours. They had been riding on Abrams tanks as they thrust their way one hundred kilometres deep into Russian-occupied Crimea.

The soldiers stood tight around Dyson's map, almost oblivious to the crumping of heavy artillery and mortars. Earth shook from the heavy Ukrainian pine logs overhead. The Ukrainians were staring at the map.

'This low ground.' Dyson pointed a blade of grass at a tree line on the folded map. 'I have a feeling the reserve is tucked in there.'

Dyson was so tired he was slurring his words.

The men were all nodding. Dyson returned the map to his back pocket and rubbed his enormous square jaw. Then he nodded, resigned.

'Get back to your teams. Mount up in the Bradleys. Stand-by.'

The men filtered out of the bunker. When they were gone, Dyson turned to Jack.

'There's now "medium" confidence.'

Dyson rubbed his chin. He never did that. He was always calm to the point of silliness. The Ukrainian Special Ops teams called him 'The Sphinx'.

Jack felt a bolt of fear. He held his body armour chest straps with both hands. Rumours of a plan for massive retaliation had recently spiked in the mobile phone intercepts.

'A human intelligence source said three artillery batteries are being escorted to the front, in self-propelled artillery. With a commissar. Saw mechanics fitting lead lining in the ammo bays of the armoured cars.'

'Still. Not conclusive, right?'

'Detection shielding material? Stops gamma rays penetrating the nuke housing. You can't detect the weapon.'

Dyson unslung his rifle and put his hand on Jack's shoulder.

'It's been an honour.' He chuckled, and Jack laughed, then shook his head.

The absurdity of war. The carnival of human torture.

Dyson left the trench and Jack followed, and as they cleared the parapet, Jack realised that no artillery had hit their position for a full minute.

Just as the thought struck him, a pair of F-16s flew low overhead and dumped a stream of flares. A concussion thump belted out and both planes pointed to the ground at the same time, as though they'd been switched off. A streak of dust or smoke poured from the fuselage as they dove.

They plummeted to earth, screeching.

A ball of fire, like a sun, appeared over the front of their position. The light was blinding, the blast thunderous. The world went silent. Jack could see through Dyson's silhouette, black rods inside red human flesh. Dyson turned, his shirt on fire as the sun expanded over the battlefield. The tree trunks were smoking and sprouting flames. Only Jack's shoulder and arm were outside of Dyson's shadow, and his clothes burst into flames.

Dyson turned to Jack and threw him to the earth, taking the force of the blast.

'Open your mouth,' he shouted. *Equalise pressure, protect the lungs.*

Then the shockwave hit them, a full body slap. The sun abated and the fire consumed their whole position, including the spot where Dyson had Jack pinned beneath him.

23

A WAVE BOOMED OFFSHORE AND SEEMED TO RATTLE THE limestone walls of the bay. Jack jolted awake in the tray of the car and sat up. The pounding waves told him he was not in Crimea, but his neck and shoulder still felt burning hot. His heart was running away with itself.

A climbing moon lit the limestone breakers and the hewed timber shelters. Booming waves. A dog somewhere. Orion falling to meet the north horizon. Jack stood in the tray and gazed up at the endless stars, then squatted and put his hand on Harry, bundled in the swag next to him. Jack felt for his chest moving, then reached down and found his warm face. He kissed his hair.

His mind turned to the mission. It was 0440.

He had to be at the precise RV point by 0530.

The pick-up could be dangerous if they were spotted. He stood up in the tray and watched the swell, eyeing the pockets either side of the bay where water was rushing back out to the ocean. He would ride in these streams out to the pick-up point.

The swell was building. Jack could clearly see the silver crests, and hear the thump and thrash of the cold water. He stepped off the tray, filled the kettle and started the gas burner.

He scooped tea leaves into the water, then when it boiled, he poured the tea into an enamel cup and let it cool. He slipped his board out of the dusty cover and weighed it in his arms, breathing in the coconut wax and salt. Bumps from pit stops in the Mentawai Islands were etched into the fibreglass rails; the last trip he took before the war. A black and red spiral spread across the face of the board, in bright contrast to its yellowing body.

Jack held the rails and gauged its heft. It was a huge board. Seven-foot-two, a big wave 'gun', with a curved rocker, and more than two and a half inches thick. It had a thick timber stringer down its centre and a triple coat of glass so it would hold together under the fifteen-foot guillotines barrelling out of the Southern Ocean. It had kept him afloat when he was at full strength: a hundred and ten kilos and muscled. He was lighter now, and he knew it would be a struggle to get beyond the break without the power in his arms.

Soon, the swell was at twelve feet, with the occasional fourteen-foot set. Jack had spotted the boiling rip alongside the limestone point. He'd let that pull him out, then he could sit on the shoulder and watch the freight train waves rattle into the bay.

He ran a wax shard over the board, working on the lumps to raise them, but it was small and too old, sand grains all through it. The hollow scratch of the wax on the board was an old memory. But today wasn't about surfing. Today, he had cargo to collect.

He inspected the lanyard and threaded it through the rear plug, then examined the full length of the leg rope. He held the rubber close to his eyes, feeling it for fractures. It was stiff, but intact.

Speckling grey light dawned out to the east, under a black cloud front. Perfect when you needed shielding from drones.

'Keep coming,' he said. Stillness fell. The wind was gone,

and the sucking low pressure was over them. The calm before the war.

Jack stepped into the stiff old wetsuit Jimbo had packed for him. When he stuck his arm in the sleeve, the shoulder joint ripped. He tore off the sleeve at the shoulder seam and slipped into the rest of the suit, then sat sipping his tea while he watched the red fingers of dawn reach above the cloud front.

Harry stirred and sat up in his swag, blinking. 'I had a dream.'

'I bet you did.' Jack turned to him. 'You okay?'

'Yup.' Harry rubbed his eyes. Jack handed him the enamel mug and he held it with both hands.

'It's got sugar.'

'Sweet.' Harry blew on the tea, then took a sip.

Jack pointed to the horizon. 'We wait for cloud cover and then we walk down. You stay under the cliff wall. Don't come out for me, no matter what. I don't care if a great white has me – stay under the cliff, under the blanket.' Jack pointed out the cave he could sit in. 'When I come back in, there'll be two of us. Then we exfil back home.'

'I knew it. Who is it?'

'You'll see.'

'Giddy-up,' said Harry. 'I bet you won't even get out the back.'

'Watch me.' Jack smiled. 'Grab the binos.'

He threw his tea dregs out and tucked the board under his arm, then the pair of them walked down the sand path to the edge of the bay, limestone cliffs towering either side.

Jack knew the asset would have been guided out of the sub by now, probably with a dive team. He would have a motorised dive propulsion vehicle, a motor the size of a small bar fridge that would allow him to transit to his RV point. Then, at a couple of metres depth he would dress in his 'cover' outfit:

wetsuit and surfboard, just before surfacing. All any drone would see was two surfers in the water.

Jack looked skyward. Nothing. There were black clouds overhead and lightning was cracking down to the water, way off to the south, against purple smudges of rainfall. A grey object sat on the horizon. A boat, a long way out. He kept his eyes pinned to the grey spot.

Harry passed the binos.

It was a grey patrol boat, heading west, tracking in low speed. There was a red hammer and sickle on its flank and no windows or portals on the boat. It was like a floating isosceles triangle.

'There.' Jack pointed and gave the binos to Harry. 'Drone ship. It's a coast watcher. Keep an eye on it. If it turns this way, signal to me.'

They skirted the cliff wall, Harry with his hoodie and blanket over his thin shoulders and a dummy timber board under one arm. He scurried under the cliff, while Jack ran for the water. He thrust his board out ahead of him and jumped on. The first batch of whitewater hit him as he paddled, and the salt over his head and hair took his breath away. It tasted amazing as it crackled on his skin.

He wobbled and slid on his board, neither true nor straight; it took him time to find the trim. He paddled hard between the sets, aiming for the troughs in the waves. Salt filled his mouth as he was pushed back. A bomb wave landed and he tried to duck dive but he had no weight to do so and was washed backwards off his board. He saw the rest of the set coming, so he ducked under the waves to save energy. His body remembered this. He had been pushed back too far, so he turned his board back to the beach and caught the next broken wave. As the board zipped in front of the whitewater Jack felt the slip and perfect trim, and the chatter of the nose on the water. He was in heaven.

He walked back up the beach towards the rip. Harry was still parked under the cliff, grinning at him.

'Doing a beach recce, old man?'

Jack flipped a middle finger at him and broke into a jog. He ran down to the water again. This time, his arms found their stride. He got a calm set and he paddled hard as the foam in the water settled.

He pushed hard and got clear of the swell, then sat right out the back on the board. His neck hurt and his arms burned. He was 300 metres off shore. When he recovered, he found the tip of the peninsula and lined up the peak of the ridgeline. His car was parked in a bay that lined up with a peak on the dune half a mile beyond it. To the west, he kept level with the mouth of the limestone bay. The intersection of those two lines was where the diver would be.

He sat in that water and waited for their salvation to surface. After two more sets of waves, a sleek black flipper kicked from the water five metres away. He was here. The asset.

The man who would save them all.

24

A SURFBOARD BOBBED UP FROM THE WATER AND SAT UPRIGHT, half submerged. It was bright and brand new, gleaming and glossy. Jack paddled a couple of strokes and reached out for it as it popped out of the ocean. He held it steady as he looked down the leg rope beneath the surface. A black duffel breached the surface, bound with nylon straps and black buckles. Jack scanned the sky, trying to conceal the sack beneath the water. He scrambled to stay upright on his board.

A head surfaced near him, facing the open ocean. The head swivelled, and the diver's arms thrashed about as he turned in the water to find Jack. The diver wore a military dive mask and coiled tubes on either side of his mouth. His wide eyes were visible even behind the misted-up goggles. He yanked his mask down to his neck, then yanked his hood back. Long black hair in a ponytail, a slender face, red loop of compressed skin around the eyes from the mask. This was no he. It was a woman, her eyes wide with fear. She reached for Jack's board, heaved once, and vomited. He looped his hand through her chest rig to hold her in place. Debris floated across the water.

He waited a moment.

'You okay?'

She held onto his board and coughed, rising and falling in the passing swell.

Jack looked up to the sky and then back to her, eyeing the new board, the black duffel. 'Where's your dive propulsion?'

'Under me. I'm holding it,' she said.

'Well, can you please descend and pack all your shit before you get us all killed?'

'Hooyah,' she gasped.

'Get into your cover outfit, please.'

She nodded, then pulled her hood and googles on and sank back under the water. She kicked on the surface for a minute, her flipper tangled in her leg rope.

'Jesus Christ,' Jack muttered.

Finally, she disentangled herself and descended.

Jack leaned over and pulled her board over the top of the duffel to cover it. He realised he hadn't even used his authentication phrase.

Jack shook his head. He pulled her board up by the leg rope and inspected the top. Firewire. Timber trim.

I bet you were 3D printed on the boat.

He inspected the nose of the board, looking for an antenna tip or a microphone or camera, but there was nothing. It was all smooth fibreglass. He turned to the beach and looked for the cliffs. At the peak of the swell, he held his arm up. Harry held both hands up, thumbs raised.

Five minutes later, she resurfaced in a wetsuit with her dive gear stowed. Jack helped her onto the gleaming new board, then strapped the leg rope to her ankle.

'Okay!' She gave him the thumbs-up, but she was too far forward on the board and the nose was sinking as she paddled. It was hopeless. Jack took the lanyard off her leg and secured her load to his arm, then pushed her into the whitewater.

'Paddle!' he yelled. She was nose-diving the board. 'Arch your back!'

She was picked up at the rear of the board by a large wave and face-planted into the water. The board shot out from under her stomach and popped up in the foam. Jack pulled up to her and they continued to paddle in with the duffel.

Jack walked her through the dumping shore break, trying to get her to lift her board, but she was too slender to do so. She fell to her hands and knees and vomited again in the shore break. Harry bolted back to the car and waited under it while Jack hauled the black duffel to the tray then sprinted back for the dive propulsion vehicle. He hauled the black cylinder onto his shoulder and was shocked at the weight. It was compact and light, with a magnetic dive board and GPS screen on the front. *At least they still make good stuff in the USA.*

Jack stood under a tarp and stowed the dive gear in the forty-four-gallon drum. The woman reached into her duffel and fished out jeans and a flannel shirt as she towelled off. Jack eyed her from the other side of the car. She had muscled arms, a tattoo of a feline skull with dandelions growing from the sockets on one shoulder. She had Asian heritage, but from where exactly, Jack couldn't tell.

'Thanks. Sorry about the pick-up,' she said to him in as plain and mainstream an American accent as you could get, with the soft twang of a west coast valley surfer girl in the vowels.

'No worries.' He stopped packing and turned to her. 'I'm Jack.'

'Amanda.' She nodded.

Jack draped the towel over the side of the car and put his hands on his hips. 'What's your real name?'

Another spook trying to bullshit me.

He was staring over the top of the tray. She kept packing her gear like she hadn't heard the question. Jack walked around to her side of the truck and stood with his arm on the tray.

'But what's your real name?' he asked again.

She looked up from her gear. 'You don't need . . .'

146

Jack didn't blink.

'Nope. I need to trust you.'

She stared back. 'Constance.'

He stepped away.

'Constance.' He strode off to the back of the tray and began throwing gear around, then stormed back to her side of the truck. 'RV drills like that will get us killed.' He gestured with his thumb over his shoulder 'This isn't Santa Monica.'

Then he returned to his packing, staring at her over the tray as he worked. Her eyes still wide, she turned back to her gear. He could tell she was calculating her position.

Jack was still looking at her.

Constance nodded and wiped her mouth. 'I hope you at least have Starbucks.'

She zipped her duffel inside an old green army bag and threw it in the tray, then turned to Jack. 'If you didn't need me, the Resistance wouldn't have sent one of the last Outriders to collect me. Right?' She pulled her shirt across her chest and folded her arms. 'So I must be a little bit important. And since the Chinese AI can replicate people's voices, laughs and tics over strategic comms, you kind of need me on the ground. Right?'

Jack huffed. 'Yes. Unfortunately.'

'And you Aussies have fought in three of our wars now.' She raised her eyebrows. 'So maybe this isn't unlike Santa Monica.'

Jack ignored her. 'Why are we all the way out here, so close to the Yard?'

'I had another job. Out west. You're lucky I hadn't infilled. We barely made it here in time.'

Out west.

She pointed towards the rising sun.

'Okay, driver,' she said. 'When the time comes, I might just save your redneck friends on that Hill – if I decide you're worth it.'

Jack heard a snigger from under the car.

147

She bunched her long hair in a towel and rubbed at it. 'Honestly, without me, without our tools, what are your chances?'

'One in three,' he shot back. 'What are yours?'

She smiled and looked across the bay, then up at the sky. 'Pretty good, actually.'

'Get in. We don't have time for this,' said Jack.

He sat in the driver's seat and Constance went to climb in the front.

'Back seat please,' said Jack. He banged his hand on the door panel twice.

Harry scrambled from under the car and jumped in the front. He turned in his seat and eyed Constance, then looked back at his dad with wide eyes.

'Constance, this is Harry,' Jack said.

'Hi, Harry,' she said, dragging out his name.

Harry beamed back. 'Dad, her teeth. They're all clean,' he whispered.

'Of course. She's a Seppo.'

They rolled out of the limestone bays and headed east, past rocks and potholes and washouts. Jack eyed her in the rear-view mirror.

'Californian?'

'San Diego.'

They drove in silence for a moment.

Jack pulled down his visor, the sun breaking over the road ahead of them as they drove.

'What's a Seppo?' Harry asked.

He looked at the boy.

'Back in World War Two in Brisbane, they called the Americans "Septic Tanks". Yanks. Seppo for short.'

'So nice,' said Constance.

'Well, we did fight in every major war you *started* in the last century. You probably owe us for that,' Jack said.

'We didn't start World War Two. But we finished it.'

'Well. Third instalment's not gone well.'

'The first few chapters could be better,' she agreed.

They drove on.

His frustration over the fiasco of the rendezvous gradually subsided. They had recovered the asset alive. It was a big milestone.

'Why can't you surf if you're from San Diego?'

'My family lived near the beach, but we moved away later. There was an accident.'

A silence settled in the car, broken only by the sound of the motor.

'Drowning?' Jack eventually asked.

Constance turned her face to the window, watching the salt-bush rushing past. Jack peeked at her in the rear-view mirror. She had soft hair, and she brushed it over her ear.

'You were a history undergraduate. Near the bottom of your class in the Academy.'

Jack frowned and returned his gaze to the windscreen. He could feel the boy's eyes on him. 'Yeah. And?'

Harry chuckled. Jack shot a look at him.

'Are you a rock collector too?' Constance asked.

Jack's brow furrowed. Then he realised what she was sitting next to. The AI mine.

'Don't touch that.'

'Oh. It's technical?'

'Correct.'

He saw her nod.

'I'm gonna need to brief you at some point. Alone,' she said.

He jabbed his thumb at Harry. 'He's cleared.'

'I can brief him, but are you sure you want him to know?'

Jack pursed his lips, resignation sinking over him. The boy was all in. It would make no difference if he were captured. His fate would be the same.

149

'Yes. Tell us both.' Jack turned to his son. 'You're about to be briefed to Top Secret.'

Harry used an invisible zip to seal his mouth shut.

'Let's drive and talk. Defence. I want to know what you have on the Hill first.'

'I'm authorised to represent the Hill Commander. You tell me what you have, I'll write it up.'

'Okay.'

Constance spent half an hour outlining the platforms they had available and some of the risks. She talked through a real operation where the Chinese AI had replicated an agent in South China, and US Joint Special Operations Command had committed a whole CAG Troop with CIA ground operators into a trap. Forty of America's best operators were captured. The AUKUS treaty had been amended to include new safe-guards, including asset control with qualified CIA operators on the ground.

Most of the assets, Jack had only heard rumours about. Weather manipulation, offensive space platforms – science fiction material.

When she was done, Jack was quiet.

'I know. It's a lot,' she said.

'I barely understood most of what you just said. But it sounds wild,' said Harry.

Jack held a finger up. 'Not another word about this. Is that clear?'

Harry nodded, but Jack was rattled. If the Yanks were sending a fraction of that much gear, it meant the forces that were coming were serious.

Constance told Jack to report it in via his end and she would do the same. Harry pulled out his tablet and held it to his father's mouth as he used AI voice dictation software to file his report back to HQ.

25

JESS WILSON WATCHED AS KAYNE SLID A SALT SHAKER BACK and forth across the mica table top. Suddenly, the screen door banged open, and the Principal appeared in the entrance to the diner, dressed in the same black overalls he'd been wearing at the roundabout.

He carried no weapon save a tomahawk, which stayed at his side as he walked over to them.

He placed the tomahawk on the table in front of them with a thud. It had a burnished handle of dark maroon timber, and rainbow hues on the edge of the blade.

The deputy with a vertical scar on his face entered the diner behind him and walked the perimeter of the room, then disappeared into the kitchen.

Jess looked up at the Principal. He was handsome, his face and jawline symmetrical. His clouded eye stared right through her as he slid into the booth opposite them.

'I was born here. Did you know that?' He reclined, fished a packet of cigarettes from his breast pocket, pulled one out and lit it. The Principal took a long drag. It smelled of cloves and menthol.

'My father bought me this axe in Perth,' he said. He placed

his fingertips on the handle. It was well maintained with a moist sheen on it, and a broad leather strap hitched around its base.

'Do you know this timber?' he said. 'This is jarrah. One of the best timbers in this land. The First Australians used jarrah to make hunting spears and digging sticks.'

He took a drag and blew the smoke away from the table, then leaned forward with the cigarette. 'Don't tell my wife,' he confided, nodding at it. 'She says that I am under a lot of stress. But this work, it makes my heart sing.' He flashed the hint of a smile.

He tapped a finger again on the handle of the tomahawk. 'This handle is from southern WA. I got the head shaped in Shanghai; it's carbon-titanium-nickel.' He traced his finger down the blade edge. 'The heat treatment gives it these stunning colours. I've kept it on me since my first deployment, to India.'

Jess looked up at his good eye. It was shining, like a wet black gem. Kayne hadn't so much as taken a breath.

The Principal went on.

'My friends laughed at me because real officers carry concealed pistols. See, in India, neither side could carry firearms to the border.' He gestured at the tomahawk with his cigarette. 'This was all we had. The other lieutenants used wooden staffs, very basic weapons.' He made a chopping motion with his hands.

Jess swallowed and looked at Kayne. Beads of sweat had appeared on his upper lip.

'Indians are great warriors. Especially the Sikhs.'

The Principal took a long drag on his cigarette, not taking his eyes off the axe handle.

'On the border the valleys are very deep. Rivers of ice water. The Indians had pushed us off a ridgeline that day.'

The deputy returned from the kitchen and placed a teacup in front of the Principal. He took a sip, then returned the cup to the saucer noiselessly.

'My company commander, a coward, refused to attack. So I gathered my troop. I walked us downstream in the dark with improvised weapons. No lights. Very quiet. The river was loud.'

Jess hadn't moved a muscle.

'I was at the front. I was very young.' He shrugged and smiled. Then he tapped the tomahawk blade. 'We found men by the river, cleaning pots. Squatting, jabbering.' He held up his cigarette stub, and the deputy took it.

'The first man,' he said. 'I hit him here.' He chopped a line over his collarbone with the back of his hand, then stared out the window for a long moment.

'We went into the river. Swept downstream. I found my feet in the boulders and I pinned him down like this.' The Principal was gripping his own hands, wringing them like he was still holding the man's neck.

'He would not drown. So I . . . used a rock. Until he stopped.'

The Principal turned the teacup by its handle.

'This is a hard memory,' he said. He stared at the teacup as he turned it.

'When I pulled him up from the river's edge, the axe was still buried down to his chest. Hence this here.' He ran his finger along the leather strap. 'That lesson almost killed me.'

'After that, I was downstream, behind the rest of their fighters. I was shivering so much, but I went to work.'

He shook his head.

'By sunrise, there were forty dead Indians in that valley. Swept down the river. My battalion sergeant walked the position holding a severed head.'

Jess winced. For so long, she had believed her side, the government, was the 'good' side. Now she wasn't so sure.

The Principal went on.

'The next time I cooked them in their tents. That was easier, but not sporting. Not for a real soldier. I regret it.'

He pursed his lips and put his elbows on the table, forearms either side of the axe.

'Attack early. When the enemy are washing their pots.'

He scanned his eyes over them, his dead eye fixed ahead, grey and milky. He spoke slowly.

'Jack Dunne and the child. Where?'

Kayne went to speak, but the Principal held up his finger.

'Lady first.'

Jess had sunk into her seat, wishing she could shrink to nothing.

'We sent a team for him. He crossed the border into South Australia, further inland,' Jess said.

'There's a pursuit team dealing with him,' her brother lied.

The Principal nodded.

'The team that was turned into dog food? That team?' There was a hard edge to his voice.

Jess sat with her mouth open, looking like a dog about to be spanked.

The Principal pushed his chair back, reached for the axe and dragged it across the mica table, the ominous grind of metal.

He holstered it in his belt loop.

'You have until sundown tomorrow.'

He walked out of the cafe, his deputy following close behind.

Jess exhaled as she watched him go.

26

THE SIGNALS SOLDIER WALKED INTO THE BUNKER WITH A printout and handed it to Dyson.

'Flash message, boss. Outrider has the package.'

Dyson took the printout and pored over the details. Then he re-read the force package, line by line.

Then he read it a third time.

He called Heads in. 'Read this,' Dyson said.

TOP SECRET / SENSITIVE COMPARTMENTED / AUKUS
INFORMATION
    SITREP:
    + Urgency: FLASH
    + TO: Resistance HQ
    + FROM: Outrider 11, via Hill HQ
    + Location: GR 52 SQS 43 23. In lying up
position 1000m off main road.
    + Status: Asset secured.
    + Offensive Support Briefing from asset:
    In Direct Support from H-Hr:
    - Air Domain (B-21 Raider with strike package

@ 90 mins notice to move. Massive Air Ordnance Blast device at 6 hours notice)

- Subsurface (SSN-McRaven: 24 × Tomahawk sortie @ 30 mins notice to move)

- Weather: 1 × HAARP adverse weather mission (8–12 hours impact)

+ Command and Control. All assets to be directed as per AUKUS Directive 611 (Ground operator available). Agent 'Amanda' is the only person authorised to direct the assets. This is a critical vulnerability. The lack of an alternative control mechanism puts defence of the Hill in jeopardy. Agent was pulled off insertion to West Australia for operations against Yard, in order to support new mission at Hill HQ.

Request additional air/ground support at border crossing to ensure safety of asset and strategic comms.

+ INTELLIGENCE:

+ Actions today: Collected asset, running countersurveillance route around CCP air assets and VMF ground raiders.

+ INTENTIONS:

- Return to Hill operations area as fast as possible. Border penetration is major risk point.

+ Quick Reaction Force: Four Horsemen on 10 mins notice from 1100–1500. Request direct fire, and airlift capability.

Code word for QRF: VALHALLA NOW

+ Request for Information:

- General: Please provide overflight of Crossing Point (Vic/SA) border.

```
    - Priority: Armour/Rotary Wing/Strike
Assets
    - Secondary: Checkpoint ──> Location/manning/
coverage/overwatch locations
    + Comments: Asset is cooperative.
Inexperienced in the field.
    Greatest threat: lack of time, and border
crossing point.
    TOP SECRET / SENSITIVE COMPARTMENTED
INFORMATION / AUKUS
```

Heads looked at Dyson with raised eyebrows. 'I'll scan his land corridor for the run home.'

Dyson clapped his hands once, then walked to his terminal and typed up his dispatch for Resistance HQ. After pecking away with his stumpy fingers for a few minutes, he read over what he'd written.

'Ack all. Task Force Leopard formation posturing out of MCG. Assess H-Hour sometime 19 Aug. Final synch session will be in 24 hours. Be back for that.'

He hit send and stood up to face Heads.

'Start prepping for area defence. Centre point on the Five Ways. It's critical terrain.'

'Copy,' said Heads. 'He better haul ass. We need him. And Amanda.'

Jack picked up speed as the sun was rising before him. They were making good time. Harry and Constance had swapped seats so Harry could rest in the back.

'How many deployments have you done?' Jack asked.

'This is my third.' She held up a finger. 'Hong Kong. Then Taiwan.'

'Taiwan. When?'

She sipped her tea. 'I got there before Z-Day.'

'Bullshit. You saw the invasion?' Jack said.

She sat still for a while.

'I didn't hear anything about your guys,' Constance said eventually. 'They pulled nine people out of the water when the *Gerald Ford* sank.'

'Nine?'

'Nine. Not nine hundred. Nine. Four and a half thousand souls lost. Life rafts with bodies in them still wash up at Diego Garcia.'

Jack winced. Two Squadron and SAS HQ were on the *Canberra*, five years ago, when two Dong Feng warheads, each a sedan-sized missile barrelling down at Mach 5 from outer space, had blown the ship into scrap parts. There were no survivors.

Jack glanced at Harry's reflection in the rear-view mirror. He was fast asleep.

'When were you in Hong Kong?' he asked.

'Two years before Taiwan.'

'Did you ever get to Singapore?'

She looked at Jack. 'I did. Jack, I spent a lot of time in Singapore.'

Jack stared back at her, reassessing.

'You're just like she described.'

Jack recoiled. 'What?'

Constance held his gaze, watching as the understanding dawned.

'You worked with Gemma?'

'I knew her well. We were friends.'

Jack was in utter shock. 'For real?'

'She's the whole reason I volunteered to deploy here,' Constance said.

'No way.' He shook his head. 'What was her favourite drink?'

'Hendriks gin, cucumber, lots of ice. She could only have one or two though.'

Jack frowned, fighting back tears.

'She told me all about you and Harry. She was so in love with you, Jack. She hated being away from you.'

Jack was shaking his head. 'How was she?' His voice was trembling. He had carefully boxed up his grief so he could do this job, and this conversation was threatening that safety mechanism.

'The best. She was the best. I loved her. Crazy Aussie.' She laughed, remembering.

She patted his arm. 'It's okay, I know she never would've mentioned me. But you're exactly what she described. Including your temper.'

She smiled. Jack was trying to hold himself together.

'It's been awful,' he admitted. 'It's been just . . .'

'I know. I heard she passed. Everyone in the Intel Community heard about it. I wish I could've been there for her.'

Jack felt like a fool. He was so hard on everyone he met, but she had been an ally all along.

'I heard the funeral was amazing.'

'It was.' Jack pulled a small jar from his door well. 'Open this, would you? Take a sip.'

Constance opened the jar and smelled the moonshine. 'Whoa.' She raised the jar in a toast. 'To Gemma.' She sipped, and coughed once, then handed the jar to Jack.

He took a sip. 'To Gemma.'

He handed the jar back to Constance.

'We spent most of our time recruiting Chinese sources. It was easy. You know, I took her out in Singapore and we drank all night and ended up in some shitty karaoke bar. She attacked a pervert with a microphone. She missed you and Harry so much.'

She chose her next words carefully. 'One day, I woke her up.

She was sick. Pounding head, buzzing noises, fainting. Agency doctors said it was one of the worst cases of Havana Syndrome ever.'

She closed the jar.

Jack stared ahead, biting his lip. No one had told him that.

'They think it was a targeting mission. Probably Chinese Special Forces.' She leaned forward.

She nodded. 'The same unit that pulled off the mission is operating out of the Melbourne Cricket Ground.'

'Tell me everything you know,' said Jack.

Constance spoke in detail for some time. Horrifying detail. The more Jack heard, the more he wanted to hurt them.

27

Jack continued east. It was still early in the morning; the patrols would be more alert. The border was a few hours away.

Transiting it would be a critical step.

'Pull over up here, will you? I want to show you something.'

Jack pulled over. Harry pulled a diesel jerry from the roof and fuelled the car while Constance booted up a small tablet, unlocked it, and handed it to Jack.

Jack looked at her long, dark hair in the morning light. She had beautiful skin, and she was much surer of herself out of the water.

'I have to warn you, it's not easy viewing.' She gestured to Harry.

'He's seen plenty,' Jack said, the hard edge in his voice unable to mask the tone of regret. He hit the play button.

The video showed a sprawling city in the desert. It had a distant quality, like satellite imagery. There was some green writing and block lines on the image.

Jack recognised it: the massive semi-circle on the Bight cliffs. The enormous ramp that opened to flood the ship holding pens. The L-shaped floating barrier in the ocean that protected the entrance. Eight cranes, and the hulking bodies of steel carriers.

It was the Yard.

'How old is this?' said Jack.

'Twenty-four hours.'

'Satellite video?'

'Classified. Sorry.'

'Jesus,' Jack whispered.

It was a megacity. A shipbuilding, war-manufacturing mega-complex. The walled yard was riddled with lights and roads and cranes. Billowing furnace stacks rose from the desert floor. This was all west of Adelaide, positioned near the cliffs of the western edge of the Great Australian Bight.

The image had boxes with annotations in them, highlighting different parts of the facility. It reminded Jack of the U2 pictures of tactical nuke sites in Cuba in the 1960s. The measurement span across the diameter was twenty-five kilometres.

Four-storey-high sentry turrets ringed the semi-circle. Beneath them, a wide channel served as a downhill ramp from the Yard into the waters of the Bight; wide as a ten-lane highway, it launched the supercarriers of the Chinese fleet. Eight cranes stood tall, their arms at right angles. The shortest one was at least a hundred metres. A dark portal carved into the cliff face, a hundred metres wide, was annotated by the tablet as 'Deepwater submarine pen'.

Harry grabbed his dad. 'That's why all the metal was gone, Dad.'

Constance spoke. 'You see the ramp for the Dreadnought Carriers? Two airstrips wide. The ship is at least 450 metres long.'

'How?' said Jack. 'How do they do it?'

Constance looked at him. 'Cities the size of Sydney have been popping up in China many times a year. In 2012 alone, they poured as much concrete as the US used in the entire twentieth century. They churn out ships like they're cars. Slave labour, led by technicians. That's how they do it.'

As parts of Australia had collapsed, the CCP had kept Victoria as a foothold and run their resources through the rest of the country. They didn't need the whole country. They just needed to harvest its key organs.

Whole cities of people were transferred to the Yard by decree. If you lived in an occupied area of Australia, working at the Yard was a life, better than the trenches in Taiwan – if you could survive the twenty-hour days.

'What are you seeing?' Jack said.

'Air-defence batteries. See the dome farm near the edge of the facility? That's a ULF farm. Talks to the submarines. Vehicle farms, air traffic control towers. Sentry towers. Missile towers.' She pointed to an airstrip on the flank. 'See that pair taking off?

'Gen 6 fighters,' said Jack.

'No,' Constance said. 'See the canards? The little wings forward of the main wings. They're J-20s. Gen 5, but still good.'

Jack shook his head.

It was way worse than he'd thought. He heard that many of the displaced had occupied the shanty towns in the free part of WA. The rumours were wrong. The Chinese had built a new industrial centre, using Australian people and Australian resources. And Australia's leaders had agreed to it. Sacrifice some to save the rest.

'Keep watching,' she said.

Three large metal gates were carved into the concrete walls of the Yard, each with rail tracks running through it. The tracks then curved and wrapped around the inside of the Yard, like a roundabout for trains.

'It's the crown jewel of the Southern Hemisphere. Three rail lines link it all the way to Darwin, Port Hedland and Victoria. It transports raw materials, food and labour,' she said.

The video zoomed in on a train that had entered through the cavernous curved doors on the east side. They stayed open while the long train circled the edge of the Yard.

'Look at the thing.' Jack counted ten carriages and then multiplied that segment across the whole train line.

'Over two hundred carriages. From Victoria.' At least three-quarters of the carriages were Connexes with slots cut into the sides. Some were lumber carriages. There were gun platforms with sandbag walls and quad-barrelled machine guns. A missile battery. Armoured cars chained to the platform beds, some twisted and charred from the frontlines. The camera slewed to civilians disembarking the trains onto the concrete platform.

With sickening horror, Jack suddenly understood what he was looking at.

He shielded the tablet from Harry.

'Look away,' he said.

Harry sat back in the seat with his arms folded.

Jack kept watching. The train moved around the inside wall of the Yard and stopped beside a concrete platform. A long line of flatbed trucks stood on the other side of the platform, each with a single trough of water mounted on the back. There were a couple of dump trucks, too.

Hundreds of soldiers shepherded the civilians off the train, one carriage at a time. Families sprinted to the trucks and fought their way onto them, ringing around the troughs like farm animals. Women plunged babies into the troughs, to bathe them and quench their desperate thirst.

Jack felt a rising bile in his throat.

'What is it?' said Harry.

'Quiet,' he admonished his son.

The feed zoomed onto a man holding a child in his arms, limp and naked. He was appealing to two soldiers. They took the child from him, holding the sagging body by the limbs, while another soldier restrained the man. They walked the body to a dump truck and threw it in. There were several more twisted bodies in the truck, all naked. The man appeared to collapse.

He was dragged to the truck by his armpits, his bare feet dragging behind him on the pavement.

Jack turned it off. He felt sick.

'This is real? This is really happening?' asked Jack. He was pale, trembling.

'I'm sorry,' she said.

Jack gripped his chest with one hand.

A gulag.

He looked out the window.

Everyone was silent for a long time.

Finally, Jack broke the silence.

'We need to get to the border.'

Starting the engine, he gunned it.

28

JACK CHECKED THE TIME, CALCULATING. THEY WERE DUE TO hit the border crossing into Victoria by early afternoon.

'That Quick Reaction Force better be ready. Pretty sure we'll be needing them,' he muttered to himself.

He turned to Constance. She was a reading a report on her tablet. Still an enigma.

'Why were you in Taiwan?'

She didn't answer for a moment. 'I was posted there. I was part of an indig deep cover op.' She looked back down. 'Once the combat phase was over.'

'Really?' Jack stole a look at her and raised his eyebrows. That meant she'd been helping lead strike operations after the surrender.

'Thirteen days for the PLA to destroy two carrier battle groups and the Taiwanese Navy. Captured a whole Marine Division. We were all still on the ground when the first wave landed.'

She had gone completely still.

'Must've been brutal,' Jack said.

Constance didn't respond, just stared straight ahead, eyes on the road.

Jack saw her jaw flexing at the corners like she was grinding her teeth.

She went back to her tablet and didn't talk for a long while.

When they were twenty kilometres from the border, they drove a fishhook pattern off the main track and stopped.

Harry prepped a compact drone while Jack went to the hilltop with Constance. The smell of dirt and musky salt-bush assailed his nostrils. Jack could hear the waves booming against the cliffs of the Bight, a few hundred metres to their right.

They eyed the approaches to the checkpoint with a thermal viewfinder. It looked bare. Quiet.

Jack licked his lips and looked at Constance.

'This will be the hardest part. We cross that border and we're home tonight. That's twenty-four hours early.'

He checked his watch.

1530.

They had until 2100 tomorrow to make it back.

Constance had her tablet open and was reviewing intel. Jack leaned over to see the screen but it was obscured from his angle.

'What's it say?'

Constance read from the screen. 'Satellite intelligence, only an hour old, have four men and two trucks parked at the border. No heavy weapons. Could be smugglers.'

Constance looked at him, brow furrowed. 'Advance party? Like a tripwire? Hit them, the main forces come. Only problem is our scans haven't picked up PLA patrols here yet.'

'You put too much faith in this crap.' Jack pointed at the screen.

Constance pursed her lips and reviewed the images.

'There are no tracks in the sand. No old heat signatures. Nothing. That's five clicks wide.'

'Well, they can bring armour in from Adelaide. They can get aircraft in here quick, too,' said Jack.

He surveyed the land again and checked his watch. 1536.

'Ideally, we're back by nightfall. That buys us a bit more time. You can fully brief Dyson, and we can re-arrange defence if we need to.'

Constance looked at him. 'Yeah. But maybe we cross further north.'

Jack tapped his foot.

Harry was launching the drone off the rear tray. Jack hissed down the hill to him. 'Harry, not behind the tray.'

'Quiet, Dad,' he hissed back.

After a beat, he shuffled away from the rear of the HiLux.

Jack looked back at Constance.

'I think we run it. I'll queue up the air support and get the Horsemen in striking range. If we hit a reserve, we just commit them to the assault.'

'The who?'

'Some air support. You might get to meet them.'

'More Aussie rednecks?'

Jack grinned. 'Maybe.'

'Alright. We go,' said Constance.

Jack put the binos down.

'We have a Maximi in the back, I'll take that. I got a pirate gun for you if you want, plus a bandolier and a few dozen HE rounds.'

'Oh,' she purred, 'wombat gun? Forty-millimetre?' She reached into her duffel and pulled out a compact launcher with a laser tube on the side, weighing it in her hand.

'I got this. Not bad. I preferred the 203,' she said, hand on the side of the sleek weapon.

Jack admired it. 'Not bad. I prefer retro,' said Jack.

He reached into the cab of the HiLux and held up his sawn-off M-79 launcher, an oversized blunderbuss pistol that fired egg-sized grenades. 'I reckon this thing pounded a few enemy positions in 'Nam back in '68,' he said, then nodded to her weapon. 'May I?'

She flipped it in her hand so it was barrel down. Jack cracked his barrel open at the breech and they swapped grenade launchers. He cracked the breech on the black gun and extended the stock. 'Fancy. Too many points of failure though.'

She flipped the M-79 lengthways and inspected the breech. It had a chipped stock and a green bungy cord. 'I kinda miss simple. What was it like in the Tet Offensive?' She smirked.

Jack frowned and took his weapon back.

'It was good. Your mum and I got together around then.'

It was her turn to frown. 'Really? Mom jokes?'

She reached into her duffel and extracted a bullet that was as long as the barrel; it was gold and sleek with a black nose. 'Pike rounds. Laser guided to 2000 metres. Ten-metre kill radius.' She handed it to Jack.

'No way.' Jack felt the heft in his hands and looked into the black nose.

'Has a rocket motor. I got two dozen rounds.' She rattled a black camouflage shoulder satchel.

They headed down the hill back to Harry, who was holding the drone controller and gesturing to them. 'Are you two done?'

Jack packed his weapon in the cab and turned to grab Harry's controller. 'Let me see.'

He peered at the screen.

'Okay. Three men. Two trucks.'

Jack showed Constance.

'Well done, mate.' He handed the controller back to Harry. 'Jump in the back seat, would ya?'

Harry headed for the passenger side.

'Not that side, mate, you're in the back.'

Harry stared at him, his hands on his hips.

'Dad.'

'You're the stepson. She's the stepmother. Play along.'

Grumbling, Harry stuffed his bag into the back seat and climbed in, arms folded.

'He's tired,' Jack said to Constance. 'Come with me.'

He guided her to the tray of the HiLux. The tailgate was down.

Jack motioned to it. 'There's a cutting charge built into this. It only works if the tray is down; it's directional. It activates with this.' He held up his wristband with the perspex cover.

He slapped a hand on a flat black panel in the rear of the tray. 'The 84mm is in this recess under the tray. Harry, load a high-explosive round dialled in for 500 metres, please.'

'I'm not your slave,' said Harry.

'You will be if you don't do what I ask.'

'That makes no sense,' Harry bit back.

Jack turned to Constance, eyebrows raised. 'They grow up.'

They hid all the gear in the truck, then talked through all the nightmare scenarios that could happen on a border crossing. Constance and Harry climbed into their seats while Jack stood by his open door, facing the checkpoint.

Constance took a drink from her water bottle, then offered some to Harry.

He ignored her.

'Shift your seat forward. My knees are squashed,' he said.

Jack stuck his head in and shot a look at Harry.

'Please,' Harry corrected himself.

'No worries.' Constance pulled her seat forward.

Jack shook his head as he tied his boot laces up and zipped his leather jacket against the breeze. He pulled his fingerless leather gloves on and flexed his hands, then stood still by the car and pulled in a deep breath, closing his eyes for a moment.

He could feel Harry's eyes on him.

Jack stood still, lips moving, eyes closed, hair shifting in the breeze. Harry watched as his father reached into the car, pulled the fist mike off the dash and keyed it.

'Border penetration commencing at 1600. Launch the Horsemen and hold eight clicks out.'

29

JIMBO ADJUSTED THE RADIO VOLUME AND HEARD JACK'S VOICE boom in from the plains.

'Copy. Wheels up in ten mins,' he responded.

He ran to the pilots' room and rapped on the door. The pilots were already half-dressed in flight suits.

'Outrider is live. See you on the tarmac.'

He ran across to the team room and rapped on the door. Loud rock music echoed around the room, punctuated by a dog barking.

'Zeus, shut up!'

The door opened and Cole stuck his head out.

'Jack's gonna cross at 1600,' said Jimbo.

'Copy.' Cole turned to his team. 'Wheels up in five. Orders in the air.'

The pilots pulled on leather jackets with filthy shearling collars as they sprinted across the airstrip to the Cessna Skycourier that sat under the corrugated iron half-dome. They pulled the wheel blocks, then climbed in and dialled the engines to life.

The four elite Resistance fighters were already at their lockers, assembling body armour and collecting weapons. Jimbo had a satchel with radios and wrist-mounted maps for the mission. He slipped a radio in the back of their body armour and entered the code fills, slapping each one on the back when they were ready.

Zeus sat in his harness at Horse's feet.

The fourth Horseman, Beetle the Sniper, shouldered a long rifle with a thick, hourglass-shaped scope and tightened the sling. The young soldier had his Sri Lankan parents' dark complexion and intense eyes, and a gregarious sense of humour.

Each operator ran an eye over their buddy's gear to check it as they prepped. Sacha's tattooed forearms strained as she and Jimbo prepped Mrs Rabbit.

'Let's move,' said Beetle. 'Engines are running.'

'Comms check complete,' Jimbo confirmed.

Each team member wore a streamlined parachute vest for low-level jumps, and carried four magazines, a pistol and an M4. Their combat uniforms were sleek and form-fitting, stretched across their broad shoulders. With the parachutes, body armour and weapons, they looked dangerous and drilled.

Cole had a black patch with four horses on his chest rig, and a black and yellow Free Australia flag rolled into a tight bundle and attached to the back of his body armour.

Mrs Rabbit was being put through its boot-up sequence. Sacha spoke commands into her earpiece to move the robot from the stand-by bay out to the tarmac. She added two heavy boxes of ammunition onto the robot's back.

Cole spoke as they completed their final checks. 'Outrider 11 is about to run a border penetration. He is mounted in a HiLux, three-up. The passenger is an asset. Extremely high value. This is her image.'

He showed them a photo on his tablet, of Constance back as a trainee at the CIA Farm in Virginia.

Beetle gave a low whistle. 'Definitely an asset.'

Sacha rolled her eyes.

'The other passenger is Harry Dunne. Jack's boy.'

'Jack, what have you gotten yourself into?' muttered Horse as he clipped a set of goggles and tiny earmuffs onto Zeus's head. The dog cocked its head to one side to make it easier to fit the earmuffs.

Jimbo spoke in an even voice.

'There are four fighting-age males near the checkpoint.'

'That's it?' said Beetle. 'Armour?'

'Two trucks only. No more sighted.' He turned to Beetle. 'Any armour presents, use top-attack 84mm. They're good up to T-100 tank armour.'

'I know it,' said Beetle.

Sacha pulled her M4 and grenade launcher out of her locker and put her head and armpit through the sling.

'Jack's definitely got his cock on the anvil,' she said.

'He can handle it,' said Horse.

'I heard he's gotten sloppy,' said Beetle. 'He lost his shit at that roundabout job.'

Cole slammed his locker shut and looked at Beetle. 'He was smacking down on Spetsnaz teams in Ukraine while you were doing TikTok videos in your dickstickers on Bondi Beach.'

Beetle frowned at the putdown because it was true.

Horse and Sacha chuckled as they fought their way out the door. As they approached the aircraft, the propellers were winding up into pre-starts. Cole spoke up as they walked.

'This is the last window we can operate in. Once we hit this job, we're back to the Hill.'

The co-pilot stood at the rear ramp with his aviator glasses on, watching the team stride across the tarmac, a ghastly crew of humans, machines and animals. Four elite soldiers with heavy weapons, a galloping, ammunition-hauling robot, and a werewolf-sized dog wearing goggles and ear protection.

Jimbo followed the group with a radio in one hand, a clipboard under his arm and a tablet slung around his neck.

The plane had streaks of black exhaust along the wings

and peeling white paint. The corners of the cockpit window were held down with thick blue tape. An aiming crosshair was scrawled on the window in red marker. The entire cargo panel behind the wing had been removed, and two 84mm composite fibre rocket launchers were stuck to a block mount and swivel out of the starboard side. The outside of the plane was adorned with a drawing of a muscular wombat holding a rocket launcher. There was a surveillance camera ball mounted at the base of the nose and a minigun mounted to the ramp, with a metal tail leading up the ramp to an olive, esky-sized ammo box.

The co-pilot waved them up the ramp and the aircraft began taxiing out to the airstrip.

Cole checked his watch. 1540. He keyed his headset.

'Best speed, Captain. If you can get eyes on in twenty mins, we're good.'

The craft lumbered off the strip, just clearing the low fences, the engines working hard to climb. They tucked up the wheels and tracked low near the limestone cliffs for a distance to test the air, then they sank below the line of the cliffs, low enough that the occasional blast of sea spray hit them.

The plane tracked the coastline, and accelerated to full speed.

30

'TEN MINUTES OUT FROM CROSSING POINT.'

Jack leaned forward, staring out of the windshield. Perhaps word of his attack on the bandits further north had never reached here.

They had enough cash and a backstory to get through the checkpoint. Any problems and they'd need to wipe out everyone in sight. It was worth the risk to get the extra time back on the Hill.

Jack keyed the fist mike. 'Trinity, this is Outrider 11, how copy?'

'Outrider, Trinity, have you five by five. Horsemen will be on station in one minute.'

Jack grinned at Constance. 'They're here.'

He turned on the tablet and linked to the Cessna video streamed from the surveillance dome. The grainy black and white feed showed tracking and distance reticules in green copy.

'Where are they?' said Constance.

'Southeast. Off the Bight.'

The view feed canted on their truck, which was parked two kilometres out from the checkpoint, behind a dune. It tracked along the road to the checkpoint, where it picked up two tents, and two trucks parked either side of the road.

'Outrider 11, we have two vehicles. Likely personnel. Scanning for weapons.'

Constance darted her eyes to Jack. 'Bait?'

Jack stared at the horizon. 'Maybe.'

They waited.

Trinity crackled back to life. 'We have blankets on long objects in the trays of both cars. Probably heavy weapons. Four alphas. I would call positive identification on those cars.'

'Read back, PID on two cars and four alphas.' Four fighting-age males. That was enough for Jack.

'Copy.'

They checked the tablet feed, both seeing the same thing. The view slewed across the brush-covered landscape to a low limestone cliff. A crop of bush overhung the cliffs. One side had a straight edge.

'Possible thermal tarp. 1300 metres north. No tracks visible. We can't see under it.'

'I'm not feeling it,' said Constance. 'Let's cross further north.'

Jack kept his hands on the wheel. 'We need to get to the Hill. What if the enemy launch early?'

Constance was taking shallow breaths. 'Jack. Think about it.'

Jack eyed Constance, then keyed the radio.

'Trinity, are you in position to interdict?'

'Affirmative. Four minutes out. Thirty minutes on station,' said the pilot.

Jack sat with one hand on the fist mike, the other on the steering wheel.

This was one of those 'fork in the road' moments in life. No matter which direction he chose, everything would change.

'Outrider, this is Trinity. Advise your course of action. We're burning fuel.'

Jack stared at Constance. She dipped her chin once.

Jack raised the fist mike.

'Trinity, this is Outrider 11.'

Jack felt sweat on the back of his neck. He looked at Harry in the rear-view mirror.

'Proceeding to checkpoint. Stand-by.'

Jack took one final look at the video feed. It was slewed back to his truck. Beside the truck, Jack spotted a black-haired woman in a billowing white robe, peering through the driver's side window, her back turned to the sky.

Jack started and looked out his window.

Nothing.

He looked back to the feed.

There was just his truck, in the desert. He picked up the fist mike.

'Trinity. Did you see a . . . person in white next to my truck?'

'Negative.'

Shit. Gemma.

'Dad. Go.' Harry jolted him out of his trance.

He accelerated off the shoulder towards the checkpoint. Constance checked the back seat and adjusted the covers over the weapons. Jack looked out the window.

Standing on the shoulder, he saw a barefoot woman in a white dress, young and lithe, pulling her hair over one shoulder. She locked her black eyes onto him as they passed.

Gemma.

31

'WE'RE RUNNING THE CHECKPOINT. GOING DARK,' SAID JACK.

He could see the silhouette of the two trucks on the horizon. A bouldered outcrop, Giant's Marbles, was the only visible feature within range of the checkpoint.

Harry squirmed in the back seat for a better view.

Constance was still, her hand resting on the black shape under the shroud by her knee.

'Remember,' Jack pointed to Constance. 'Stepmother.'

He went on: 'First layer of our cover: We're VMF, dropped a weapon consignment into Ceduna. Second layer: We're located on the Hill and we are sources for VMF who work in the Resistance.'

Jack went on.

'Deep breathing. Do not touch your face.'

Jack kept the car at an easy speed.

'And do not go anywhere near the rear of the vehicle,' he added.

'Dad, concentrate,' Harry said.

'Sorry,' Jack said.

They were 200 metres short of the cars and already two men on the checkpoint were setting up. One had his arm held high, signalling for them to stop. The other ran to a low table with a long weapon resting lengthways on it, a camping chair behind it. There was a single tall tent behind him.

No one else was out there.

'The other two will be in the tent,' said Constance.

On the road sat a yellow box with a single lamp that glowed red. Jack slowed the car and stopped at the light. He raised his hands above the steering wheel. Constance copied him. Harry held his hands out the back window.

A hundred metres away one man was perched behind an oversized sniper rifle with broad scope. The soldier behind him scanned them with binoculars.

The light turned green.

'Here we go. Nice and easy,' said Jack.

He looked in the rear-view mirror. Harry was breathing fast and his eyes were wild.

'We're fine,' said Jack.

Fifty metres out.

Jack rolled the car forward at an idle, keeping both hands flexed open at the top of the wheel.

A long row of metal spikes on a welded chain spanned the road. A HiLux technical with a mounted machine gun was parked side-on to the road. It was a safe distance back from the checkpoint, about forty metres, and was unmanned.

The soldier with the binoculars sauntered to Jack's door. He wore the ragged militia uniform of work boots, a peaked cap and jeans.

Jack inhaled through his nose and nodded to the man.

The soldier was built like a racing dog. He wore a baseball hat with the Adelaide Crows logo on the front. An old leather strap across his chest, like an officer's trench belt. A silver revolver with a pearl handle drooped low off his hip in a leather holster, worn down and black.

Jack felt a tinge of déjà vu. At least the approaching man wasn't wearing an akubra.

The man cast his eyes over the car, then looked in the back seat. He leaned over the door.

'Where ya headed?'

'Mate, we're headed back to Vic.'

'Oh yeah? Where to?'

'Yarra Valley.'

'Yeah? Love the Valley.' The lithe man kept his eyes on Jack a beat too long.

He stooped to look at Constance.

'Hello,' he said. His teeth were a row of yellow and brown stains. He turned and spat a stream of brown fluid onto the ground.

Constance kept her eyes ahead.

The soldier who had covered them with the sniper rifle was standing up now, carrying a broom pole with a mirror taped to the end, similar to the device Jack had seen at the roundabout. The soldier walked around the truck, holding the mirror to its underside. His tongue stuck out the side of his mouth as he studied the reflection.

The guy in the hat spoke to Constance. 'You're not from here. How long you known this bloke?'

'Since January,' she said, in the best Queensland accent Jack had heard.

He nodded. 'Look at you.' He turned his attention to Harry. 'Hey fella. This your old man?'

Harry nodded.

Jack beckoned the man closer and lowered his voice. 'We're doing source work.' He showed the man his palms. 'We can't be stopping.'

The man spat another stream of nicotine juice from the side of his mouth without taking his eyes off Jack. It ran down his red beard.

He turned and drew his pistol without making a sound, and pointed it at Jack's eyeball.

'Steady,' said Jack. He felt the hot flood of fear wash through his chest. The scoring and dents on the end of the barrel and the dull grey heads of the bullets in the cylinder filled his view.

The nose of the gun tracked between Jack and Constance. Jack could hear someone pulling the tarp off the tray.

The man kept his eyes on them.

He pointed at Jack. 'You first. Hands on your head and look up.'

He opened the door for Jack, and as he stepped out of the car the man swung his weapon stock right into Jack's mouth.

Jack heard a crunch. The impact sent pain from his jaw down to his toes. He collapsed to the bitumen on his knees, then lay face down on the road. He spat once, and two white molars tumbled from his mouth in a river of blood.

The man cuffed Jack's wrists behind his body with cable ties and yanked hard on them so they bit into his skin. Jack felt his heart rate climb. He could hear a scuffle on the other side of the car, then he heard the thud of metal on bone, and the unmistakable sound of Harry crying out in pain.

An unnatural poison shot through Jack's veins. His body burned and hummed, but he took a deep breath and kept his hands clasped behind his head. The only thing on Earth that scared Jack was his son being harmed.

You just killed yourself.

Today or later, it made no difference to Jack.

His only hope was that the Horsemen were watching this unfold. If so, they would intervene before they could be extracted to the Yard.

The men hadn't searched his body. He could feel his belt and grenades at the top of his left buttock, under his jacket.

Harry moaned. Jack heard a body thud on the bitumen and turned towards it. Constance was pulled from the vehicle and dragged by her armpits away from the car. Jack heard a man speaking with Constance, then her saying something in response.

Then there was another thud against Jack's skull, and he heard nothing more.

He must have lost consciousness. Jack was lying on his side, facing south towards the Bight. He saw a brilliant white horse standing on the plain, its mane rippling in the wind.

Jack could hear men conferring at the rear of the HiLux. He turned his head towards the car. On the far side he could see Harry's hoodie, and the brown suede of a hiking boot. Constance. He flexed and twisted his wrists in the cables, pushed one thumb up his forearm, under his jacket sleeve. Nothing. He reached further up his forearm, straining against the cable ties, and his efforts were rewarded. He circled the velcro band with his thumb, the plastic cuffs now cutting into his wrists. Finally, he felt the smooth plastic cover of the electronic fob.

Jack's index finger clicked the cover off the fob. He felt the raised button on the surface.

He pushed the button three times.

Nothing happened.

He swung his head further around, caught a glimpse of a pair of boots at the rear of the truck.

Jack probed again with his finger, then pushed the same button. Once, twice.

Three times.

There was an eruption from the truck, a mule kick that bounced Jack off the bitumen.

Debris rained across the position, and Jack heard two men screaming, like wounded dogs.

'Constance, go!' Jack shouted.

He rocked to his side, then onto his feet and ran past the

bonnet of his car to see Harry, in the foetal position, covered in black powder and metal dust.

I'll get you mate. One second.

Jack stepped around the rear of the truck into the acrid blast cloud.

He was greeted by a smoking torso, still holding its rifle, legless. An unrecognisable pile of uniform, bone and cauterised flesh. Coiled wet matter spilled onto the road. The scrawny man was still intact and standing, but a broad disc of bone protruded from his eye and his shirt had been reduced to a few shredded strips hanging off his body. He was staggering in a circle with his head tilted back like he was looking out from beneath a blindfold.

Hell in a tailgate.

Jack opened the driver's side door. Constance had already uncovered her carbine and turned for the checkpoint. 'The tent!' he shouted. Constance fired a full clip into the olive tent, just twenty metres away, brass shells sailing through the sky. She ran to the tent, solo.

'Clear! They're not here.'

Jack turned to check on the scrawny man. He was walking around the truck like a lost man, pistol still in his hand.

Jack stepped forward to scoop the dead man's carbine off the ground, but brass rounds tumbled from the base of the magazine, sheared off by the blast. Despite his cuffs, he stepped towards the tottering man and wrenched the silver pistol from his hand. Jack pulled the hammer back and shot him in the side of the head. He crumpled to the ground, kicking his legs.

Jack thought of Harry and a white-hot fury surged through him. He wanted to see the eyes of the man who had hit his son. He ran around the truck to Harry.

'Sit tight.'

Constance was by his side, facing out towards the tent.

'Covering!' she shouted. 'Tent's empty. I'll cover the technical, you get Harry.'

Two men unaccounted for. One probably injured. They were close. He could feel it.

They had harmed his son.

Jack rolled back onto his buttocks, scooped his wrists up to his boot heels and squatted hard. The plastic bit into his wrists, but he pushed down with all his strength, feeling the skin at his wrists separate. Howling in pain, he pushed once more and the cuffs clicked and broke at the join. He reached into the truck and yanked his carbine out of the footwell.

'Coming up!' he shouted.

He stood up, holding his weapon level, blood flowing from his wrists.

With one arm, Jack dragged his son to the rear of the truck and examined him. His hair was bright red and wet, his ear partially separated from his scalp.

'He hit me,' Harry said, the voice of a child.

'I know.' An unnatural anger swept through Jack, the fear disappeared. Jack pulled him into the tray of the ute and slapped his shoulder.

'Stay here. There's two more left.'

Harry slid to the rear of the tray and pulled the tarp across his body, eyes wide with fear, but still thinking, still acting.

Jack ran towards Constance, grabbing her M320 grenade launcher on the way. He draped the weapon sling across her shoulder as she covered the trucks.

'Constance, hit the cars. I'll get the Horsemen overhead.'

Constance shouldered her rifle and swung the grenade launcher up, knelt off the flank of the truck and fired a single round at the technical fifty metres away. The round penetrated the windshield and blew all the windows out in a yellow and black flash. She had the weapon opened and the spent shell ejected before the round even hit the truck.

She paused to inspect the destroyed truck.

What they'd thought was the weapon system was actually two welded axle tubes mounted on an old engine block. A belt of carved wooden ammo was draped across the weapon.

'Decoy!' Jack spat.

The whole checkpoint was bait.

It's a trap. There's a reaction force nearby, I'll bet my life on it.

Constance was reloading as she spoke. 'Get Harry. We gotta move to that outcrop.'

Jack helped Harry into the back seat, then jumped into the front. He picked up the fist mike, which was already transmitting from the Cessna.

'This is Trinity, we have picked up four armoured vehicles leaving a hide, 1300 metres to your north. What's your intention?'

Jack keyed his microphone handset.

'Valhalla now.'

32

'VALHALLA NOW,' SAID COLE TO HIS TEAM AS THE CESSNA tracked hard towards the target.

'Armour leaving a hide. 1300 metres north. Two tanks, two armoured carriers.' Horse read the feed like a football commentator. 'Jack is mobile. He's heading for that bouldered outcrop.'

'We're on.' Beetle talked to himself as he opened the side panel of the plane, which was loaded with launchers with anti-tank rounds behind stowing nets. Sacha was kneeling behind the minigun, and Horse was seated at the video scan, calling targets over the radio. Zeus sat between his legs with his ears up, also watching the feed.

'Checkpoint engaged by Outrider,' said Cole. 'I think they killed two already.'

'Naughty boy, showing off to his new buddy like that,' said Horse over internal comms.

Cole gave his fire orders.

'Beetle, heavy rounds onto the tanks and carriers. Carriers first, then the tanks. I want the infantry taken down.'

Beetle gave him the thumbs-up from behind his rocket launchers.

'Sacha and Horse, you'll be first chalk. Secure the outcrop and give us overwatch.' They nodded.

'Beetle and I will engage from the air, then jump to your position.'

He clicked over to internal comms.

'Pilot, put in jump profile over the outcrop, then make a pass on the armour.'

'Copy,' said the pilot.

Cole checked the video feed. Jack's truck had pulled up, and three dark silhouettes were scrambling up the outcrop.

Cole pointed. 'That's them. Get into position and secure them!'

The plane accelerated over the ocean, rushing alongside the limestone cliff. The pilot climbed to 1000 feet above the ocean, into radar range. It tracked along the bitumen road heading west and then accelerated. The propellers bit into the air.

On its first pass above the checkpoint, the plane rolled to starboard and circled hard over the position. Sacha had turned to Mrs Rabbit, the electronic coffee table now rising to its legs as she held her ear and shouted into a jaw microphone. The device rose back legs first, then front, like a camel, stepping high on the spot and turning for the rear ramp. Sacha, Horse, the robot and Zeus shuffled down the narrow body of the Cessna to the ramp.

The light on the rear panel turned amber and they steadied themselves at the back ramp, checking helmet straps, chest straps, static lines and personal weapons. Horse scooped Zeus against his chest and clipped the dog to his harness. He adjusted the dog's earmuffs and checked his goggles. Sacha slammed her fist down on Horse's shoulder.

'Go!' she screamed.

The signal light turned green, and Cole chopped his arm at the ramp.

Sacha shouted at Mrs Rabbit and the robot galloped

forward. As it reached the threshold, it hopped over the edge, tumbling into the void. Sacha walked behind and jumped, head first. Horse shuffled forward with Zeus on his chest, sat at the edge of the metal ramp and slid out into the air. Cole checked the dispatch of parachutes as he reeled in the static lines.

The pair landed short of the outcrop and the dog yelped as it landed, begging to be released. Horse unclipped it and it sprinted for the boulders. The robot landed with a thud, its hydraulic legs cushioning the impact. It righted itself, sheared the parachute cords and galloped to the outcrop, following its canine sibling.

Sacha's voice boomed through the comms, breathing hard. 'On the ground. Heading to Outrider.'

Beetle had locked the anti-tank rounds in the rocket chamber. He shouted, 'Gun up!' over the intercom. By now, Cole was on the ramp behind the minigun, covering the road.

They flew in low over the holding position. The troops from the armoured hide had climbed onto the tanks and carriers. There were four vehicles in a tight line. There must have been a whole platoon riding atop the armoured fleet. Dark red and black Chinese uniforms could be seen on two of the cars, and the ragged VMF troops were visible with their green bands over their limbs and helmets.

The pilot turned into the next orbital pass, exposed in the daylight to the armour.

Beetle aimed the first recoil-less, guided round onto the Chinese troops on the first carrier. The computer had recorded the shape, size, location and heading of the target.

He pulled the trigger.

The weapon tonked and a long round slid from the tube. It fell twenty metres before the rocket motor engaged and swept the round towards the target.

The first round struck true in a shower of sparks and brown smoke. Half a dozen bodies were jettisoned from the carrier.

'Scratch one!' Beetle shouted to himself. He turned to the pilot. 'Pull us higher, I need a better arc!'

'You got one more pass,' the pilot shouted.

As Beetle reloaded, he tossed the casing and pulled a fresh round from the holding recess.

'Gun up!' he yelled.

The pilot pulled into a hard right-side bank, circling high above the armoured formation that had burst across the red desert in a panic.

The co-pilot on the ground side of the cockpit called the targets out to the Cole, but he was already on it. He gripped the handles of the minigun and pulled the twin trigger. The six barrels spun to life in a continuous rip. He cut a line of tracer across the exposed troops. Some tumbled off the tanks in the melee, providing easy targets. Cole wasn't aiming, he just walked the ripping tracer across the uniformed soldiers in long bursts. Beetle reloaded his rocket and watched Cole as he knelt and fired, the brass and link tumbling from the gun and off the ramp.

The aircraft circled a hard left around the formation again, jockeying above the first T-100 tank. The tank commander was already swinging his crew machine gun into the sky to shoot at the Cessna. A trail of red tracers whipped past the craft.

'Hurry!' the pilot said.

Beetle released another round. It popped out of the tube and arced down, missing the rear of the tank.

'Shit!' yelled Beetle.

The tanks had broken formation and one was making a break for the bouldered outcrop. Beetle reloaded. Second-last round.

'Gun up! Firing now!' he shouted.

The round arced down and slammed into the turret of the tank. A puff of smoke snaked out the end of the barrel. The tank commander slithered from the turret hatch and sprinted away. Beetle yelled and looked down the aircraft for confirmation from the pilots as he loaded the final round.

The burn hatch flipped off the rear of the turret and a column of flame billowed into the air. More figures slithered out of the hatches onto the red earth, limping for cover.

Cole fired a continuous burst from the minigun down onto the soldiers. He walked the tracer streams across the toy soldiers and they collapsed onto the deck, showered with earth and lead. He fired through a 200-round belt, filling the rear of the aircraft with the smell of burning metal and acrid cordite.

'That's Winchester on the 84mm,' Beetle shouted, making a cutting motion across his throat.

'Next pass, we're gonna jump,' shouted Cole.

Beetle clipped his static line to the wire overhead cable of the aircraft and clapped the pilot on the shoulder.

'Thanks for the shit flying, we're out.'

Cole disconnected his headset and clipped onto the overhead wire, then turned to the video feed. He saw Jack, Harry and Constance firing from behind the boulders at the remaining infantry.

'Bring me back over the drop zone! Co-pilot, take the gun,' Cole shouted. The co-pilot unbuckled himself and climbed to the rear of the craft, his aviator glasses askew, sweat on his brow.

The plane levelled off, and the engine revs dropped as they washed off speed. Once they were 300 metres short of the outcrop, Cole gave a chop of the arm. Beetle ran off the ramp and howled into the wind as he dove out.

Cole watched him jump, then followed suit. It was time to enter the fray.

Jack had taken up a position on the rear of the outcrop and hidden Harry in a small nook. His ear was bleeding badly, and he was pale and faint from blood loss.

'We'll get you patched up soon, mate.' Jack held his son's hand for a moment, then went to search for Constance.

He climbed to the top of the outcrop, where Constance was raining pike rounds onto the infantry troops that were only a few hundred metres away. Rounds were whipping over the outcrop, and bullets pinged off the granite boulders.

Constance was weapon up, shooting at all angles. She didn't blink as she fired, and her white teeth were locked together against the rip of the rocket-powered 40mm rounds as they ripped across the desert.

They had killed or wounded close to two-thirds of the troops. Most of those kills were thanks to the rain of fire from the Cessna overhead.

Jack climbed up next to Constance and was about to fire when in the low ground behind the boulder he saw two humans, a robot and a dog closing on his position. Only in occupied Australia would such a sight surprise no one.

A robot, a dog and two Horsemen ran into a checkpoint . . .

He could hear the hydraulic pivots of Mrs Rabbit closing on his position.

Sacha and Horse gave no greeting, just mounted the boulders and went to work. Constance shouted target indications while they fired long bursts.

Zeus crouched next to Harry and rubbed his nose in the boy's face. The robot swung itself rearwards and scanned.

Jack called to Sacha, 'I need Mrs Rabbit!'

'Go ahead,' said Sacha.

Jack pulled his headset arm from his jacket and activated it.

'Authorise: Jack Dunne, Outrider 11.'

'Access authorised. Can I help?'

Jack slung his weapon and ran to the truck. He pulled the AI mine out of the back and examined it quickly. It was undamaged.

'Link to recovery platform. Run mine to nearest target. Engage and kill all enemy.'

'Copy. Link confirmed,' said the steady female voice.

Jack ran back and lay the AI mine on the robot's metal panel. A graphene panel as wide as his hand extended crossways over the mine and locked it in place.

'Targeting parameter: Prioritise command elements. Kill chain authorised,' said Jack.

'Parameters understood. Moving.'

Mrs Rabbit sprinted across the desert towards the enemy, clouds of dust rising behind it, the rock mounted to its back.

The robot covered 200 metres before Jack had sprinted the twenty metres back to the outcrop. He clambered up just in time to see three columns of black smoke rise from the low ground. The enemy fire dropped to a dribble.

'Look!' said Sacha. She pointed at a dust cloud galloping towards them from the opposite flank, the brushed metal of the robot shining in the sun.

'Damage assessment: four infantry KIA. One was ranked major.'

'Yeeewww!!' screamed Sacha.

'Jesus,' said Jack. 'How do you know?'

'Cross-reference from open-source intelligence and social media; 99.9 per cent certainty.'

Jack shook his head. 'Treat Outrider Junior. Prepare for evac,' he said to the robot.

Mrs Rabbit galloped back over to the outcrop and lowered itself to the ground next to Harry. It discarded the spent mine to one side.

'Wait there, Harry, I got you,' the machine said to him.

Harry crawled onto the machine. Jack reached over and squeezed his hand. It was cold. He was in shock, but still functional.

'We're leaving. You did great.' Jack kissed his son on the

forehead and smiled at him. Jack locked eyes with Harry, his son's pupils like pin-pricks. He tried to smile but grimaced in pain.

Cole and Beetle were jogging over to the outcrop. The Horsemen helped Jack and Constance off the position towards their HiLux, still parked fifty metres away.

Sacha shouted into her mouthpiece. 'Take the patient to the pick-up point. Staple him on the way. Stay next to Jack's truck.'

Cole called into his throat mike, 'Target secured. Moving to evac point.'

'My son . . .' said Jack.

'It's okay Jack, we got him. Mrs Rabbit will fix him up.'

Cole called into his headset, 'Trinity, wheels down on the highway, best speed.'

'Copy. Inbound. Interceptors have been launched from the Yard. Merge in four minutes. Wheels down in two minutes.'

'Get in the HiLux!' screamed Cole. 'Interceptors are coming. We got less than four minutes to get under the cliffs.'

Cole ran his hands over a bunch of grapeshot holes punched into the side of the car, flakes of paint missing.

'Your car's hit. Get in.'

Jack climbed into the rear and Constance drove, Cole sitting beside her. The rest of the Horsemen and Zeus jumped in the tray.

Mrs Rabbit ran alongside them, Harry curled up in the foetal position. Jack watched the robot galloping beside the car. A motorised arm squirted saline into Harry's wound, then pinched and glued the wound shut. Harry didn't wince. A roll of gauze appeared in the bot's hand and made the final wraps on the boy's head. Jack leaned out the window with his arm outstretched, and the robot elevated one side of the table as it ran so Harry's hand could touch his. This thing was another species entirely; it had compassion.

Cole pointed out the Cessna, which was circling across the ocean to line up a final approach.

'Cessna will pick us up, and we'll sneak out alongside the limestone cliffs. Let's just hope they miss us.' He pointed at the ocean.

It was high risk.

Jack looked at his son, strapped to the top of a robot, plasma and blood running from his sealed cut.

Another day in paradise.

'Go,' shouted Cole as Constance brought the car to a stop. They jumped out and knelt off the side of the road, covering all directions. Jack and Harry stayed in the centre of the circle.

'Watch and shoot,' Cole called to the operators. 'Mrs Rabbit, air defence scan.' The robot repeated the call and its head swivelled 360 degrees to cover all directions. The Cessna was completing a slow turn low on the horizon. It lined up on the road and dropped its flaps. The landing gear was lowered.

'When wheels are down, get straight into the aircraft and put a parachute on,' Cole said.

The Cessna made its final approach. As the wheels touched down and the ramp was lowered, the team sprinted across the blacktop, through the propeller wash and up the ramp. Jack took one last look at the HiLux as he went. It had served them well.

Jack and the robot ran up the ramp, Mrs Rabbit still carrying Harry.

The plane taxied and the pilot was revving the engine before he raised the ramp. They bumped down the highway and lifted into the sky. Jack's stomach lurched. He had not been in an aircraft in years.

He was scanning the horizon, looking for aircraft. The robot scanned out the windows to the south and east. It crackled to life: 'Bogeys, three o'clock high, eight miles. Vector speed: 900mph.'

Cole stooped to look out the ocean-facing windows. Jack followed his gaze and saw the twin black crosses with shimmering exhaust contrails in the blue sky.

J-20 fighter aircraft. Two of them. Swooping low into attack formation.

33

'Sir, looks like we have Jack Dunne with a team of Horsemen on the ground at the decoy checkpoint. They're pinned. We have armour on them.'

Kayne turned to the blue force tracking screen, Jess looking over his shoulder.

'The border checkpoint?' he asked.

'Yessir. Confirmed at the checkpoint. With air support.'

'Are they alive?' said Kayne.

'Yessir. He's not responding now, but the last update was from the Squadron Commander two minutes ago.'

Kayne looked at Jess and grinned. 'What did I say?' He slammed his fist on the desk and hooted. 'He fell for it. We got him.'

He slapped the radio operator's shoulder. 'Tell them to hold them in location. I want our team in there quick before those idiots try to take the credit.'

The radio operator had sweat on his brow and upper lip. 'Sir, we're having trouble raising the checkpoint.'

'Tell them to hold, we'll fly in with the Principal,' said Kayne.

The operator shifted in his seat. 'Sir, we got a report from the intel cell at the Yard that they picked up,' he read from his notebook, 'fixed wing aircraft providing direct fire support.'

Kayne turned to his sister, then back to the radio operator.

'Resistance don't have air support.'

He snatched the handset.

'Checkpoint West, this is Cranbourne. Send sitrep.'

Static.

Kayne repeated his call. More static.

The radio operator was sliding further into his seat.

'Jesus,' said Kayne. 'Get the Principal.'

34

JACK'S STOMACH LURCHED AS THE CESSNA DROPPED A FEW hundred feet in a matter of seconds and pulled up just over the frothing ocean. The pilot slammed the throttle forward. Through the windows at nine o'clock, Jack could see limestone caves and cliff and rocks and sea spray. They weaved along the coast, the engines screaming. Jack surveyed the cliffs but there was no beach, just jagged limestone boulders being pounded by twenty-foot swell.

Cole was scanning the water to the south as Jack pulled two reserve parachutes from the seat lockers.

'Bogey still closing,' Cole said.

Jack followed his gaze and saw twin contrails and the lumbering bodies of two J-20 fighters appear from over the ocean. One ripped high over the tail of the Cessna in a show of force. Low enough to the surface for twin coils of spindrift to whip up from ocean. The warplane was enormous. Slate grey like a shark.

He turned to Harry. Mrs Rabbit had wrapped his ear neatly, but bright red already blossomed through the field dressing. His skin was still pale, and there were blue veins just visible at his temple.

'Anything happens, jump out that door.' Cole pointed at the back ramp, then slapped the metal T-bar on the parachute. 'Pull this handle. Get out. Gravity will do the rest.'

Jack nodded. He knew if they jumped into that water, they were dead. He grabbed Harry's shoulder and pulled him up in his seat. He was limp and clammy, but his eyes locked onto Jack's.

'Put this on. We might be going for a swim.' Struggling to maintain his composure, Jack pulled off Harry's jumper. He thought for a moment, then removed his leather jacket and put it on his son, remembering the automatic buoyancy cell in each arm. He zipped the jacket up then pulled the harness over the boy's head and put his hand on the release handle.

'If we go out, pull this. Don't pull it until you're in the air, okay?' He tugged Harry forward into his chest and was hit by a surge of deep sorrow. This could be his last embrace with his son. Through the fall and drift of the craft and the roar of the propellers, they held each other. Jack took his son's face in with both hands, so they were nose to nose.

'If you go in the water, stay calm.'

Harry nodded, but his eyes were red. He could barely swim in rough water and they both knew it.

'I love you.' Jack kissed his forehead.

He knelt and pulled on his own harness.

Constance already had her chute on and was looking out the side of the aircraft, scanning for the enemy. The pilots were sweating and wrestling the plane as close to the cliff as they could. Cole turned back to Constance and Jack.

'Okay, jump, we'll follow.'

Shit.

Cole pulled Jack and Harry to their feet and shepherded them down the ramp, which the pilot had lowered to level. The rear ramp window looked like a bright plasma TV showing limestone cliffs, shadows that reached beyond the whitewater, and twenty-foot waves thrashing the cliffs. Jack's heart was pounding as he pulled Harry upright and turned him to face the rear opening. 'We're jumping!'

Harry held his arms across his front and stood still as Jack checked his chute straps. The other Horsemen were scanning the ocean.

Jack looked at Cole, hoping for a last-minute reprieve, a stay of execution.

Cole was grinding his teeth while looking at the co-pilot.

He turned back to Jack, then pointed at the ramp like a maniac.

'GO, GO, GO!!!!' He shoved Jack and Harry towards the ramp. Constance followed behind. The nose of the craft pitched upward, trading speed for height. Harry and Jack both collapsed to a crouch on the ramp as they shot skyward, their legs buckled under the force of the climbing plane. Ocean filled the plasma screen. The pilot was heading to jump altitude. Jack looked out the ramp and saw a red earth headland, the cliffs beneath him.

'GO!' Cole pushed Jack. He held Harry's arms and they rolled off the ramp into air.

Jack pulled Harry's chute as they fell into the roaring void.

PART THREE

THE RETURN

35

JACK'S HARNESS YANKED AGAINST HIS BODY AS HIS PARACHUTE unfurled. Harry was a short distance away with his chute already open. Jack checked his risers and looked back for Constance. Instead, he caught a yellow column of flame streaking across the sky towards the headland.

'Jump!' Jack shouted at the plane, willing them to get off in time.

The Cessna was tilting wing down in an unrecoverable dive. As Jack watched, it slammed into the headland, a billowing explosion of yellow and orange.

Jack knew the Horsemen hadn't got out. He hadn't seen Constance bail out either.

They had cleared the headland, but the ocean was a hundred metres below. Jack was falling faster than Harry, so he pulled hard on the forward risers of his parachute. Air spilled from the rear of the parachute and he drifted towards his son. Jack was thirty metres below him.

He looked down. Pure emerald ocean. He braced his knees and shut his eyes.

He plunged deep into the roiling waters of the Bight and his clothes flushed with cold water.

He reached for the surface and when his head broke through, he drew his knife from his belt and cut the risers away. The swell was bucking and rolling; it was like dropping five metres into a valley and then hurtling back up the hill. He spun around, searching for his son.

The shadow of Harry's chute passed over him. He turned, shoved the knife into his chest belt and began to swim towards the splash.

His legs were still jelly from the adrenaline, but he pulled his breaths long and slow, working to calm his mind.

Just like being sunk underwater in helicopters for escape training.

His boots were slowing him, and he felt like he was swimming in treacle. In the rise and fall of the swell, he could see Harry flailing in his parachute risers. The arms of the leather jacket had inflated and he was propped up clear of the water, but he was coughing and his eyes were wide with terror. He held his arms out for his father.

'Help me!' he screamed.

'I'm coming!' Jack was thrashing towards Harry with powerful strokes. Harry disappeared in the trough of swell, his arms were limp from burnout. Jack kept swimming.

He lunged for his son as he closed the distance.

'I got you. It's okay. We're okay.'

Jack pulled the knife from his chest strap and began to cut Harry's riser. A wave crashed over them and he held Harry's vest with one arm. Another wave hit, and the knife was snatched from his hand. Harry vomited a thick stream of seawater as the wave subsided. Jack pulled him onto his back and supported his neck with his arm.

'Hold onto me. Hang on.'

Harry gripped his arm, but was still throwing up white foam and rasping between breaths.

'Rest. Let the ocean do its thing.' Jack looked around at the cliff face that towered a hundred metres away. 'Yeewww!' Jack called as a thick wave washed over them. 'Look! Nice ocean, big cliffs. So cool, hey?' Jack remembered his surf instructor speaking to him like this when they were caught in double overhead waves at Margaret River and he was convinced he was going to die. The words had calmed him then.

There was a ripping streak overhead and the water vibrated into foam. Two jets circled around the Bight, a long way out.

If there are jets, there are helicopters too.

They had to move.

Jack watched the base of the cliffs in the rise and fall of the swell. He spied a pale band in the middle of the bay, maybe crushed rock or sand. Crevices and caves dotted the fifty-metre-high cliffs. The limestone shelves overhung the water. They sat in that shadow, the sun now low to the west. Harry had stopped vomiting and was now paddling with one arm, the parachutes and risers trailing them. Jack pulled the risers up and looped his arm through them.

'We both live, or we both die. I'm not going anywhere without you, mate.' Harry's dressing had come off. The cut over his ear was clean and stapled, but it had an ugly swelling to it. His forehead had an avocado-sized contusion in it and the skin around his eyes was turning black and blue from swelling. The water washed pink off his head.

Blood in the water.

'We're gonna get washed in. Relax. The waves will take us in.'

If the sharks don't get us first.

'Dad,' Harry spluttered. 'I love you.'

Jack's voice turned ragged. 'I love you too. We're gonna make it. Okay?' Jack felt a little surge of hope.

They rose and fell ten plus metres from peak to trough as they faced the cliffs. Jack sunk under the water and drank half a litre of saltwater. He surfaced again, vomiting foam. He was getting weak. Jelly in his arms and legs.

Another house-sized wave pitched them into the air.

It's getting shallow. Waves are popping up.

The waves rolled past them. From behind they looked like enormous monsters, bent forward and throwing everything in their path high into the air.

They were in the impact zone.

'Stop swimming. Deep breaths now.'

Harry was sucking in deep breaths, copying Jack.

The ten-foot face reared up and they became weightless.

Jack sucked in a breath and they pitched forward.

Wrapping his arms around Harry, he locked him in tight with the last of his strength.

36

THE WAVE PITCHED UP AND SLAMMED THEM INTO THE WATER so hard Jack's eardrums collapsed from the pressure.

His limbs thrashed about at odd angles.

Jack tried to still his mind. Years earlier, he would feel for his leg rope in this moment and climb onto his board, but not today. Harry had slipped from his grasp, but he felt a thrashing on his left arm, and a web of thin ropes across his neck.

Parachute cords.

He might have lost his grip on Harry, but those parachute cords held his son. He opened his eyes in the whitewater and scooped upwards to the pale light, knowing the next wave wasn't far away.

As his head broke the whitewater he inhaled deeply and looked for Harry, but there was just a sea of boiling foam. Jack faced the surf. It was fizzing and quiet, until the silent guillotine of a wave attacked him from above. He sucked in another quick breath and submerged as the wave detonated across the water.

Another thrashing.

His lungs were burning now, and he had pins and needles in his hands and feet. Stars in his eyes. His ears had compressed from the barotrauma and he guessed he was a storey or more underwater. He wrenched away the parachute cables and paddled for his life. He clamped his jaw shut as his diaphragm convulsed. A tingling spread to his feet and hands.

He breached the surface again, coughing.

'Harry!' he bellowed.

Nothing.

A wave exploded behind him, and as the tower of white-water came for him, he turned and pointed himself towards the beach, letting the swell carry him forward. His feet hit the first rocks of the shore.

He climbed to his feet in the shallow water and turned, screaming for Harry. The boy had almost certainly had a two-wave hold-down. That was two minutes underwater in a boxing match. Most top surfers struggled under that.

He checked the foam and spied the green shadow of Harry's parachute in the break. Jack stood knee-deep in the whitewater and cupped his hands to his mouth.

'Harry!'

He scanned the edge of the bay, where the water met the limestone and there was no beach. There, tucked under a lime-stone ledge, he could see a leather-clad arm and Harry's pale upper body bobbing in the whitewater. He'd been swept across the bay, pinned to the cliff wall.

'Harry! Wait!' Jack screamed. He began stumbling over the rocks towards Harry, then turned back for the beach. He waited for Harry's parachute to be swept in and bundled it in his arms.

'Stay there!' He swept the sopping bundle up and clambered over the narrow beach towards Harry. As he went, he rolled some fist-sized rocks into the parachute to make a heavy point. A slab of whitewater hit Harry and sunk him. As Jack watched, terrified, he bobbed up again in his jacket, spitting seawater.

Jack stumbled over the boulders. When he got within twenty metres of Harry he swung the rock in the parachute around his head and slung it to Harry. The first throw fell short. Jack walked

waist-deep into the water and swung again. This time, the parachute landed closer. Harry let go of the cliff and dog-paddled to
the parachute. When he had hold of it, Jack pulled him through
the swell into the beach. Weak and struggling, Harry lost his
grip ten metres off the shore. Jack swam into the whitewater
and scooped his son up in his arms. His head lolled back, white
skin and blue lips, his body limp from fatigue, near death.

Jack pulled Harry onto the rocks and tipped him on his
flank. He pressed on his chest near his armpit and foam and
water ran from his mouth. He started coughing. As another
wave washed into them, Jack hauled him up by his armpits and
dragged him clear of the whitewater. He was breathing again.
Jack collapsed with his back against a limestone slab.

He pulled Harry into his lap and they sat there, in the shade
of the cliff, for a long time, watching the hell from which they
had swum. Jack couldn't move his limbs. After forty minutes of
combat and another twenty minutes in the ocean, he was spent.

Harry coughed and spluttered and the colour slowly returned
to his skin. Harry's shoes were gone and his pants had been
stripped off him in the whitewater. All he had was his under-
wear and his dad's jacket.

'Never again, Dad,' said Harry and they both began to
laugh, giddy at having swum with Death and slipping his bony
grasp. Jack hugged his son for a long time, savouring the taste
of fresh air. He'd watched his son sink under the ocean; he'd
accepted his certain death.

So close to death, but so alive.

'I know you're tired but we have to hide.'

Jack stood and walked along the bank of the beach. There
was almost no way up the cliff face, save for a single seam of
rock that led five metres up to a shallow nook. Just a handhold,
but it might do.

Jack combed the tiny beach and collected two armfuls of
wet seaweed. He bundled it into the parachute and clipped the

harness to his chest, then began to free climb as Harry watched him. Five metres up, he found a sinkhole in the wall of dissolved limestone. It was a wide nook with bird droppings on the floor, large enough for them both if they sat one in front, one behind. Once he had reached the nook, Jack lowered the harness to Harry. Harry shouldered the harness and climbed the seam while Jack pulled. He had no strength, but Jack was able to get him to the rock seam. He put Harry in the cross of his folded legs and then wrapped the parachute around them both, pulling the seaweed bundle to their front. Jack was parched, shivering in the cave recess. He remembered Jimbo talking about the emergency beacon in the jacket. It would have self-activated in the water jump.

'Did anyone else get out?' asked Harry after a long silence.

'I don't think so,' said Jack.

They listened to the crashing waves.

'They saved us,' said Jack.

'Yeah. They did,' said Harry. 'Did Constance get out?'

'I don't think so.'

Everything I touch turns to shit. Good luck holding the Hill if she's gone.

Jack felt a sense of helplessness. He could barely protect his own son, let alone save the Hill. Harry had been bashed, shot at, pushed out of a plane. Drowned. For all that had passed, they were empty-handed.

Except for each other.

37

AMONG THE SMOKING RUINS OF THE CHECKPOINT, DINGOES fought over the remains of the bodies. A wedge-tailed eagle, a full three feet tall, sat on the chest of a fighter and picked through the mess. It raised its wings as it saw the Dragon VTOL jet, matte black and barely audible, circle the battlefield. The eagle chewed a strip of skin and watched.

As the jet found its mark, both engines swivelled forward. The Dragon descended to the road, among the smoking cars. Debris and rock, car parts and dingoes all scattered as the jet settled on the blacktop and a large ramp folded down. A whirly whirly crossed the road and disappeared into the desert.

The Principal walked off the ramp before it had touched the ground, a tiny black carbine slung across his chest. He scanned his surrounds as he strode down the ramp. Jess and Kayne fanned out behind him, weapons up.

'Christ,' Kayne muttered to himself as he stepped around a torso laying on the bitumen.

The Principal scanned the shattered trucks and walked past several of the dead fighters. A skinny man was propped up on his elbows in the centre of the position, a look of abject shock on his face; the hole through the side of his head a blackened stain with a trembling mass of flies on it. He gurgled as the Principal squatted in front of him and inspected the wound on the side of the man's head.

'Comrade, that's no good.'

The man began to shudder and sob. Tears ran from his eyes. The whites of his eyes were deep red from broken capillaries, his pupils wide and black. The Principal wiped a tear from the man's cheek and gripped his jaw, summoning Kayne and Jess with his glare. They stood behind him.

'You missed him. You missed everyone.' He scanned the horizon, then stared back at the man's eyes. 'You could've been a hero.' The Principal stood up and turned to Jess, nodding back to the man. His meaning was clear.

Jess didn't move. Kayne stepped around Jess and shouldered his carbine, but the Principal raised a finger, his eyes not leaving Jess.

'No.' He pointed at her. 'You.'

She exhaled, stepped astride the man's legs and pointed her rifle at the crown of his head.

The shot bucked across the saltbush plain, and the eagle flinched and crouched. The man's head bounced as it struck the blacktop. Jess lowered her rifle as she stood over the man and looked at him. He was gone. Kayne stood motionless. Jess turned and faced the eagle, and the eagle stared back at her.

A small mercy, perhaps, she told herself.

Kayne spoke first.

'Dunne was kitted up, decent weapons. That HiLux further down the road? Looks like the rear tray was rigged. Ripped two blokes in half.'

The Principal faced him, his good eye probing. 'You continue to use the incorrect tools for the job,' he motioned to the dead man, 'so I am forced to intervene.'

He stared at Kayne, then turned and walked towards the

bird as the jet wound up. He boarded, then leaned into the comms bay of the aircraft.

'Tell Task Force Leopard we missed their target; they're now the main effort. Get objective Outrider, the boy, and the woman.'

'Capture?' said the radio operator.

The Principal shook his head. 'Kill.'

38

THE DRAGON JET FLEW IN LOW OVER THE MCG AND NAVIGATED its way between the towering light poles that had once lit winter sports games. The towers were now painted red with a yellow stripe down them. Bunched at each light array were a cluster of cell antennas, thermal cameras and video capture devices.

A formation of five drones smacked into a broad mesh net that ran between two of the lighting towers. Men in climbing harnesses scuppered out to the drones like spiders after their prey.

The MCG was now the largest forward operating base in Victoria.

Electronic banners wrapped the playing field. They used to show game footage and statistics. Advertisements for new cars. Reminders to report anti-social behaviour.

Now, motivational banners for the PLA whipped across the screens. Young men and women in flying helmets. Soldiers in combat fatigues, their rifles held high, charging through the jungles of Taiwan, blood running from their bayonets. J-20 formations on bombing runs. An astronaut saluting a red flag on a red planet, three more figures on the ridgeline behind, a cylindrical buggy behind them.

A scanning code for reporting insurgent information.

The old scoreboard was a screen the size of a house and it dominated the stadium walls. Emblazoned across it was footage of a listing aircraft carrier, the USS *Gerald Ford*, apocalyptic fires bellowing from its underdecks, the on-board phalanx raging against incoming hypersonic missiles. Sailors jumping into the water from the high deck. Jet fighters sliding off the runway into the ocean and the hardtop sunk into the water line.

Jess took a long breath.

We should've stayed the hell out of this war.

The Yarra end of the stadium was covered over with a board awning, sectioning off an area for maintenance and medical centres. At the opposite end were a dozen aprons of crushed rock with concrete blast walls where helicopters took off and landed. A regiment of 400 soldiers sat in the stadium seats before a dropdown projector that showed a terrain map of Mount Dandenong.

The aprons were packed with helicopters; soldiers with forklifts loaded missiles onto the wing stubs.

The Principal, Jess and Kayne, who had just touched down at the MCG, disembarked from the vertical take-off and landing jet and strode across the airstrip towards the stadium.

Kayne returned the chin nod of his fighters as they walked to the stands. Jess followed, staring around her at the nightmare of this once-beloved childhood location, grotesquely transformed.

They passed twelve men in armoured suits, titanium matte metal struts reaching up their legs and spine and arms. The ballistic glass situational awareness overlay shielded their upper bodies, checked by technicians in white overalls. Two operators in suits thrust and parried, using metal pikes that extended from their forearms.

'The suits will make all the difference,' said the Principal.

Kayne grunted.

They crossed the VMF section of the oval.

There were twenty HiLux trucks with the Cranbourne Boys and their pig-hunting dogs in cages on the back. The boys wore tattered football jerseys from the old times. Pistols in leather holsters and long knives ran down their thighs.

They followed the Principal to the members' section, where he swiped his ID card against the secure access door. Inside, maps, models and comms terminals lined the room.

The Principal booted up a terminal and three images appeared on the screen.

The heading, in Chinese with English subtitles, read: 'Joint Prioritised Effects List'. The Principal turned to Kayne and Jess. 'These are your targets.'

The first photo showed Constance in a black pants suit and dark glasses on a city street. Not Western; probably Hanoi or Singapore. Her hair was tied up, but she was unmistakable: sharp edges, immaculate skin, dressed to kill.

'Objective Nunchuck: aka Constance Lang. CIA. Offensive Fires coordinator for the Resistance. She served in Taiwan as a Talon Commander supporting local forces. She is a strategic force coordinator.'

'Can you elaborate? Force coordinator?' said Kayne.

'CIA only allows ground operations officers to call in fires. It's the only way allies can use supporting strategic weapons. They must have Outrider escort and protection,' the Principal said.

Kayne looked at Jess.

She stared at the screen, eyes unfocused.

'If the Americans introduce their best assets, they can hurt us,' the Principal said.

Kayne went to speak, but the Principal cut him off.

'I've sat under US B-21 Raider strikes. They can kill thousands of troops in just one pass.'

The second photo was an image of Jack Dunne, bearded and smiling in the breaks at Kabul airfield, dressed in jeans and a long-sleeved shirt with his sleeves rolled up. Body armour and a pistol belt. He was standing with several Afghan soldiers in similar dress.

'Objective Outrider: Captain Jack "Damage" Dunne. One of the foremost unconventional warfare operators in the Australian military, with extensive experience in discrete reconnaissance, counterintelligence, improvised weapons, sabotage, explosives, marksmanship. Completed a doctorate in Counter Insurgency at UCLA. Led a recovery team in Kabul, 2021. Deployed on an undeclared mission to lead a Ukrainian Special Ops battalion. Awarded a Ukrainian Medal of Honour and a Medal of Gallantry. He has two Distinguished Service Medals.' The Principal looked up; his good eye tracked the two of them.

'The Hill is his home. He's protected by the locals. He's a direct report to the Hill Commander, Dyson Carr.' A grainy image of Dyson shot up, a towering man with a bull neck, standing on the ramp of an M1 Bradley in a poppy field in Ukraine.

'Interesting twist about Dunne: his wife was an intelligence officer, Objective Mace, aka, "Gemma Dunne".'

The Principal smiled. 'My task force was credited with her incapacitation.' Jess filed that little fact away.

A picture came up of Harry, Gemma and Jack standing together at a beach in Perth. Harry was beaming a big smile, one front tooth missing.

The Principal pointed at Harry.

'Objective Pike. This is Jack Dunne's son. Eleven years old. Trained by his father and considered dangerous. Taskforce lawyers have approved him as a combatant target.'

Jess shut her eyes and took a deep breath.

He's eleven. You sick bastard.

The next photo showed four Special Ops soldiers atop horses in the middle of a rock desert. They looked like the sort of gang that would hold up your horse and carriage.

'Objective Pestilence, Plague, Famine and War. The Four Horsemen. Indicted war criminals, already tried in absentia by the CCP. They have a lot of blood on their hands.'

Bit rich to call them war criminals, Jess thought.

'They were at the checkpoint today, and they killed your team, plus one of my armoured units,' said the Principal. My guess is they're still alive.'

Kayne nodded.

'Your mission: destroy Objective Outrider no later than 0300 tomorrow night. After we achieve that, the whole Leopard Task Force and a Chinese Regiment, with VMF clearing force, will be over the Hill.'

The Principal stopped pacing and moved to stand directly in front of Kayne and Jess.

'We might get one more shot at Outrider before he hits the Hill. Launch your air assets and your best team and hit him before he gets the asset there.'

Jess and Kayne looked at each other.

'Kill them all,' said the Principal.

Jess piped up. 'The kid?'

'Especially the kid.' He stormed out of the room.

Jess stewed in her seat. She had heard enough.

What if your creation turns on you?

39

Jack jolted awake.

Beneath the sound of waves pounding the beach, he heard the sound of rubber scraping on rocks.

He woke Harry with a gentle shake.

'Listen,' he whispered.

They sat with their eyes open and mouths closed, listening intently. They heard a rock tumble on the shoreline.

Jack peered forward over the edge of their nook.

Two figures in black were hauling a zodiac rubber boat onto the shoreline.

'Dingo. Dingo. Dingo,' came a whisper from below.

'Dingo,' Jack whispered down to them, flooded with relief.

One soldier slapped the other on the back.

'Jackpot. Call it in,' he said.

He called up to Jack. 'Let's go, Jack. We're taking you back to the Hill.'

After thirty minutes in the zodiac, a squat, angular vessel appeared in the ocean. It had no windows and no deck space, and the sharp edges of an iceberg. When they circled the vessel from the stern, Jack was astounded. It was a stealth raider. All smooth edges, slate grey, with block panels of radar-absorbing material on its exterior.

A narrow door raised on the leeside of the craft and they drove the zodiac into the bay. The door slid down behind them, and another rose from the bottom of the craft. Inside was a wide loading dock bathed in red light.

Jack helped two men pull Harry from the boat, then he collapsed back in the boat, unable to move again.

He fell into a deep black sleep.

A doctor stood over Jack and watched as a mechanical arm with narrow forceps fished around under his skin. The pan clanked as the hand retrieved a sliver of bullet fragment from Jack's forearm. The arm moved twice as fast as a human, and it was completely silent. Jack felt no pain, only the pressure on his shoulder, and he watched the arm working on him with no hesitation.

The doctor looked over his glasses at Jack. Jack tried to sit up, but the doctor put a hand on his chest.

'Your boy's okay. Nearly lost his ear. We got him hooked up to a bag. He's fine. You were all badly dehydrated.'

'Anyone else?'

'The boys found a woman in the bay next to you. Nearly dead. She lost a hand. She was in the water a long time.'

Jack winced. He turned to the robotic arm and watched it parse his flesh.

'A surgeon in Boston is doing that.' The doctor nodded to the arm.

Jack stared at it, marvelling at its movements, fast and fine.

'Constance. The woman. We need her on the Hill.'

'I know. We got her a new hand. Cybernetic motors. They printed it on the sub, and this little sucker,' he patted the arm, 'fixed it back on.'

The doctor pulled his mask down and tabled his glasses.

'Okay. You're clear. We'll glue you up and get you some antibiotics. Your son is in the next bay.' The doctor held Jack's hand. 'I was a regimental doctor.'

'Thanks, doc,' whispered Jack.

'It's my honour.' He shook Jack's hand.

The doctor supported Jack as he sat up carefully, breathing through the pain. The doctor handed him a fresh t-shirt, which he pulled on gingerly, then they walked to the next room. It was a recovery room, with light blue walls and benches mounted to the bulkheads and a booth where you could sit.

Harry was laid out under a foil emergency blanked with a cannula in his wrist. Jack put his hand on Harry's forehead then leaned down and kissed it.

'Hey, little man. You're okay. You're alright.'

Harry's eyes wandered across the room before they locked onto Jack.

'I wanna go home. I want Mum.'

Jack winced. 'Me too,' he whispered.

'Where's Constance?'

'She's alive. She's here.'

Harry smiled.

'What are we gonna do?'

'We need to get Constance to the Hill. If we do that, we might be able to stop it getting rolled. Then we can get out. For good.'

Harry nodded. 'I'll help you, Dad.'

A man in blue overalls stooped as he entered the room. He had a thick black beard and carried a steaming enamel mug in each hand, which he placed on the galley top. The man smiled, showing a gold incisor. Jack stared at him in shock, then pulled him close and hugged him.

'Slater? I heard you were dead.'

'That's how I like to be,' said Slater.

'This is my son, Harry,' Jack said. 'Harry meet Slater. We go a long way back.'

'G'day, Harry.' Slater handed a mug to each of them. 'Drink up. Hot chocolate.'

He went on. 'Only a few of us got out of the Pacific. We were in the lifeboats for a month. Fisherman picked us up. Once we got back to Darwin, they hid us away. Kept us dead.'

'They wanted a network that didn't exist,' Jack surmised.

'That's right,' said Slater. 'And here we are. We run all the offshore missions.'

A ghost force of special operators. Totally off the books.

'Who else?' asked Jack.

'You know Carson's team? All of them.'

'I don't believe it,' said Jack. 'Where are they?'

Slater grinned at Jack. 'Around. You'll see them sometime.'

'What were you doing out here?' Jack asked.

'Well, we had work further up the east coast, but were diverted to here once your mission kicked off, in case you needed support.'

Jack shook his head, realising how little he really knew about this war.

Slater went on. 'You did great. We were sure you were gone. We picked up the girl and the rest of the team in the bay next to you. They were stuck to the cliff face. You were lucky to get ashore. You should both be dead.'

'Bullshit.' Jack felt the rush of hope. 'All of them?'

Slater's face turned grave. 'No. Horse is gone.'

Jack's heart sank.

'Died saving Zeus. Tied his life vest to the dog after they hit the water. The dog survived, but Horse drowned. We got his body.'

'Ah.' Jack shut his eyes for a moment, fighting a rush of feelings. 'It was a day.'

'I bet it was.'

'Pilots?'

Slater shook his head. 'The pair that picked you up checked the site.' He glanced at Harry and whispered, 'All they got were some charred teeth and a melted watch.'

'I heard that,' said Harry, without looking up.

Slater flinched. 'Sorry son,' he apologised.

Jack folded his arms and looked down. That pilot had pulled them above the clifftops so they could jump. He'd known it would get him killed; he'd done it anyway.

The silence in the room said everything. Slater went on.

'They cleared the site. They're looking for you and the asset. Your boy. Probably all of us now.'

'I have to get her back.'

Slater checked his watch. 'It's 9 pm. We're gunning it for Victoria. We'll have you offshore at Kilcunda by daybreak.'

'Kilcunda? That's another hundred kilometres from the Hill.'

'Actually, it's further. They're gonna pick you up offshore.'

'How?' said Jack.

Slater smiled. 'You'll see.'

He looked over at Harry, bundled up under a blanket, sipping his chocolate.

'What if we just send her back?'

'We can.' Slater held his hands up. 'Man. There's no way in shit I would wanna go back to that Hill after what you did. And with your kid?' He whistled and shook his head. 'You can only circle the flame for so long.'

Jack let out a long breath. *If I don't complete the mission, I have no way of getting out. I have to take Harry west.*

'Someone has to get her there in one piece,' Jack said.

Slater leaned in towards him. 'They'll be on that Hill by tomorrow night. You gotta get her there. Everyone is cheering for you. We want to see them get their asses handed to them.'

Jack frowned.

225

'I'll get her back, but after that, I'm done. We're heading west. Dyson gave me his word.'

Jack stared at the floor and rubbed the back of his neck.

'Tell him I'm good for pick-up, but only with an *UGLY* escort. Get me to the comms room.'

Slater nodded. He helped Jack up the stairs to the comms room.

Jack sent a long message to Dyson, outlining his instructions for the pick-up and dispatch to the Hill. He signed off with one final request.

'Tell Jimbo to get his fox tail. He's on the team.'

40

DYSON LIMPED UP THE CAVE TUNNEL, CROSSING THE METAL matting and stooping under the thick timber frame of the tunnel. Heads was crouched over the blue force tracker with a headset and a microphone. Radio chatter permeated the room, different formations reporting their preparation levels.

The tracker showed the real time location of his own troops and any known enemy forces. There was a series of blue dots and targets south of Victoria, but nothing but red dots surrounding the Hill. One pocket of blue sat at the southern edge of the Hill, protected against the cliff side. A massive red splotch sat over the MCG.

'Jack better deliver the asset or I'll be selling my house to a Chinese officer and his family. How's the cordon strength looking?'

Heads pointed to a gap in the red, just to the east of the Hill.

'Lillydale Lake is looking like a decent gap. My guess is they assume no one would try to infiltrate the Hill from there. It's a natural obstacle.'

'Good. I'll let Jack know,' Dyson said.

Another analyst walked in from the comms room. 'Sir, Outrider on HQ main.'

'The devil himself,' said Dyson.

The operator handed the set to Dyson and he keyed the radio. 'Send.'

He stood and listened.

'Approved. Send grid for the RV. We'll winch you out. Reinsert and infiltrate the Hill via Lillydale Lake entry point. I'll get Jimbo to meet you at the lake.'

Dyson handed the phone to Heads.

'Launch the recovery team. Pick-up offshore near the *Coral Snake*. Jack has the asset, but they're all injured. The asset's lost a hand. Horse is dead.'

Heads winced. 'Crap.'

Dyson went on. 'Tell Jimbo to get up here. Jack wants him promoted. It's not his call, but he's right. I'm badging Jimbo. Time for the squire to be knighted.'

The radio operator guffawed.

Dyson limped off, then stopped and turned.

'One more thing.' Dyson pointed his mangled finger at the radio operator.

'Yessir?'

'Launch the *UGLY*.'

Two pilots in black aviator sunglasses, leather jackets and sneakers sprinted out of the rocky hillside cave to a matte black helicopter gunship. It had dual missile packs on the wings and a 30mm cannon on the nose, like a mechanical anteater. One rack of air-to-air Stinger missiles, four in total. The pilots shouldered leather holsters as they ran, and each had a slung carbine. The lead pilot wore an old AC/DC shirt. One carried a map board against his thigh as he ran.

The craft sat on a pressed rock tarmac hidden among a cluster of gum trees. The rock wall of the mountain hugged the craft. Two support crew pulled the thermal matting and camouflage off the helicopters and tugged the engine covers down. One pilot scanned the opening above for fallen branches. The tree tunnel about them was as wide as the aircraft. It required true vertical ascent or you would be trimming eucalypts. The other pilot was pulling the red tag of the arming pins from the missiles and yanking each one on the pylon to ensure it sat true.

The red strips on their sleeves were visible as the pilots reached up for the engine controls. The craft was spartan. Bare. You could see the bent legs of the pilots working the pedals, hand on the collective arm. The nose of the craft was painted to look like a bunyip mouth, all sharp teeth and fur and webbed feet on the underbelly, a VMF soldier in its teeth. The word *UGLY* was painted in white letters on the tail fin. As the aircraft whined through its start-up sequence, the pilot tested comms and checked in with the Blackhawk that was starting up just a hundred metres away.

As the Blackhawk pilots prepped for launch, a tall, thin soldier trotted past on horseback. It was Jimbo. Back straight, chest out, dressed in full battle order: chest rig, carbine, ballistic helmet and gloves. One black stallion and a white mare in battle order trailed behind him. The horses were shrouded in thermal blankets that covered their heads and chests in multicam.

Jimbo sat easy in the saddle, his carbine slung on his back. Each horse's saddlebag bulged with ammunition. Jimbo had a single fox tail hanging from the side of his pistol belt, a tribute from any new Horseman to a fallen one. A tiny koala clung to Jimbo's saddlebag, looking unimpressed by the commotion. Jimbo held his gloved hand up at the roaring helicopters and his horse shimmied and trotted away from the aircraft. The pilots waited for the horses to clear the LZ, then hauled up into the blue sky.

The bird lurched above the green expanse. Thousands of

white galahs scrambled and screamed as they headed south, away from the rattling aircraft. From the canopy of trees, a hundred metres away, a squat black Apache gunship emerged like a wasp. Its wings bristled with missiles.

UGLY was headed for Jack Dunne.

41

JESS STOOD AT THE FLOOR-TO-CEILING WINDOWS OF THE pavilion and stared across the MCG. Where a hundred thousand locals once cheered their teams, foreign troops and the Aussie VMF units now moved in all directions. Helicopters lifted off in pairs, heading east. Troops in lines of fifty did kit checks.

Kayne fidgeted with his iPad, then lay it on his desk. 'I've kept Lillydale Lake clear of forces. Might present an attractive infil route we can target.'

He looked to Jess. 'Did you see the suits? The strike unit taking the Hill has the new ones.'

Kayne's hand flexed on his pistol handle.

Jess stared at him, trying not to let her frustration show.

'That's right. Imagine what we could do with them. Hours of endurance. Lift trees, carry artillery shells, heavy weapons, bodies, climb a thousand metres in two minutes. Imagine the arses we could kick.'

Kayne stood beside her and put an arm around her shoulder. He was taller than her by a foot.

Jess kept her eyes locked onto the dozens of CCP troops in woodland camouflage boarding the helicopters. Another few hundred were boarding a stack of armoured personnel carriers.

'People say this war might never end.'

Kayne scoffed. 'Every war ends, unfortunately.'

'Maybe this one won't,' Jess said.

Kayne's phone rang. He eyed the number for a second, then answered it.

'Copy.' Kayne hung up and turned to Jess. 'They picked up rotary wing assets from the Hill. Headed to the south coast. We're gonna track them.'

'Why don't you go with the Principal? I'll lead a ground element in case they sneak through.'

Kayne rubbed his stubble with his hand.

'You know what? Lillydale Lake is clear. If they infiltrate there . . . you know, take the bait. This could be your chance,' he said.

'Maybe I can get a bomb car rigged, at the block position.'

Kayne nodded. 'Good thinking. Better than a whole company sitting in a cordon like fools.'

Jess smiled. *Like I'd want to kill a kid. A bomb car is a nice hedging bet.*

'Take the driver,' said Kayne.

Jess shook her head. 'I won't need him, I'll do it.'

'Take the driver,' Kayne repeated. 'I'm not asking. You guide him out. You control the detonation,' he said, turning for the exit.

'Kayne,' Jess called. 'You're doing great. This is gonna get us in a good spot,' she lied.

The beauty of working with a suicide bomber was that if she changed her mind, there would be no one left to snitch.

Jess stood in the operations room waiting for the truck driver. She scanned Kayne's desk. His tablet was still turned on. Unlocked.

She picked it up.

The screen displayed a military overlay of Melbourne. It showed the Hill, with a blue circle over the MCG and a series of blue rectangles at the side with circles in them. It was the overlay of the clearance plan. The route tracker for the convoy of over a hundred vehicles led directly from the MCG to the Hill.

The route cut directly through a hill on the approach.

They're using the Mullum Mullum Tunnel.

Tanks, personnel carriers, fuel trucks, ammo trucks, all squeezing through a six-lane tunnel stretching just short of two kilometres.

The wheels turned in her mind.

She looked out onto the oval, where a VTOL jet was landing, and watched Kayne jog out to it.

He looked good, like a real soldier. Like the one he had been.

The Principal exited the Dragon in full combat gear, and Kayne fell in beside him. They strode towards a pair of helicopters, jumped on the deck and hooked on with lanyards. The packet of four helicopters rose in unison and sped off to the east.

Off he goes, like a loyal dog.

There was a rap at the door.

She turned and was greeted by a scrawny man in tracksuit pants with a backpack in one hand, a lunch bag and a bottle of water in the other. He had a long, matted mullet of black hair. She smelt the pong of old unwashed clothes.

For a reformed meth-head though, he appeared to be in functional order.

'Reporting for duty.' The driver saluted with a filthy hand.

'Let's go.' Jess walked him out to the medevac tunnel, where a medium-haul truck, like a removalist truck, was parked. 'Jump in. I'll guide, you drive. It's a jamming mission.'

'What are we jamming?'

'There's a Resistance unit near the Hill. We're going for them.'

The driver started the truck and guided it out of the MCG, heading east.

Dyson shouted across the command dugout. 'Fill your coffees, everyone. Wake the shift crew. I want all hands.'

Heads spoke up. 'We have four bogeys that lifted off from the MCG, headed southeast. My guess is they got the radar track for our birds and they're moving to intercept.'

Dyson nodded. 'Okay. Let 'em know.'

Dyson picked up his binoculars and walked down the tunnel through a hessian sheet and out into the dugout that faced south across the Hill. He glassed the ridgelines to the south, looking for an approaching storm. There was a solid, ugly black shelf of sheet lightning and swirling storm heads taking shape.

Right on time.

He smiled and went back into the dugout.

42

Jack helped Constance into the zodiac. Harry held her saline bag on her good arm as she climbed in and lay flat in the bottom of the boat, her head resting on a life jacket. They were still in the interior of the ship in the launch bay. On the other side of the ship, three Horsemen and their driver prepped the boat.

Slater appeared and shook Jack's hand.

'We'll transfer and winch up. Can't have the rotary wing coming to us, sorry.'

Jack shook his hand. 'Thanks. For everything.'

Slater looked into his eyes and grinned, his gold incisor shining. 'We'll do some work together in the West,' he said.

'I'm retired,' said Jack, smiling.

Slater laughed. 'We haven't authorised that.'

Jack settled into the boat. The ramp door beeped twice and slid open, ocean to the south and low cloud across the horizon.

He checked his watch.

10.30 am.

'Copy.'

'Where's Horse?' came Constance's voice from the bottom of the boat.

Jack looked down, rested his hand on her shoulder.

'He's gone.'

She closed her eyes.

Jack watched her laid out on the bottom of the boat and felt a growing sense of unease. Her fingers extended from a thick bandage on her new hand. A silver medical blanket had been draped over her, and there was a line of saline leading to her good wrist.

The image brought Gemma to mind. Gemma, lying on a stretcher with her ears bleeding after the Singapore mission.

Jack looked away. Instinctively, he searched the horizon for the helicopters, his blue eyes ablaze with focus.

After a thirty-minute drive they hitched the boats alongside each other and waited in the ocean. The driver had a radio clipped to his belt and he called the approaching helicopters. The Blackhawk and Apache flew in a tight formation, straight for them, just clearing the wave tops.

Must be Christmas; troop lift, with an attack helicopter, thought Jack.

The Blackhawk flared as it approached them and the *UGLY* circled nearby, a terrible insect waiting to kill. Jack admired the painting on the nose of the aircraft.

'Dad, look!' Harry pointed it out, a beautiful, terrifying machine. The Apache was a show-stopper on the battlefield. Sidewinder missiles, 30mm cannon shells and Hellfires – it could tip the balance of any contact.

'She's a ripper, hey?'

After years of hiding their air assets from the enemy, the Resistance had revealed three within the space of a day for this mission.

Harry gazed at him as though seeing him for the first time. 'You must be important, Dad.'

Jack gestured at Constance. 'It's all her. We get her to the Hill and she'll make *UGLY* look like a plaything.'

The B-21 sortie alone would stop the Chinese and VMF in

their tracks. Weather modification and cruise missiles would be most unpleasant for an assaulting force.

Jack scanned the *UGLY* weapons loadout. He counted four stumpy AIM-92 Sidewinder missiles, a thin, agile missile for targeting enemy aircraft.

Jack looked south. A huge storm front, black and grey with cracking lightning, was building out of the south like an omen.

The Blackhawk swooped in low over the boat and the water churned. The load master ran the winch down to the zodiac and collected everyone in three lifts.

Jack hoisted Harry onto the deck and Constance sat over him, nestling him between her shins, and held him in place. The Horsemen and Zeus entered last. Sacha immediately jumped on the twin Mag 58 guns mounted on the side door, while Beetle climbed onto the minigun and squealed like a kid as he swivelled it left and right, making a 'Brtttt' sound as he raked some imaginary targets. Cole shook his head as he clipped onto the deck.

'Mrs Rabbit?' Jack asked Cole.

Cole shook his head. 'Lost at sea. She was waterproof, but I don't think she was designed to survive ocean swells like that.'

'Damn.'

When everyone was secure, the aircraft lurched forward, nose down, pinning the team to their seats, and they swung low over the zodiac boat drivers. They waved as they shot back to the *Coral Snake*.

Jack pulled on a headset and checked in with the pilots.

'You know where the drop point is?'

'Yeah. Lillydale Lake. A guide will meet you on horseback.'

'Copy. Is that what Heads recommended?'

'Affirmative.'

That's all I need to know, thought Jack.

'He said don't go uphill until nightfall. I hope y'all are well rested. Tomorrow should be a doozy,' said the pilot.

'I'll bet my life on it,' said Jack.

43

HARRY, WHO'D BEEN STARING INTENTLY OUT THE SIDE OF THE Blackhawk, suddenly yanked on Constance's trouser leg.

'Helicopters.' He was pointing out the left side of the aircraft. Constance tapped Jack's shoulder, held her thumb downwards and pointed out the window. Jack looked in the direction she was pointing, but couldn't see anything.

Frowning, he spoke into his headset. 'Check ten o'clock, low.'

As he spoke, he saw two pairs of aircraft tracking just above the treetops. They were big. They were a couple of miles away. They had turned and were tracking towards them, their profiles growing.

Jack leaned into the cockpit, grabbed the pilot's shoulder and pointed them out. The pilot startled when he saw the formation, he pulled the controls right, pitching the aircraft onto its side. He reported the aircraft on the flight network.

'Four bogeys, bearing two-niner-zero. Two miles. Z-20s.'

The pilots were talking fast now, and moving even faster. The helicopters were closing.

'Put us down.' The lead pilot pointed out a clearing in the scrub where the single-lane road widened on a hairpin turn.

The Apache descended into a clearing a hundred metres ahead of them.

'Check for wires,' said the lead pilot as they descended into the opening. It was tight. The trees were all around them, and an old power pole rose up beside them, wires sprouting from it like guitar strings.

'You wanna insert here?' the co-pilot said to Jack.

'No. You need to engage.' Jack checked the wing stubs on the Apache, hovering only thirty metres away. The four narrow Stinger missiles sat in a quad pack on the wing stub.

Constance grabbed his arm. 'They're looking for us.'

The look on her face told him what they had to do. Cole pulled him in by his shoulder. 'They don't have escorts.'

Jack swallowed and keyed the fist mike. 'You think we can engage?'

The pilot nodded. 'You can approve. Cleared and armed to fire?'

Jack responded. 'Cleared to fire.'

The pilot radioed the command.

'Roger. Contact. Judy.' The pilot radioed to the *UGLY*. The Apache confirmed the plan

'Copy. Contact two-eight-zero. My bogey.'

Jack reached over to Harry and pulled hard on the strop attached to the helicopter. He pointed to the missiles on the Apache wing pod and held his hand to his ear.

Harry did the same, he knew what was coming.

Constance sat upright in her seat and yanked the IV cannula from her wrist. Beetle put his hand on her chest to restrain her, but she pushed his arm away. She climbed to her knees, stowed the silver emergency blanket under her seat and pulled her body armour on, wincing from the pain in her hand.

Jack and Harry grinned as she clipped her helmet up. Her new hand was an adjustment, the neural pathways were activated during the transplant, but like any new machine, she was getting used to driving it. Harry leaned forward and clipped her chinstrap on.

The only thing this superwoman can't do is paddle into a wave, Jack mused.

He chuckled as he watched Harry hand her a spare carbine and wrap the sling over her shoulder, like a war caddy. She pointed her weapon barrel down between her legs. Catching Cole looking at her, she frowned and pointed at her eyes and then out of the aircraft, towards the enemy.

Cole was shaking his head. He was a hard man to impress.

You couldn't keep a good asset down for long.

44

THE PILOTS WERE GOOD, BUT THEY WERE RUSTY.

Not much opportunity to keep flight hours up in a fuel-rationed Resistance.

Jack hung on the wire frame of his seat and felt the helo clip the tree branches as they descended out of sight to the road.

He watched Sacha shoulder her twin Mag 58s, while Beetle cranked the actuator on the minigun and swivelled it.

'One helicopter is four kills,' shouted Sacha. 'I get me a chopper and I overtake you for kills this week.'

Beetle rolled his eyes and shook his head. He tapped Harry's leg. 'These losers keep coming for me. But all I do is win.'

Cole pointed out the door.

'Stand-by. Bogeys are closing fast.'

The UGLY climbed from its hover and pitched over to the left, above the line of trees and out of sight. A screech of rockets could be heard over the din of the rotors.

'Splash one!' The pilot bucked in his seat. 'Two bandits down!'

Beetle banged his fist on the doorframe and hissed.

The pilot went on. 'Winchester on Fox2s.'

Cole issued his commands to the pilots.

241

'No missiles? We can switch to guns. Get close.'

Jack sucked in a deep breath and closed his eyes. Beetle yipped and bobbed in his seat. The aircraft cranked its revolutions and ascended from the clearing. As the Blackhawk cleared the vegetation, over Beetle's shoulder Jack saw two Z-20 helicopters bearing down on them, only a few hundred metres away. Their wheels were brushing the treetops, screaming across the canopy to escape the Apache that had destroyed half their chalk.

Beetle had already swung the minigun to lead them, and the whine of the barrels echoed through the Blackhawk as they spun to life.

Constance covered Harry's ears and watched the minigun go to work.

The Principal pointed out the doorframe at the Blackhawk that had just surfaced from the trees, side on. Troops seated on the skid of the helicopter raised their weapons at the Blackhawk, the shock of the close contact on their faces.

'Bogey! Eleven o'clock!' the Principal shouted as he slammed his door gunner on the shoulder. He stared at the rising Resistance helicopter, only a hundred metres off.

Side-on, he could see into the doorless Blackhawk. A child sat on the deck; a black-haired woman had her arms draped around him. A bearded man in a leather jacket pointed over the gunner's shoulder. He saw the spinning barrel of a minigun, the treetops billowing around them.

The VMF pilot screeched and pulled the stick left to avoid the gunfire.

Jack was pointing at the enemy helicopter and saw the man in black pointing right back at him. Jack flinched as his door gunner's minigun erupted into a stream of red tracers. The grinding whirr of the six-barrelled minigun and the heat from the flames reached Jack's face. He saw the trace rounds miss the black tail of the Z-20, and as it flared left and presented its belly to them, Beetle walked the rounds onto the tail boom of the chopper.

Metal sheeting peeled off the lead helicopter and a helmet popped off one of the troops seated on the skid. The helmet still contained most of its wearer's head. The gun whined at a terrible volume; shells pounded the floor of the aircraft.

The Z-20 dropped like a brick into the tree canopy. Beetle whooped a rebel yell and held up his arm in a flex.

He'd missed the trailing Z-20. Travelling a hundred metres behind the first one, it had peeled right, trying to get around the other side of the Blackhawk. But Sacha was too quick. She swung the Mag 58s forward and fired with one hand on the butterfly lever, spewing twin tracer streams at the fleeing Z-20.

Smoke billowed from the rear tail boom and Jack saw sparks striking it. Hydraulic fluid streamed from the aircraft body. It began to auto-rotate, the body of the craft spinning in slow 360-degree movements in an attempt to stay airborne.

The stream of pink fluid caught fire and the helicopter became a flying ball of yellow flame and smoke. Two flaming bodies swung out of the chopper, tumbling into the air. They didn't seem real to Jack. He saw the slung weapon of one flying in the breeze, still attached to the man, his outstretched arms searching frantically for handholds.

The Blackhawk pilot thumbed the stick and turned the aircraft in a full bank. Two columns of black smoke rose from the canopy near them. The UGLY had circled up a hundred feet higher than them, and was raking over the top of two other smoke columns with 30mm cannon fire. Black puffs of smoke came shooting from its nose, spent cases tumbling to the earth like little gold flakes.

Sacha and Beetle screamed and pumped their fists.

Their first ever air-to-air kills.

Cole spoke to the pilot. 'Put us down. We'll exploit the crash sites. Might be some prisoners or some good intel.'

He turned to Jack. 'I'll call it in to Dyson.' He slapped the pilot's shoulder. 'Take these guys to Lillydale Lake. Jimbo will be there. We'll see you on the Hill for orders.'

Jack agreed, and the pilots swung the craft round to the first downed chopper.

The Principal's chopper copped the full force of a minigun trying to cut the aircraft in two. The Z-20 cockpit exploded into sparks and a tracer bullet bounced around the interior of the craft. The engine whined and the helicopter shuddered. The pilot screamed over the sound of the rotors and slammed the collective down to flatten the rotor blades. The aircraft lurched, nose down. The Principal clawed his toes into the hard deck of the aircraft as it sank, watching the pilot's shoulders heaving as he pulled the collective back to right the nose.

They were dropping fast. Too much damage.

The pilot wrestled the aircraft into a flare as it dropped into a tree canopy. The rotors clipped the flank of a eucalypt tree, tipping the aircraft on its side. It dropped the last ten metres to the ground, chewing up the vegetation as it fell.

The rotors screamed and battered themselves to shreds on the forest floor. The Principal blacked out, and came to slumped against the side of the helicopter. He could smell jet fuel and smoke.

The pilot and the loadmaster were already climbing out of the craft. As the Principal, Kayne and the aircrew ran for the tree line, the black Apache belted over them, empty wing racks, 30mm cannon sweeping for more targets.

The flames were now roaring high up the side of the craft. Undeterred, the Principal bolted back to the airframe, climbed up the side and reached in with one arm, peeling a long ammunition belt out of the flames. As he jogged back to the others, ammunition belt dragging in the dirt behind him, another volley of cannon rounds thundered through the gum trees, obliterating the shell of the craft.

The Principal dumped his booty at the foot of the berm and looked up through the treetops.

'At least two aircraft still up. Theirs.'

He pulled his sleeve back, revealing his forearm. A jagged shard of white bone protruded an inch from the skin under his wrist. He grunted, gripped his thumb and wrist with his opposite hand and pulled hard. Kayne winced as the bone retracted back into his forearm. Blood oozed from the cut. The Principal twisted his wrist once and the bone clicked, set in a straight line.

He pointed at a map case in Kayne's trouser pocket.

'Give me that.'

Kayne passed it to him.

The Principal wrapped the map case around his wrist, then pressed it against his thigh, holding it in place. He pulled a field dressing from his shoulder pocket, ripped it open with his teeth, then wrapped the green tape the length of the map case up and back. He tied it off and inspected the dressing.

'Solid,' he said.

Kayne was pale. 'Did you see that missile? Damn near hit us.'

'Forget the missile. Jack Dunne was in our sights.'

The Principal patted down his own arm and then checked for the Apache. 'Well played, Dunne. I'm actually impressed.'

He turned to Kayne. 'Take the gun. We move.'

'Where?' Kayne was shocked.

'Canterbury Road, Bayswater. The assault force will assemble there.' He checked his watch. 'It's 1300. We have seven hours. I'm pretty sure this is Churchill National Park, I saw the lake.

We're about thirty kilometres south of Bayswater road. Hurry. The enemy will exploit these sites.'

The Principal kept the sun on his left shoulder and with his rifle in both arms he walked into the scrub, looking for animal trails.

Kayne stared after him, still absorbing what had just happened.

Shaking himself out of his stupor, Kayne rounded up the aircrew, collected the still-warm machine gun and ammo belt, and they followed the Principal into the dense forest.

Jack looked out the flank of the craft and could see a fine mist spraying off the side of the Blackhawk. The Apache was circling over a low hill, mopping up forces with the 30mm cannon. They had destroyed four aircraft, but they had sustained some damage in the process.

Four columns of smoke billowed up from the green canopy only a kilometre away. The Blackhawk tracked over to one column and landed in a wide clearing beside one of the Z-20s. It was in parts, and burning up. Cole grabbed Jack and shouted in his ear. 'Walk in from Lillydale Lake. See you on the Hill.'

Cole, Sacha, Beetle and Zeus all leapt from the helicopter when it was still a metre off the ground and made for the craft.

Jack shuffled over to the minigun and Constance took the Mag 58s. They checked the clearance, and then their aircraft ascended. They skirted east to avoid the built-up zone, and then turned north for Lillydale Lake. This was the last major infil. After that, they would be home, but with real trouble coming for them.

After all that, I get you home in time for an armoured battle.

Jack turned to Harry, who held his arms out to his dad.

Jack left the gun and knelt beside him as Harry wrapped his arms around his neck and pulled him in. Jack leaned into the hug, locking him into his arms. Constance left her gun and hugged them both.

This was the endgame.

45

Five miles south of Gakona, Alaska – University of Fairbanks

A LAB TECHNICIAN SAT AT HER DESK WRAPPED IN A PURPLE wool cardigan with an oversized coffee mug before her. She blinked and stretched, gazing out the window. She had slept in the lab overnight, so she'd had no trouble getting there. She was restless, expecting more work.

Urgent work.

She looked through the triple-glazed windows, out to the expansive antenna farm. The 180 antenna units were densely packed over sixteen hectares. It was the largest facility of its kind, charged and live.

During normal working hours, she was Dr Ameda Vishay, university lecturer in Quantum Entanglement and Ionospheric Research majoring in Airglow and Meteor Tracking. She loved the study of 'spooky things from a distance', as Einstein called them. She felt they could explain many of the mysteries of the universe.

Outside of lab hours, she was a contractor for the Central Intelligence Agency. Dr Vishay was the primary field controller of one of the most secret weapons ever developed; the spookiest strategic weapon ever made. She led operational tasking of the High Frequency Active Aural Research Program: HAARP.

It was the only weather modification device in the known world.

She pushed her spectacles up her nose and checked her email headers. Her heart skipped a beat as an email came in with the subject 'Exam Prep'.

She put her coffee down and checked the room.

That subject indicated it was top secret, compartmented information. She typed a series of prompts into the computer, activating the covert communications program. A very low energy Bluetooth beam activated in the terminal and connected directly to her glasses. A miniaturised projector in the rim of the glasses coded a delicate image to the retina of her eye. Instructions from CIA Headquarters, Langley, Virginia.

With the highest level of authorisation.

The green text appeared in her right field of vision. She read with great care; she could access this information only once, and could not write it down.

```
Designator: FLASH
FROM: POTUS // SECDEF // SASC approved
TO: SOUL CATCHER NINER
Request: Weather Modification: Counter-
Mobility Operations
Location: -37° 49' 31.19' S / 145° 21' 21.59'
E (Mount Dandenong Ranges, Victoria, Australia)
Duration: 1800-0600 18-19 August 2034 AEST/
AEDT
Effects:
Priority: Visibility reduction to 10 metres.
Secondary: Hail. Precipitation set to
maximum. Lightning strike volume at maximum.
```

Customer notes: URGENT. In direct support of
National Objective.

Cover story: no change.

She blinked hard once and the image cleared. Then she began entering the keystrokes, initiating a sequence of activations that would assess the best position for the ionospheric heating over the Victorian region. She settled on a weather system a hundred miles off the south coast of Victoria.

Thirteen minutes later, the antenna arrays began to emit a low hum. At 35,000 kilometres a second, 300 megawatts of VHF radio waves shot from the facility at a shallow angle, bounced off the ionosphere in low space over Alaska, and deflected south to the ionosphere over southern Victoria.

The sky and the upper atmosphere began to boil and thrash as the ions were agitated over Australia's south. Black, vicious clouds billowed, and a storm front as wide as Tasmania began to brew.

Dr Vishay closed her eyes and prayed for the poor souls who would feel the full impact of her actions.

46

JESS PULLED UP AT THE ROUNDABOUT AT THE FLANK OF Lillydale Lake, the last major access point to the Hill. If you were headed to the Hill, you came through here. Otherwise, you had to deal with the camps and the displaced that ringed the suburb, risking time and possibly your life if you found a roving bandit group that wanted your wheels. They'd deliberately left it unattended, making it an even more attractive insertion option.

The Golden Gate. Always ambush the entry point. Even the Romans knew that tactic.

Jess scanned the intersection. There were metal stumps where traffic lights once stood, among a rubble of blackened and pockmarked cinderblocks. A crater full of muddy water in the road. Clusters of burnt vehicle shells, tyres melted down to the bitumen with skeins of wire bundled around the rims. Pale white ribcages and spines sunk into the seat springs, and black shell casings littered the ash and rust floor.

A pack of dogs sniffed the air and howled from the ridge overlooking the lake. Jess pointed out the car park as they approached.

'Pull in here.'

The driver turned the truck in. It groaned and rocked as it crossed the speed humps.

'This jamming gear must be heavy!' said the driver. He was a cheerful man.

It's heavy alright, thought Jess.

The driver reversed into a spot and turned the motor off.

The car park was butted against the rail line on the far side of the lake. This was the cleanest approach for a team on foot, if you could stay clear of the trains headed west.

There was every chance Jack and his crew would come right past her.

47

CONSTANCE TUCKED HER HANDHELD COVERT COMMS UNIT into her pack and they watched the dusk. The Hill protruded from the dense tree line. They sat in a creek line in a circle, back to back. They had landed ten kilometres short of the lake and hiked in the last bound. They hid upstream from the lake at dusk, waiting for nightfall. They were within striking distance, but they had to wait a couple more hours for full dark to marry up with Jimbo. He'd be out there somewhere, waiting for them to hit the RV.

'Langley have our location. I've requested a strike package from the USS *McRaven*; it'll be on stand-by.'

She looked at the Hill. 'We're close. So close.'

'Looks like I could've stayed behind, Dad.' Harry chuckled to himself.

'Don't even. We're lucky that Hill's not already crawling with VMF,' Jack said. *And I mightn't have made it without you.*

Jack was parched and eager to get to the playground. He hoped the drinking taps still worked.

Finally, darkness descended across the lake. The smell of wet reeds and soil.

'Let's go,' said Jack. They stood up one at a time, very slowly, and Jack led them single-file towards the playground. They melted back into the bushes and watched it for five minutes. It was completely dark now; only the low moonlight illuminated the playground.

Harry pulled at Jack's sleeve.

'Dad. Can I drink from the lake?'

'No. Come with me.'

Harry had not complained once since they had driven off the Hill. Jack's mouth was dry as sandpaper; he knew Harry's would be the same.

The playground had been reduced to stumps, though the old plastic slide was still in place – and so were the taps, much to Jack's relief. He slammed his hand down on the stainless-steel button and water dribbled off the top of the water fountain. Harry slurped away desperately. Jack surveyed the park, ghostly in the bone-coloured light, as his boy drank.

'Do you recognise this place?'

Harry looked up. 'No.' He went back to drinking.

Jack often brought him here in the summer with Gemma. Harry would run under the water fountains and shiver away under the streams running from the water towers. He would come here no matter the weather.

Jack remembered as though it was happening in that moment. He could feel the sun on his face. See the prams lining the path, mothers trotting in athletic wear. Ice cream and coffee trucks lined the car parks. Dogs yapped and chased ducks. Runners lapped the lake in visors and earphones. Trains clacked on the far side of the lake, busy commuters heading to the city.

Jack was still leaning on the bubbler. He took a long drink and then looked at the top of the Hill.

'Dad, they're coming in the morning, right?'

'Yeah.'

'So if we get Constance there, Ed can give us a chance to leave?'

'Yes. Dyson and Ed have to approve,' Jack said. 'It's a long way west, though.'

'How long?'

'Four days driving. Way past where we picked up Constance.'

'That's so much petrol. Dyson must need a lot of help.'

'Well, actually, I owe Dyson a favour.'

'Why?'

'He saved me. In Ukraine.'

'Was that how he got burnt?'

'Yup.'

Jack exhaled a ragged breath. 'The Russians used a big bomb. Dyson covered me. He got burnt. I didn't.'

'Why did he do that?'

Jack was caught out by the question. 'Because he's a good man,' he said. Tears welled in his eyes.

'He's scary.'

'Yeah. He is a bit.'

'Why will he give us a car then?'

'Well, because he keeps his word.'

Jack pointed at Constance, who was drinking from the bubbler.

'We get her up there, we can leave.'

Harry looked at Constance. He cupped his hand to Jack's ear and whispered, 'I like her, Dad.'

'Yeah, I do too. She's a good person. She worked with Mum. A while back.'

'Really? Overseas?'

'Yes.'

They eyed the silhouette of the Hill for a moment. Harry was quiet.

'Do you think Mum is watching us?'

'I do.' Jack put his arm around his son, trying to ignore the sting in his heart. 'Remember that photo of me in Afghanistan? She was at the airstrip; that's where we met.

'The following year, I asked her to marry me, and then we had you.'

They both stared up at the Hill. Harry was wiping his eyes. Jack pulled him close and kissed the top of his head.

'She's here. I can feel it. She's proud of you.'

Jack checked his watch: 2007. Jimbo was seven minutes late.

A wild dog sniffed around the low reeds and howled. The sky was still, not a single satellite or falling star. A shelf of black cloud sat on the horizon, bursts of sheet lightning within.

'Jack, where are they? We need to move,' said Constance.

'He's watching us now,' said Jack.

Mist was settling in the low ground, illuminated by the moonlight.

On the high ground beside the lake, Jimbo emerged from the tree line on horseback, two more horses in train. He trotted over, and Jack could see his smile in the moonlight, the thermal covers on the horses, and inhaled their sweet smell as they closed in on them. Jimbo dismounted and rubbed his horse's jaw affectionately.

'Sorry, Jack. Been tracking you. Had to make sure you were clear.'

Jack pulled him in for a hug.

'You guys have had an adventure,' he whispered.

He reached for Constance's hand and held it in both of his. 'What an honour. Thank you.'

Constance smiled back. 'Anything for the Hill. The whole world is watching you.'

Jimbo reached for Harry and shook his hand, bending forward as though meeting royalty.

'I hear you've been saving your old man. Well done, squire.' Jimbo said.

Jack ran his hand along the fox tail at Jimbo's pistol belt. 'Well done, mate. Vale Horse.'

'Vale the big man.' He dipped his head, then gathered

himself. 'How did the car go? Heard you made good use of the tailgate.'

'We did. You saved us,' said Jack.

Jimbo got down to business.

'Well, let's see what we can manage now. Harry and ma'am, you're on Sherman.' He patted the black horse's flank and it shimmied its head. 'Jack, you're on Patton. We're gonna follow the rail line for two miles and then it's straight uphill.'

'Where to?'

'Pig & Whistle. Orders at 11 pm. H-Hour is likely 5 am.'

'Good. I could use a beer,' Jack said.

They mounted the horses and headed for the high features of the Hill.

✕

They were making good time. A mile down the train line, they were still flanking the lake. Jimbo held up his hand at the front and cupped it to his ear. There was a faint clacking on the rail line. They all heard it. Jimbo broke track and rode towards the lake's edge. Constance and Jack followed. The scrub was thin and the mist had become fog.

Jimbo dismounted and guided his horse into the reeds. The horse clopped into the muddy water, blustering at the cold. It was chest-deep for Jimbo, and the horse sank to its haunches but kept its head clear of the water and sat still. Jimbo motioned for them to join him. 'Get in.'

Jack followed him in, guiding his horse behind him. The water was cold and the shock took his breath. He motioned to Constance to follow.

The clacking was getting louder.

'I can stay here,' Harry said to Constance, gesturing to the edge of the water, sounding panicked.

'It's okay. No waves here. I'll hold you,' she said. Constance dismounted with Harry and all four of them clustered together in the black water, the three horses beside them, breathing their sweet breath across the water.

The rattling of the tracks was loud now. A dull red light flitted through the scrub where they'd come from. It lit the fog up like something supernatural.

'Don't move,' whispered Jimbo.

The first carriage came into view, a trundling dark box in the fog, red lights at the flank. A red curtain of light strobed through the scrub. It was a sixty-foot-long Connex, battered, patches of rust, with bright red flood lamps on each corner. A single portal was cut into the Connex, lengthways. Barbed wire mesh traversed the length of the portal. The silhouettes of the inhabitants were visible through the side of the train, bathed by an interior red light.

As the train rumbled past, bare arms clawed through the windows, some reaching for the tree branches, others for the rising moon. Hundreds of limbs, reaching for the fresh air and for the land they once owned. Some were clearly dead, hands closed onto the barbed wire by rigor mortis, like dead vines. Moans echoed over the rattle and clacking of the wheels. Foul fluid dripped from the corners of the Connex.

The train rolled past for twenty minutes; a hundred carriages, carrying hundreds of souls per carriage. The odd lumber stack. Odours of excrement and vomit settled across the lake. A human cattle train. You could smell its oozing juice from a hundred paces.

Jimbo held his head in his hands and Jack heard him sobbing. The horses blustered at the disturbance. Jack had pulled Harry in and put one hand over his eyes. As the train rattled past, he whispered to Harry about the warm sand on the beaches in the West, desperate to drown out the moans. Harry was trembling, whether from cold or shock or both, Jack wasn't sure.

Finally, the last carriage rolled past and the moans receded.

They sat, shaking, immobile, their clouding breath across the water the only clue that time still passed. Finally, they climbed up the bank on their dead legs, mud sucking at their boots. Jack stood in the dark, dripping and shaking, and stared at the fading red lights along the track.

There was a fate worse than death, and for the first time he had seen it.

Constance put Harry on her horse, then turned to Jack and grabbed him with both arms.

'That's what you're fighting for,' she hissed, pointing at the Hill.

Jack looked at Harry and then back to her.

'No more. It stops now,' he said, mounting his horse.

'I'd rather burn than get on that thing,' said Jimbo. 'Let's roll.'

They clopped into the darkness, a fire blazing in Jack's chest. He squeezed the leather reins tight and set his jaw.

He wanted the enemy to come to the Hill.

All of them.

You take one of mine, I'll burn a hundred of yours.

48

JESS STOOD BESIDE THE TRUCK IN THE DIRT CAR PARK AND watched the train rumble past, a ghost ship on rails. The bitter, acrid stink drifted past her, the moans from a thousand souls echoing over the clatter of the wheels on the tracks.

She could hear the shrieks of children as they passed the lake, and pinned her hands over her ears, desperate to block them out.

'By God,' she whispered.

After the first fifty cars she could take no more. She climbed into the truck and dug her fingernails into the dashboard. The driver sat in his seat and stared at the train.

'Ship those pigs off to the Yard.' He made an oinking noise and then a wheezing laugh.

The red light of the carriages flashed across her face.

She looked across at the driver, then wiped her eyes with shaking hands and pulled her ponytail tight.

No more.

'Stay here,' she said to the driver.

She put her carbine down and took off her pistol belt, then walked out to the tracks, out of view of the truck, and held her hand against the warm metal rail.

She could still feel the vibration of the train beneath her fingertips.

That was no dream. She put her hand on her mouth and sobbed.

She walked to the lake's edge and squatted, watching the ripples of breeze across the lake in the moonlight. She thought about the Principal. The MCG. Her brother. Her lost childhood.

She knew what she was going to do. What she *had* to do. She ripped the single star patch off her chest, and tossed it.

Jess strode back to the truck, grabbed her night-vision binoculars and scanned the service road coming from the east side of the lake. She could see the party of ghost white figures only a hundred yards away. Three horses. Four people. One horse had two figures on it.

She picked up the initiator box from the driver's side door, pressed her index finger to it. The device ran a bio scan and clicked open. She engaged the button release activation, then squeezed her thumb down on the button.

Dead man's hand. You shoot me and it's over for all of us.

Holding it in one arm, she stood at the side of the trail, watching her new allies approach.

Jack squinted. A woman on the trail beside the tracks, unarmed. He had seen the truck first, but when he focused he saw the woman. He dismounted his horse and knelt, locking the IR laser on his weapon onto the woman. Jimbo had done the same, and together they patrolled towards her, the dots of their carbine lasers dancing on her chest.

The woman stood still and had no weapon, but she was holding a device in one hand.

Jack and Jimbo stopped thirty metres out. Their faces would be impossible to make out in the dark.

'Don't shoot. I need to speak with Jack Dunne,' she said.

'Put your hands on your head,' said Jack.

She did.

Jack looked at Jimbo, who shook his head once. Jack checked the tree line that bounded the car park. Nothing.

A trap. Surely.

Jack did not take his eyes off her. Jimbo ran his laser across the tree line and then looked overhead for drones. The air was a thick blanket of blue and black cloud.

Constance and Harry were fifty metres back, kneeling beside the horses.

'Who are you?' asked Jack.

'Jess Wilson. From the VMF. Cranbourne Boys. I need Jack Dunne.'

Jack slung his rifle.

'What for?'

'I'm defecting,' she said.

Jack looked at Jimbo. 'Okay. Talk.'

'They're coming to clear the Hill, through the Mullum Mullum Tunnel. Over a hundred armoured vehicles.'

'How do we know you're legit?' said Jack.

'You'll know when I hit them going through the tunnel. Which I'll do – for a price.'

Jimbo spoke. 'Bullshit. Why would you do that?'

'Did you see that train?' She pointed at the tracks.

'Yes.'

'That's not the half of it,' she said.

They all stood in the dark. Jack wasn't sure what to make of this.

Jimbo shook his head at Jack, his green laser dot resting on her face.

'If you're VMF, Cranbourne no less, why don't I just drop you right here?' said Jack.

'Two reasons.' She held up the switch. 'One is that when my

hand comes off this switch, a thousand kilos of bang in that truck will kill all of us,' she said. 'And number two, you won't, because you know I'm speaking the truth.'

Jack walked towards her. Jimbo kept his laser trained on her face.

She whispered, just loud enough for Jack to hear, 'I want immunity, and I want whatever vehicle I ask for, and enough resources to get to the border.'

'Talk,' said Jack.

She outlined the Principal's plans, and told him about the Cranbourne team led by her brother. About the assembly area at the MCG, and the armour. Jack asked where her brother had served, and when she told him, Jack knew she was telling the truth, even in that darkness. The even pace of her voice. Her lack of 'tells'. She didn't shuffle, blink or touch her face.

'Let me take this truck down to the tunnel.' She jerked her head towards the truck and the driver. 'I can put it to work on the main body of their assault.'

Jimbo and Jack weighed her words in the dark.

'How do we know we can trust you?' Jimbo asked.

'You don't. Judge me by my actions.'

'Alright. Well, in the event you deliver, we will offer safe passage. Only approach the Hill from the south tourist road. Our checkpoints will stop you. Tell them who you are.'

'Okay,' she said. 'Tell them not to shoot.'

She held her hand out to Jack, and Jack shook it.

She turned to walk back but stopped and faced them.

'One more thing. The Principal killed Jack's wife. He bragged about it during a mission briefing.'

The world around that lake was still. Jack felt the million puzzle pieces of his life lock together.

Jimbo looked at Jack.

'We'll pass it on.'

Jimbo and Jack walked back to the horses, Jimbo put his

arm around his shoulders as they walked. 'Sorry mate.'

Jack was silent.

Constance had mounted up and was holding Harry to her front.

'We heard it all,' she said. 'I pray we meet him.'

Jack climbed onto his horse. He felt light.

'We will.'

49

JESS PUT THE DEVICE BACK TO HER FACE, UNLOCKED IT, AND closed off the switch. She checked twice before releasing her hand.

As she walked back to the truck, she looked at the cab. The driver was slumped over in his seat. She could hear him snoring through the closed doors.

She opened one of the rear doors of the truck and climbed in, then activated the red downlights inside and pulled the door shut behind her. Finding the internal lock, she clicked it shut.

She stepped up to the four bags of fertiliser. Reaching into each sack in turn, she lifted a detonator from the centre of each, then reinserted it against the outside edge of the sack. It took a moment to reset each detonator. She ran her fingers along the detonating cord, then sealed the bags and ran her hands over the lids of the aviation fuel drums.

Jess heard the door crank open.

She gasped. The driver stood at the rear door, rubbing sleep from his eyes.

'Where's the jamming gear?' he said.

Jess stood, scanning his face.

He spotted the nitrate bags and the detonating cord coiled above them.

He punched his fist into a fertiliser sack, and his tone darkened. 'What?'

She checked over his shoulder and then motioned to him with two fingers. 'Step up. I'll brief you in,' she said.

'You're damn well right you will. What the hell is –'

As the driver put one knee up on the tailgate and reached for the door handle, Jess reached into her sleeve cuff and then slammed the side of her fist into the driver's neck. He gagged and stepped back, both hands to his neck. A matte black handle protruded from behind his jawline. Jess already had a small tomahawk in her other fist and was bringing it down on his temple.

The tomahawk sheared through the side of his head to the bridge of his nose. Blood ran from the axe handle, looking black in the bright red light.

The driver slumped into a pile on the bitumen, a long wheeze exiting his body as he fell.

Jess stepped off the back of the truck with clenched fists and checked over the car park. She checked the driver's body; his eyes were rolled back and he wasn't breathing. She extracted her weapons from his body.

Walking to the cab, Jess pulled an old rag from the door well and returned to stand over the dead driver. He lay in a square patch of red light from the truck, black blood pooling under his prostate body. She wiped her blades down and eyed the dying man regretfully.

'You had to look,' she whispered.

Pocketing her weapons, she closed the truck door and felt for the activation switch in her pocket. Then she climbed into the truck, drove it out of the car park and headed to the Mullum Mullum Tunnel.

They walked the horses up from Lillydale Lake through the shallow river bed that would lead them to the Five Ways. They travelled on horseback for another hour. It was 2247.

Jack was coming to the end of an epic seventy-two-hour journey. And that was just the beginning.

Constance pulled her horse up alongside him.

'Think eight of my nine lives are gone,' he said.

'You're gonna need that last one in the morning.'

Jimbo rounded the bend and joined them. The sky was starting to whip and leaves were falling all around them. 'There's a storm coming from the south. It's a big one from the look of it. We need to move.' He led his horse into the river.

It was running quick from the rain northwards, chest-deep to the horse.

'We're ten minutes out,' said Jimbo.

They followed him across the river. On the far bank, a weeping willow, thirty metres tall, draped its arms across the river eddy.

The sight of it stunned Jack. He had not expected it.

'We cremated Gemma here,' he whispered.

Constance paused, taking it in. 'It's beautiful.'

Across the river, they traced the same steps Jack had taken to the pyre at the Five Ways.

Another kilometre up the road, the pitched roof of the Pig & Whistle came into view. They hitched their horses outside and walked towards the entrance, dripping wet from the waist down.

Jack took a deep breath. 'The last supper,' he said, and pushed the door open.

50

THE BARMAN RANG THE BRASS NAVY BELL THREE TIMES AND the crowd fell silent. Jack stopped in the threshold of the bar, Harry pressed against him. A hundred pairs of eyes locked onto them.

'Welcome home, Jack and Harry. And welcome to our new friend.' The barman raised a glass of whiskey and nodded. 'Y'all lookin' rough.' The room erupted with laughter.

Jack raised Constance's arm. 'This is Constance. She's a pipe hitter.'

Men yowled and cheered and asked to see her bad hand. The barman poured a beer into a child's sippy cup and passed it to her. She nodded, graciously accepting the attention she got from the oversized team leaders.

They were in a much better mood than Jack had anticipated. *Pre-battle high.*

Jimbo was smiling as he walked through the crowd, people ruffling his hair as he passed. The men all yanked at his fox tail and he pushed their hands away. Jack made his way over to Heads, and filled him in on the meeting at the lake.

Suddenly, a voice boomed over the commotion – the only voice Jack knew that could stop a room dead still.

'Sit!' boomed Dyson. 'It's 2302.'

Eighty team commanders gathered around the pool table, which had become a scale model of Melbourne and the Hill. The first row sat on milk crates, the second row on chairs and the third row stood behind them.

The room smelled of woodsmoke, sweat and stale beer.

Jack, Constance and Harry stood to the flank. It had been an hour since their encounter with Jess Wilson.

The Four Horsemen, complete with the addition of Jimbo, stood nearby with Zeus at their feet. Heads moved to the head of the pool table beside Dyson, notebook in hand.

The room fell quiet as Dyson took the floor, cigar in the corner of his mouth. In the three stumps of his right claw he held a pool cue. He steadied himself in the silence, then motioned for Constance and Jack to step forward.

'Outrider, you have the con.' He passed the pool cue to Jack.

Everyone in the room turned their attention to him.

Jack looked at Constance.

He raised the pool cue and cleared his throat.

'This is Constance. She's a friend.'

Silence. A wolf whistle came from the back row, then some chuckles.

Constance took the pool cue from Jack and moved forward. Jack raised both his hands and stepped back, to more laughter.

She took the floor.

'At first light tomorrow, the main force of the Chinese Online Combat Brigade will hit. The VMF will likely form the vanguard of the assault.'

Several men hissed.

Constance raised her voice, pointing the cue to the circular field of the MCG.

'Expect a pre-dawn, ground and air-based insertion of the vanguard. It will comprise the Cranbourne VMF Regiment as the first wave, backed by a Snow Leopard Regiment as the reserve.' The group murmured and shifted. Constance went on. 'The main assault force is this Battalion Tactical Group you've highlighted. Divisional artillery, including thermobarics, heavy tanks, light tanks and infantry.'

It was a strong force. The biggest group they had defeated was ten per cent the size of this one.

Heads stepped forward with his notebook raised, nodding to Constance.

'If I may?'

She stepped back obligingly.

'Command and control elements for each force are experienced fighters. Quick readout on each element: the VMF leader of the Cranbourne Boys is Kayne Wilson.' Heads held up a photo showing Kayne leering at the camera. 'His unit comprises 300 fighters, mostly escapees from the Barwon Prison outbreak. They're loyal to Kayne for his leadership during the breakout. His fighters consist of rapists, murderers and paedophiles.' Heads looked up from his notes. 'He answers to the Chinese Expedition leader. Kayne is thought to have narcissistic personality disorder. He was jailed at Barwon, seven years, for war crimes.'

He held up a photo of Jess Wilson, hair tied back, dark uniform, black aviator sunglasses and a scorpion tattoo on her scalp.

'His sister, Jessica, supports all his operations and is tactically very capable. A smart and strong fighter.'

Jimbo, Constance and Jack exchanged a look.

Next, Heads held up a grainy image of the Principal out the front of a market stall, maybe in Hong Kong or Singapore. He wore a tailored blue suit that framed his perfect V-shaped upper body, dark hair combed over with a neat part.

'The Principal. He'll likely lead the Leopard Regiment by proxy. He's top of our targeting list.

'By morning, 500 of the most advanced soldiers on Earth,

with one hundred heavy fighting vehicles, will lead the clearance of this Hill.'

The room was silent.

'I asked the Yanks if we could borrow their Strat Air Force but they told me to piss off.'

The men burst into laughter. Jack looked at Constance, smiling. She stepped forward, still holding the pool cue, her voice puncturing the air like a laser.

'We have high confidence that the reserve has robotic infantry. Mech suits.'

The lead row of Resistance fighters leaned back in their seats and exchanged looks.

'They'll climb the Hill and get behind us,' one said.

'We'll need more armour to deal with that,' came a voice from the back row.

Jack clapped his hands to calm them. 'Well, you better put the chainsaws to work because those fifty tonne ironbarks are about the only thing that's gonna stop 'em. Get cutting charges set and ready.'

Jack swept his hand across the Five Ways Lookout.

The Five Ways, where he had cremated his wife three days earlier. He ran his hands across the low river system that ran adjacent to the area.

'We channel them here. Make it a full engagement area. I guarantee it's either a control point or a control boundary for the Regiment. That means we use ambush. Wire traps. Tree hides.'

Dyson held his palms out, cigar red and smoking in his mouth. 'No one is coming. It's up to us.'

A team leader interjected. 'Can we do this? Maybe we make our way out through the Grampians and reconstitute. If we leave soon, we can get out through Lillydale Lake.'

All eyes snapped to the team leader. He'd just put voice to the question they dared not ask.

Constance stepped forward.

'It's too late.'

She stared the room down.

'You run and you'll lose everything. The high ground, the forest. The ammo, the fuel, the cars.'

Several of the team leaders were nodding.

The lead trooper in the front row stood up. He turned to the men.

'They have all that firepower, and we're not even talking about evacuating? I reckon it's suicide.'

The room quickly erupted into pointed fingers and shouts. The crowd was divided. Half the commanders wanted to evacuate. The other half wanted to fight on the Hill and make it their last stand.

A gunshot erupted in the din. The team leaders ducked and reached for their pistols and the chatter stopped dead. Harry clapped his hands over his ears.

Constance was anchored to the centre of the room, pistol raised, a trail of dust leaking from the roof. The barman leaned out from behind the bar to inspect the roof.

Constance holstered her pistol, her eyes on the crowd.

'We stay.' She pointed to Jack. 'I didn't risk my neck to have you chicken shit out at the last minute. We stay.'

A man with an eye patch spoke. 'How?'

'I've been allocated strategic assets at the order of the President.'

The team leaders exchanged a look. There were murmurs at the back of the room.

'What assets?' said one, with his arms out.

'Strategic air,' she said.

Cole scoffed at her. 'Bullshit. B-21s? They won't send strat bombers this far south.'

She went on. 'They're enroute right now.'

This news sent a ripple through the crowd. Cole looked at

Jack for confirmation and he nodded, despite having no clue if Constance was telling the truth.

'And take a look out the window. A category five storm, hail the size of golf balls, will be here in two hours.'

Cole shook his head. 'Thanks. But the weather does what it likes.'

'No, it does what I tell it to do.'

There was laughter from the benches, but it quickly died off. Constance did not move.

'No way,' said Cole, hands on hips.

Constance nodded.

'There's more. A potential cruise missile sortie. It's still being worked on.'

'We need each other,' Constance continued. 'We lose this, you lose the state. You lose the state, and we open the country up to the Chinese. The calculus has changed. You fight, and we'll bring the rain. Literally.'

'Listen up,' Dyson silenced the room and began to issue a series of orders, covering all entrances to the Hill and distributing the Resistance's strength and resources according to areas of risk. After a few minutes, he turned to Jack.

'Most likely, they will attack south to north, using the tourist road as their axis of advance,' Dyson said, as Heads pointed out the road on the map with the pool cue.

'Use it as a wedge and separate their forces. Jack, you lead the area ambush at the Five Ways. We got a head start, so we rigged some of the trees up there already. The Five Ways is ringed with the tallest trees on the Hill. Fifty metres tall, two metres thick through the trunk. No tank can clear that. Use obstacles to separate infantry from the tanks. Cut them to shreds from there. Constance, stay with him. We'll need updates as to when your toys are coming into play.'

Jack and Constance nodded.

'We don't have much time,' Heads said.

Dyson clapped twice. 'Go.'

The room jostled and the team leaders all shook hands and embraced. Jack knew that by first light, they would be in hell. The barman had eighty shots lined up in a straight row on the bar, and in the dim light, eighty glasses were tapped against the Victorian Ash bar before being raised in a salute that rattled the windows.

'The Hill!'

51

AMID THE ENSUING CHATTER, THE SPECTACLED BAR OWNER strode over to Jack and Constance and shook their hands, then motioned for them to follow him; Harry, too. They walked through the rear of the kitchen and over to the freezer, then he pulled the three different deadbolts on the door and entered. On the left was a wall of shelving laden with chips and frozen vegetables.

On the right was a gun locker with a dual-glazed perspex frontage. Behind that perspex was the most modern arsenal of carbines, grenade launchers, pistols, thermobaric grenades, rocket assemblies and smart munitions that Jack had ever seen.

The bar owner's keys jingled as he unlocked the cabinet.

'First pick, mate. The rest is for the boys.'

Constance nodded, eyes bright in the pale neon. 'This is more like it.' She reached into the cabinet and pulled out a stumpy M320 grenade launcher, with a six-shot breech and collapsible stock. The bar owner handed her a bandolier with long rounds in it. She draped it over her shoulder.

Jack reached in for a compact M-79 with an elastic bungee on it.

Constance looked at him. 'You're not serious? No way you're taking that antique again.'

275

'Pretty handy in close quarters.' He reached for a second bandolier and clipped it to his waist, then took a stripped-back M4 with a seven-inch barrel and handed it to Harry, along with three magazines stowed in a chest rig. 'Action up, mate, that's yours. Safety first.'

Harry lowered his black hoodie and reached out for the carbine, holding his father's gaze. He took it by the stock and felt the weight in his hands. Then he flipped the weapon, cocked the action, inserted a magazine, cocked the weapon once, and clicked the safety post to safe. He put his body armour on and slung the weapon over his neck.

Jack pointed to some drab olive satchels that looked like heavy bombs. 'What are these?'

The barman pushed his glasses up his nose.

'Fuel air explosive rounds. Good for buildings, trenches.'

'I'll take a dozen.' Jack pulled a whole box off the wall.

There were four hatchets mounted on wood racks. Each one was matte black with hatched jarrah handles. Brand new.

'These, too? I left mine in the car,' Jack mumbled to himself.

The bar owner pulled two off the walls and added the holding sheath to them. He passed one each to Constance and Jack.

Jack caught sight of a compact shotgun. 'You know what?' He reached for a bag of blue phosphorous rounds, fed one into the breech and six into the magazine of the weapon.

The barman was cautious. 'Watch those inside, brother. They burn pretty good.'

Constance was checking the laser sight on her grenade launcher and caught him eyeing the shotgun.

'Seriously? You a duck hunter?'

'Get hit by one of these and you'll be quackin' alright.'

They walked out of the refrigeration unit with two weapons and a hatchet each, as well as a milk crate full of bombs.

Jack collected a multicam shoulder satchel and bundled the

rounds into it. He slung his shotgun, his M4 and his grenade launcher. The M4 had iron sights.

Constance slung her grenade launcher, a SCAR 150 rifle and her grenades over her shoulder. In her form-hugging Arc'teryx pants and pistol belt, she looked like a video game heroine.

Harry had his body armour, three magazines and his carbine slung over his back, his tiny shoulders offering just enough room for the sling. Jack checked the seating of his body armour and tensioned the side straps to keep it snug to his body. He held his son's shoulders in the cold air and smiled at him.

'I'm proud of you, Harry. I'm proud to be your dad.'

They walked out of the freezer and into the threshold of the office. Jack hugged Constance, long and hard. Harry leaned in and hugged her too. Breaking Jack's embrace, she put her hand to his face and nodded to him.

The spectacled bar owner pulled three crystal tumblers from his office shelf, and a bottle of whiskey with a faded label that said 'Macallan's 1964'. He pulled the cork and moved to pour them each a glass.

'No,' Jack protested, and the bar owner stilled his hand. 'Bring it to me when this is over.'

The bar owner corked the bottle and pointed it at Jack.

'You got it.'

They walked out to the horses, warm under their thermal camouflage coats. The air was beginning to whip and stir, and leaves thrashed across the car park as the team leaders loaded up and headed to their positions. Four compact earth movers were trundling out to the tracks to keep digging trenches and fighting pits.

It was just after midnight. By first light, the Hill would be alive with the grinding tracks of the assault forces. They mounted their horses and rode over to their holding position a few kilometres down the bitumen to the Five Ways junction.

The place where they had cremated Gemma.
Because of one man.
The Principal.

PART FOUR

THE
HILL

52

'TIMBER!'

A forty-foot-high tree groaned and fell, thrashing through the scrub and across the access road to the Five Ways. The ground shook as the tree crushed the bitumen and bounced. Cole clicked his stopwatch.

'Nine seconds to ground contact.'

Jack and Cole inspected the tree. Even lying on its side it was over head height, and Jack was six foot four.

'We'll need lots of these,' said Jack.

Jack and Harry took in the scene. Belaymen stood at the bottom of each tree, shouting guidance to the tree fellers. A small back hoe was being used to clear out the chest-high fighting trenches along the shoulder of each road. Men and women crossed the Five Ways with double armloads of ammunition boxes.

Sacha and Jimbo stood in the middle of the Five Ways. Sacha was clutching a SCAR 150 and checking firing distances into the valley beside their holdout.

Jack strode over to them.

'Dyson's been busy. This is a solid position.' Jimbo swept his hand across the raised point of the Five Ways. 'Overlapping arcs of fire. All round defence.' He pointed at the bunker entrance dug into the ridge. 'Depth positions. Plenty of ammo.'

'Five roads are each rigged with tree explosives. They'll be handy for armour.' He nodded at the roadsides. 'Fighting trenches, too.'

A quad bike rattled up the Five Ways. An old man sat astride it wearing a black ten-gallon hat. In the trailer of his quad bike was a rattling box of moonshine jars. A large silver urn with a tap on its side was tied down in the corner.

'Ladies and gents, good evening. Bit of Dutch courage for ya.'

The fighters cheered at the sight of the quad bike. It reminded Jack of an ice-cream truck. As he walked over to view the merchandise, he recognised the craggy face and the ten-gallon hat.

It was Ed, the old Defence Council member Jack had been trying to get to the day of the roundabout showdown that had kicked all this off.

Jack embraced him.

'I heard you've been up to mischief, mate,' said Ed.

'A little bit. I'm glad you got here. I heard you were running the rest of the Resistance teams off the Hill.'

Ed gave him a wry smile. 'I'm keeping busy, mate.' He took a sip of moonshine. 'I'll join you on their approach. About time we gave them a touch-up.'

Fighters gathered around the quad bike, loaded up with axes and chainsaws and heavy weapons. Each man was given a jar of moonshine, and they raised their drinks in the dark and took a long pull. Jack sniffed his jar and took a gulp. He held his hand to his mouth, shoulders convulsing.

'Phew,' said Jack.

'You run out of fuel, just use this.' Ed let out a long wheezing laugh. Fighters poured coffee from the urn, drank from the mason jars, and watched the lightning roll in and the trees whip around them.

Cole fronted Jack.

'If we get trouble up here, I'll be blasting the approaches with trees. You'll need counterattack teams. Be ready to leave the trenches and take their flanks.' He checked his watch. '0200. We have thirty minutes, an hour max, until H-Hour. They'll be here before sun-up.'

The teams started packing up and soldiers headed to their positions.

Jack walked to the command bunker with Harry and looked to the east. The scant moonlight was smothered by the gathering storm. Gusts of wind whipped across the Five Ways and the trees started to rock and scream. Lightning forked across the sky. Jack pulled Harry under his shoulder and felt the strap of his armour over his thin shoulders.

He could feel Gemma with them, watching them both.

Give us strength.

53

'HERE WE GO.' JESS LOOKED AT THE IMMENSE TUNNEL IN AWE. It was a perfect ambush site. She knew its dimensions by heart: it was 1.6 kilometres long, and ran uphill at a seven per cent gradient, over eighty metres of vertical climb.

She pulled over at the first bend of the tunnel and parked the truck in the emergency lane, flush to the tunnel wall, then turned on the hazards and climbed out.

She slammed the door shut and the noise echoed around the tunnel.

Not a soul around.

She ran to the back of the truck and pulled out five road cones, placing them in ten-metre intervals behind the truck. This was it. After this, there would be no returning to the Cranbourne Boys. If she set this truck up to blow, she would be on the run forever.

She would be free.

Jess tipped the bonnet housing forward off the front of the truck, then pulled out a toolbox, put it beside the front wheel and activated the AI camera trigger concealed within. She had built it herself. Machine learning from a petabyte of field imagery told it when a Chinese fuel or ammunition truck was in the viewfinder. The AI was fast enough to identify a quadrillion trucks per second. It would send a tiny charge down the line when it spotted an enemy truck.

She pulled her rifle from the truck and walked backwards, assessing the scene she'd created. It looked good. A broken-down truck in a tunnel, cones and a toolbox for props.

By the time they realised there was no driver, it would be too late.

54

'WHAT A SHITSHOW,' KAYNE WHISPERED. HE HAD A GOOD view from the turret of his carrier, and what he saw of the CCP convoy did not impress him. 'Where did these idiots learn convoy discipline?'

The road out of the MCG was packed with rolling armoured vehicles of all types and sizes.

Hundreds of them.

The vehicles drove nose to tail, braking and swerving around each other. The accordion-like movement of the convoy infuriated Kayne. One armoured personnel carrier had broken down in the middle of Punt Road and the whole convoy was slowing to weave around it. Getting to the freeway and heading into the eastern suburbs had taken an excruciating amount of time.

The air was still and warm; the lightning ahead of them bathed the sky in cracks of white light. He checked his phone, but Jess hadn't called. Probably still in position at Lillydale Lake, waiting to hit any patrols escorting Jack Dunne to the Hill.

He looked down the six-lane highway, warm wind in his face. The last of the VMF trucks were far ahead of him, gunners and infantry in the trays, driving in clear convoy. The expend-ables of the assault.

A monstrous B-double fuel truck ran beside Kayne's armoured car, only a metre away.

He waved it off with a sweeping movement, then shouted into the internal microphone.

'Driver, pull ahead of these logistics vehicles. They should be up the rear of the convoy.' Kayne's vehicle pulled ahead of the fuel truck. The car approached the broad opening that was carved into the cliff wall. The words 'Mullum Mullum' were printed in metal letters over the top. Kayne looked across the six lanes of the tunnel. The giant extraction fans that lined the roof sat motionless. The emergency exits were all bolted shut. Swirling patterns of graffiti lined the walls.

A choke point.

They entered the mouth of the tunnel and the roar of the traffic grew to a vibrating howl.

Around the first corner he spotted one of his cars inspecting a broken-down truck. They didn't look worried; the gunner wasn't even covering the truck.

The car commander waved to him, but he was focused on the bunched-up vehicles.

Kayne waved him off and continued his advance.

Looking ahead, he could see the end of the tunnel a few hundred metres in the distance.

55

A DOZEN VMF VEHICLES THUNDERED TOWARDS THE OPENING of the Mullum Mullum Tunnel.

Three hundred metres uphill, the first HiLux cornered the bend and was greeted by road cones and flashing hazard lights fifty metres ahead.

'Broken-down truck, left emergency lane. Stay right.'

The HiLux stopped a short distance behind the truck.

The car commander stepped out of his HiLux and waved the remaining trucks ahead. They howled and screamed at him as they ripped past, paying no mind to the truck. He lit a cigarette as he hopped out of his vehicle. The gunner on the HiLux had his arm draped over a 50-calibre Browning machine gun.

'Hurry. We'll lose our spot,' he called out.

'Wait.' The car commander blew smoke in the air as he appraised the truck. He got down on one knee and stooped to look underneath it, then turned back to the gunner, who only shrugged. Running a hand through his bushy red mullet, the man drew his pistol, then walked around the front of the truck and pulled the driver's side door open.

Nothing.

The first few armoured carriers passed them, the turret commanders not even glancing at the truck. The man spotted Kayne Wilson in the turret and waved both his hands at him.

Kayne waved back.

'Stop, ya silly cunt!' he shouted after him. He turned to his gunner. 'Cover me.'

The gunner swung his weapon onto the truck and waved off the convoy driving past him. Diesel fumes were filling the space as the armoured cars downshifted into low range to climb the long tunnel. More armoured cars passed them.

The red mulleted man moved to the back of the truck with his pistol out and reached for the metal lever on the rear door. One of the double doors was ajar. He pulled it open and lifted his pistol in one motion. Red light flooded from the back of the truck, illuminating four bags of explosives, four drums of fuel, and a line of detonating cord snaking from a junction into the top of each bag.

'No,' the man whispered.

He turned and sprinted for the HiLux, waving futilely at a fuel truck that was just about to pass him.

The elongated fuel truck, with two trailers full of aviation fuel, entered the viewfinder of the AI camera. The computer overlayed a social media image of that exact truck taken by a PLA transport corporal at Essendon Airport two years earlier, which he had erroneously texted to his girlfriend. In a fraction of a second the AI matched the image and sent a signal to the IR switch inside the truck. The charge ran down the cable and exploded four priming charges, detonating a tonne of fertiliser diesel explosive mix.

The shockwave of plasma and heat energy carbonised the red-haired man, his HiLux, his gunner, his driver and the fuel truck beside them. The fuel in the drums atomised into a fine mist, which ignited in the heat of the explosion. The fuel truck detonated in a massive secondary blast in the confined tunnel, sending a wall of flame shooting several hundred metres in all directions.

The blast wave hit an ammunition truck carrying mortar shells. The four tonnes of artillery detonated at once, shooting a dozen armoured cars out the mouth of the tunnel. A second ammunition truck was hit by the blast and immediately combusted in a ball of flame. Three pallets of artillery shells exploded seconds later.

Another fuel truck was just half a kilometre into the tunnel, but the overpressure collapsed the tank like a coke can under a sledgehammer. The fuel cells ruptured at the weld seams, and 10,000 litres of jet fuel exploded. Bitumen melted, metal caught fire, and concrete shattered in the heat.

Kayne felt the heat on his back first. When he turned in the turret he saw a tidal wave of white and yellow flames barrelling up the tunnel, engulfing the vehicles in its wake.

'Button down!' the Principal screamed at Kayne, who had already dropped from the turret and was closing the hatch. The explosion rocked the carrier. It smelled of burning metal, plastic and humans.

'Get clear of the tunnel! It's a chimney.'

The HiLuxes in the tunnel spluttered to a halt, starved of oxygen. BMPs – a Soviet-made armoured personnel carrier – and tracked cars slammed into the stopped HiLuxes. A Cranbourne Boy sprinting uphill was thrown into the bitumen and sucked under a BMP. One armoured car accelerated over the rear of a HiLux, crushing the gunner.

Kayne's carrier cleared the tunnel and stopped. He exited the rear ramp with a fire extinguisher and doused the burning camouflage netting at the top and side of the carrier.

He faced the tunnel, pitch-black smoke and flames billowing from its mouth.

A BMP rolled out of the hellish opening, its wheels aflame, the burning skeleton of a crew commander seated bolt upright in the turret. His blackened, shrivelled face was still on fire, his lips drawn back over his teeth in a macabre grin.

Kayne ran to the rear of his carrier, where the Principal now stood, surveying his burning armoured unit.

The Principal shook his head and looked away from the flames spilling out of the tunnel.

'Keep moving, the storm is coming.'

Kayne radioed his squadron commanders. Only one of the four answered. The other three were missing. He was sucking breaths in, trying to control the flood of adrenaline in his body.

Kayne closed his eyes and took a deep breath.

'Any cars or units that are still alive, muster at the line of departure for new taskings,' he said, his voice ragged.

The rear ramp closed as the Principal climbed back into the carrier.

'Move. We have work to do.'

56

Dyson brushed the hessian curtain aside and stepped into the command post. 'Fire detected in the Mullum Mullum Tunnel. The main assault force was in transit.'

Heads locked eyes with Jack. 'Is it her?'

'I reckon so,' said Jack.

Heads brought Dyson up to speed.

'She stopped Jack at the lake, said she had a truck bomb. Offered to hit the main body in the tunnel. My assessment: she's turned, she's unlikely to be a double.'

Dyson folded his arms and absorbed the turn of events.

'She told Jack the Principal killed Gemma,' said Heads.

Dyson guffawed. 'What?' He looked at Jack and slapped his shoulder. 'Whoa.' Dyson shook his head.

'He better stay away. Last time I saw that look in Jack's eyes he salted the fields after he'd killed everyone.' Dyson laughed.

Jack's face was set in stone.

Jimbo ran into the CP. 'We're set.'

Jack came back to life. He pointed at Harry. 'Can you please make sure he stays in the CP?'

Jimbo nodded, and his radio squawked.

'We have a walk-in. Main approach. Says her name is Jess. She asked for Jack.'

Jimbo keyed the mike.

'Search her, then bring her to the command bunker,' said Jimbo.

Minutes later, a fighter pulled up in a HiLux, dragged a body from the front of the tray and set her upright on the tail-gate. She was powerfully built, her wrists zip-tied behind her narrow waist and an undercut on one side of her head revealing a scorpion tattoo. The fighter placed a tomahawk, a sawn-off double barrel holstered to her belt, a knife and an SR-75 sniper rifle next to the CP entrance.

'This is hers.'

Jack stood in front of her and looked her in the eyes. There was no fear in them. He walked her into the command post; Constance and Dyson followed. The post was lit by a single light bulb.

Dyson studied her, drumming his three fingers on the desk.

Jimbo snipped the ties off her wrists and handed her a can of coke. She sniffed it once, looked at Jack, then drank the whole thing in one go, never taking her eyes off him.

She put the empty can down and rubbed her wrists.

'I hit the main body.'

'How many?' said Jack.

'Don't know. It's not a huge tunnel and there were fuel trucks in there. They were meant for you.'

Constance shook her head.

Jess nodded. 'We spare no expense. Not for Outriders.' She lifted her chin to Constance. 'You too. You're on the kill list.'

Constance ignored her. 'How much armour?'

'A lot were hit. The blue force tracker was only showing half the units.' She held her eyes to Jack. 'But there's still enough of a force to take this place.'

Dyson stood up and looked to Heads, 'Is that true?'

'Yes.' said Heads.

Jess went on. 'If my brother is alive, look after him. I want my weapons, a car and 500 litres of diesel.'

Dyson sneered. 'How about a full tank, but your brother comes, he can die up here with his mates.'

She pursed her lips, and he went on.

'You're free. We'll load your weapons before you leave. If you want to stay, you're welcome to, but you'll be in here, in cuffs.'

Jess stood, frowning. 'Chinese troops might be standing in here, drinking your rum by sundown.'

She eyed Jack, studied his leather jacket for a moment.

'Why don't you come? I'm heading west.'

Constance moved to stand behind Jack. 'Thanks. We're staying.'

Jack escorted Jess outside to her truck, among the earth-moving gear and chainsaws.

He watched her check the car out.

Harry walked behind her with his carbine slung. Rain pattered across the position and drummed onto her muddy black HiLux.

Jess checked her weapons and started the truck. She turned to look at Harry, who was standing by, watching, in his body armour.

She reached into the car and pulled out her utility belt, a sawn-off shotgun hanging from the holster. She draped the belt over her left arm and presented it to Harry.

He shot a look back at his father.

Jack nodded once.

Harry slipped it off her arm, beaming, and tied it around his waist. He snapped the buckle down. The overlap was long, but it sat true and level, and the weapon looked right on him, even though it was a foot long. He kept looking down at the weapon that hung off his waist.

Jack smiled at him. He was looking at himself at that age.

The naivety of youth. There's plenty in him to salvage.

The rain was starting to sheet in hard.

Jess climbed into the car, adjusted the seat and called out to Jack.

'Sure you wanna stay?'

Jack didn't move. She shrugged and took off down the bitumen. She was free.

Heads stepped up next to Jack. 'I got tracking and listening devices in the car and in her rifle. We can keep an eye on her.'

57

60,000 feet in the airspace over Kaui, Hawaii

MAJOR SEAN 'TIEDOWN' DANOWSKI SCANNED THE SITUATIONAL Awareness Displays in the cockpit of his B-21 Raider and rubbed his eyes. He was tired. Fourteen years he'd been flying, four of them in stealth bombers; the sleep deprivation didn't get any easier. He had just taken on fuel from the enormous KC-150 jet. Danowski flashed his nav lights twice and peeled away from the plane. 'Thanks for the gas,' he radioed to the refueller.

They were completing the final refuel profile on the sixteen-hour journey from Whitman Air Force Base, Missouri, to the bottom of the globe. Once each plane had sucked onboard fifty tonnes of fuel, they would commence their final run through the Chinese air defence networks.

Their destination: Victoria. The last bastion of the Aussie Resistance was about to be wiped out, and they might be the only force that could prevent a Chinese victory.

His watch showed 0410 Pacific Time; the darkness would hold as they chased the night.

Three of the four bombers had finished refuelling. The final one was lining up for the boom.

'Rampage flow direct to waypoint 220.'

'Trinity, copy,' the Airborne Early Warning and Control aircraft radioed in. It would track the craft during their transit and make sure they were safe from enemy interceptors.

Danowski looked up, taking in a stunning view of the night. The inner arm of the Milky Way shone, and the Belt of Orion stood out as gems on the black sky.

Danowski manoeuvred his craft into box formation. He was trailing the pair that were one nautical mile ahead of him, but they would let him push ahead and lead the box. His wingman would refuel and then race to catch him. For now, they were in a tighter group than he preferred. Danowski could feel the sweat in his gloves.

'Rampage, commence weapon checks at the final control line. See you there.'

'Copy, Rampage 1,' came the call from the plane ahead of him. The eight pilots and navigators had spent two days in a vast lecture theatre at Whitman Air Force Base, rehearsing every aspect of the mission. Danowski kept the reminders going anyway. Humans got tired during these missions.

Each B-21 Raider carried forty 500-pound bombs.

Their mission: vaporise a whole Chinese Regiment and an Aussie Militia unit.

Danowski tracked the pair of pale white slits above the horizon, his lead pair. The internal network crackled to life.

'Hey Tiedown, for this weekend I'll trade my two best wide receivers for your running back,' said James 'Jumbo' Nellis.

'Not happening. Not surrendering pole position,' said Danowski.

'True, but when you pay me, I want ten dollars – whoa! Rampage check right, break . . .'

Two green streaks of plasma ripped downwards from the heavens through the pair of white dots on the horizon. The projectile moved faster than Danowski could track with his eyes.

One bomber exploded in a ballooning flash of yellow. The second was engulfed by a long streak of flame, arcing downwards.

Danowski pulled his aircraft nose up and to the right and scanned high. 'Trinity, this is Rampage. Defending. Orbital strike.'

'Read back, orbital strike. Stand-by,' said Trinity.

'Rampage 1 egressing north. Engage active camo.'

Danowski flipped a switch, activating the onboard camouflage system. Light-emitting polyaniline composite panels sensed the light signatures around the aircraft and projected light from the underside to the top of the craft. The 140-tonne bomber disappeared from view, merely a smudge in the sky.

Danowski slammed the engine power up and pulled a hard bank back to the north, dropping altitude but presenting a narrow profile to the heavens. A green streak whipped from above his cockpit, missing his bomber by a wing length. The shockwave thumped the aircraft.

'Rampage break right ninety. Tally one, three o'clock, two miles. Height uncertain, probably orbital.' It took all his self-control not to scream into the radio.

'No radar lock. Rampage 2 and 3 are hit,' he said.

He was pulling hard, and chaff billowed out the underside of his bomber in long streaks as he swung his aircraft around on its wingtip. As he tracked his turn north, a long curtain of flames reached down towards the earth, where the fuel tankers had positioned. Four columns of flame and debris in total. His onboard cameras caught the tumbling grey cockpit.

'Whale call signs are down. Both refuellers are down.' There was an edge in his voice now. His legs tensed and cramping from strain.

Danowski scanned the stars overhead. He did not see the metre-long tungsten rod coming from low earth orbit, skewering the atmosphere at eight kilometres a second.

The rod punched through the last third of his wing tip and sheared it off. He felt the immediate tilt towards the damaged wing. Counter thrust activated automatically and tried to right the craft, but there was a long streak of white hot flame trailing from the fuel tank.

'Rampage 1 is hit, I'm going down.'

Fuel cells exploded one after the other into blue flames, creeping up the wing towards him.

A cool woman's voice spoke to him: 'Eject. Eject. Eject.'

He reached for the yellow T-bar between his legs and pulled the handle hard.

In a fraction of a second the canopy's explosive bolts blew the cover off the cockpit. Two spring-loaded arms shot forward from the ACES 5 ejection seat and clamped his helmet onto the headrest. Then the rocket fired Sean Danowski into the sky. He blacked out as twelve Gs of force compressed him into his seat, and unconscious, he sailed into the thin air over the dark Pacific Ocean, his bomber flaming through the sky as it disintegrated.

Ten minutes later, the cov com unit in Constance's pocket beeped.

She stepped out of the command bunker and opened the unit. After it verified her bio signature, the high-priority text flashed on the screen.

Raven strike cancelled. No comms with USS McRaven. *Stand-by.*

She closed her eyes and held her head in her hands.

'Fuck.' She turned down the hill, where she knew the attacking force would come from.

The submarine USS McRaven *is our last hope.*

58

'THE RESISTANCE HAS NOT USED A WEAPON LIKE THAT.' THE Principal's gaze burned into Kayne.

'True. Very unusual,' said Kayne. He looked at his phone. Nothing from Jess.

He sucked his teeth and surveyed the roundabout where they had established an armoured hide.

This is where Jack killed Stevie Adams.

The Principal was scanning the ridgelines of the Hill with binoculars. He lowered them and turned to Kayne.

'Switch to alternate entry point. Inverness Road. Main objective, the Five Ways. Advance to contact in two minutes.'

As he picked up the fist mike to issue the command, the Principal looked at Kayne. 'Suit up. You'll need it.'

'Should we save it for when we commit the reserve?'

The Principal stared back. 'We are the reserve.'

'Okay. Just a thought,' Kayne said.

'Suit up.'

Kayne watched the Principal walk to the back of the carrier and haul his suit out of the wall-mounted charging rack. He stepped into the thick metal leg struts, clipped the matte titanium hip actuators to his groin and flanks, and pulled the

titanium arms and spine over his back. Retrieving his tomahawk from the car, he slid the head into a sheath on his thigh.
He rolled his arms over in a shrug and drew his tomahawk in
one fluid movement.

Kayne watched the Principal.

The man lived for the hunt.

The prize barely mattered; it was the struggle that fuelled
him.

The Principal slapped his fists together. 'When the battle
starts, I'll go with the mech unit. You press forward with the
VMF. Call it in.'

'Copy,' said Kayne.

'This weather is going to complicate things. The forecast
wasn't this bad earlier,' said the Principal.

'That's Melbourne weather for you,' Kayne said bleakly.

The remaining twenty vehicles and HiLuxes all ramped
down and rolled out towards Inverness Road.

Next stop: the Five Ways intersection. The heart of the
Resistance.

59

JACK KNELT IN THE BUNKER AND HUGGED HIS SON. HE HELD him for a long time.

'Stay,' Harry said. His voice trembled.

Jack pulled his face away and held Harry's in both his hands. 'We're gonna win. I'll be here by sun-up.' Harry nodded, his lips shaking, and Jack felt the pull in his heart. The same any parent feels when they step away from the most precious thing: their child. Jack slapped his son on the shoulder, stood up, and stormed out of the bunker with Constance in trail. He didn't look back.

Through the driving rain, Jack gazed at the willow tree he had stood under four days ago while he watched Gemma's body being washed. The black water coiled and thrashed around the rocks, and the willow had spread its arms across the river. Lightning cracked overhead, illuminating the draw in white light.

Jack approached the trenchlines and dumped his heavy weapons and ammo in the fighting trench. He scanned the trees with thermal binoculars.

Enemy were driving up Inverness Road, winding uphill through the ironbark trees. The vehicles' white against a black background, the car commanders' heads swivelling in the turrets.

Jack felt the climbing dread in his stomach as he listened to the low rumble of the gears. He had always dreaded the hour before battle.

The Resistance fighters were already dialling the ranges into their rocket rounds. The stayed low in the trenches, which were now ankle-deep with muddy water.

Ed grinned at Jack as he walked past with two armfuls of rocket ammo, making no effort to stoop below the parapet. The old man's eyes held the glint of a young man with a purpose.

'Ed!' Jack said. 'Get low, they're right there.'

The old timer grunted and waved him off. 'They can't shoot for shit. This is your fault, anyway.' He chuckled.

'I told you to live on the Hill. How many times did I say it?' said Jack.

'You did. Still your fault though. Take this.' Ed passed him a green block with buttons on it. It was a remote firing device for explosives rigged in the trees. The buttons were numbered one through eight.

'Cheers,' Jack said.

'You do fire control. I'll follow.' The old timer shuffled down the line into the dark, boots sloshing in the trench water.

Jack lay the Carl Gustav 84mm rocket launcher on his knee and opened the breech. He pulled a rocket from a tube and began to insert it into the launcher. The rumbling of the tanks in low gear was getting louder.

The rain was still barrelling down.

Constance ran down the trench behind Jack and knelt next to him.

'Bad news. I think the –'

Jack cut her off.

'They're right there.' He pointed down the hill. 'Stand-by.'

'Jack, hurry,' Constance said.

He slammed the launcher closed, but it jarred on the back of the round and stayed open. It was jammed.

'Quick.' There was an edge in her voice.

'I know. Take the shrike.' He passed her the green box.

Lightning crackled over the flanks of the hill and hail started to bounce off the ground, pounding them and reducing visibility even further. The sound was incredible. The sort of thrashing weather that could stop technology dead in its place.

'Four hundred thirty metres,' she said.

Jack shifted the round a quarter turn in the breech and it slammed home by a half inch. He closed the launcher and pulled his night-vision goggles down, then hauled the rocket launcher onto his shoulder and activated the infrared laser beam mounted to its flank. Through his night vision, the white aiming dot of the laser danced across the green background. A light-green armoured hulk, the crew commander's head and shoulders, was visible through the scrub.

'They're at the first fallen tree obstacle. Three hundred metres,' said Constance.

Scanning the road, Jack could make out the turrets of the first three tanks. The lead tank was whining, pushing against the fallen tree. Cracks appeared in the branches, but the tree didn't budge. A moment later, a conga line of helmeted heads bobbed past the front of the tank, heading for the obstacle.

'Dismounts!' he said.

Six enemy troops stood at chest height at the front of the formation. They had chainsaws – electric chainsaws, judging by the low whir.

'Suits. They're in suits,' Constance hissed.

'Bullshit,' said Jack. She passed him the thermal viewer. The six troops had the unmistakable black metal struts on their limbs, and they were chainsawing and hacking out the tree.

'Oh.' He passed the viewer back to her and keyed his mike.

'All call signs, first three cars, 300 metres. Anti-armour and anti-personnel rounds. Fire on my mark.'

Jack trained the white dot of his launch laser onto the tree obstacle. He checked the ground to his rear, then flicked off the safety on the rocket launcher.

He tensed his hand on the foregrip and rested his finger on the trigger.

60

'THERE'S A TREE ACROSS THE ROAD. WE CAN'T SHIFT IT. Engineers dismount,' the carrier commander called from the road.

The trees were swaying and rolling in the crackling light. Hail was belting off the hull of Kayne's carrier. He could feel the rapping on his helmet.

Going uphill in this is a fuckin' nightmare.

The engineer team commander walked to the tree and ran his hand over its six-foot-high flank.

'We'll use cutting charges,' he declared.

Kayne had heard enough. He ripped his helmet comms off, stormed out the ramp of his carrier and gripped the engineer's chest strap.

'Cut a section out! We need to move,' he shouted.

A pair of engineers stepped forward, each carrying an olive crate with cutting charges in it.

'Don't blow it!' Kayne screamed. 'You want to tell everyone up there where we are? Shift it. Use your suits.'

The team leader called the rest of his operators forward.

'Okay, let's do a lift. Get ready to drive forward to shift it.'

The Principal's voice hissed in Kayne's earpiece.

'Get moving.'

Kayne rushed them along. The suits had rammed their lifting pikes into the tree, and each sat in a squat position, readying to lift the tree.

Jack had locked the rocket onto the lead tank, where the bulk of the dismounts were.

Constance held the shrike in two hands.

'Number seven. Hit number seven when I shoot,' said Jack.

Her finger hovered over the button.

'Prepare to lift . . . lift!' shouted Kayne. The suits groaned as they took the strain. The hydraulics whined, and the biting noise of metal on bitumen came from the suits. The tree shifted and cracked, then lifted a foot off the road.

A long rectangle of bark casing tumbled from the front of the tree onto the suited arms of the lead engineer. He peered into the carved hole, but the recess was dark. A crack of lightning flashed overhead and in the white light he saw eight olive explosive Claymore mines with orange detonating cord snaking from the tops.

He stepped away from the tree, eyes wide.

'It's rigged, it's rig–'

Constance jammed her finger down on the number seven. An orange and yellow hydra exploded from the fallen tree and consumed the engineers standing in front of it.

Jack squeezed the trigger, and his rocket flew off his shoulder with the force of a mule kick and arced over the vegetation towards the dismounted troops. It exploded over the top of them in a burst of orange sparks. They heard one soldier howling in agony from the blast.

Constance scanned the obstacle. There were no troops left, just white-hot fragments of metal, tree splinters and strips of human flesh.

Kayne was thrown onto his back. He climbed up and staggered back to the rear of his carrier just as his crew vehicle opened up with the clattering flash of 30mm rounds. Something was stuck in his face. His hand probed a foot-long shard of Victorian ironbark sticking out of the side of his jaw. As he climbed into the back of the carrier, the Principal barely glanced at him.

'Fire mission, danger close: ridgeline on top of Inverness Road, grid 3472. White phosphorous, airburst.'

He put the handset down and turned to Kayne, sitting slumped beside him, blood pooling across the nape of his flannel shirt. The Principal bunched Kayne's shirt up in his fist, gripped the sliver in his other hand and in one smooth movement, pushed Kayne's body away and yanked the sliver of ironbark from Kayne's mouth.

Kayne howled. Red foam bubbled from the hole in his cheek.

The Principal threw the stake away, then pulled his face up to Kayne's and spoke through gritted teeth.

'Stand up and watch.'

He pulled Kayne up by the shirt to the turret hatch and held his head up as the first white phosphorous rounds sailed overhead. The smoky white fingers of burning phosphorous sprinkled onto the ridgeline ahead.

'See that? Head towards it. We will begin our flanking manoeuvre,' the Principal said.

He looked around and saw the one VMF soldier in a mech suit. The others in suits had been killed by the explosive traps laid by the Resistance.

'You,' the Principal said, pointing at the suited-up man. 'With me.'

Kayne watched the pair head off. The Principal looked too eager to get his hands dirty.

A hailstone the size of a golf ball smacked the top of Kayne's helmet, drawing his gaze back to the slope he had to lead his forces up. He wished he had a bottle of whiskey to hand.

Kayne jumped in the hatch of the nearest tank heading towards the crumping bursts of shells over the ridgeline. He knew death was likely up on that hill, waiting for them.

61

'GOOD HIT,' SAID JACK.

Jack scanned the waist-deep ravine of volcanic rock behind the trench. He wagered it could carry them to the top of the position in protective cover. The 30mm cannons of the armoured cars opened up, showering the trees and rocks in their position with exploding sparks. Tree branches and leaves rained down on them amid the rain. They ducked in the covered draw and waited.

'After we fire eight, we scoot back to the position.' Jack pointed up the draw. It was his only way back to the command post. To Harry. Constance and Ed nodded and crouched lower, ready to move.

Jack pointed to the firing device.

'Fire eight.'

Constance hit the remote. There was a high explosive crack from the ravine as shaped beehive charges exploded along the track.

Rock, dirt, metal casings, compressed gas plasma and molten copper slugs burst from the road embankment. Three armoured cars were penetrated diagonally through the hull, the molten slugs cutting through with ease. A plasma jet of gas and metal cut through the troop-carrying trucks, shearing through the arms, legs, hip bones and heads of the infantry stacked up inside.

Some of the other Resistance's planted charges went off in the distance. Constance looked up and saw the first tanks exploding as the ammunition lockers cooked off, burning up a flue of white-hot gas that reached two storeys into the night sky. One crewman took off down the hill at a full gallop, on fire, the trees either side of him glowing as the human torch tried to outrun the flames that engulfed him.

Three tanks appeared on the next ridge. They swung their turrets to the hillside and began to fire along the ridge.

Jack stood up in his trench, exposed from waist up, rocket launcher at his shoulder. His infrared laser dot found the turret flank of a T-90 tank. He flicked the safety off and pulled the trigger. The rocket screeched between the tree trunks and slammed into the angled turret. The round skipped off the metal and tumbled into the night.

'Ricochet!' Jack squared and cranked the lever once more, and a smoking shell jettisoned out of the launcher. Constance put her boot on the parapet and fired a single pike round. A black and yellow explosion rose above the rear of an armoured car where troops were dismounting. They could hear muffled howls in the rain. She reloaded.

Ed stood up with his rocket launcher and Jack saw him brace as he fired. He sent off a single round with a crack, and as he swung his rocket launcher to his side, his helmet popped off the top of his head. Ed crumpled in a heap in the trench.

'Ed!' Jack called.

Jack stalked down the trench and pulled him to his side. His eyes were still open in shock, but one hemisphere of his head had been pulverised by a bullet.

Jack's brain stayed in a surreal autopilot. He had felt this before; the mind cuts off inputs that are too extreme.

He turned back to Constance.

She kept her foot up on the parapet and continued pumping out rounds towards the enemy. The tanks had closed now; they were only one hundred metres away. The white streak of a tank salvo ripped through a metre-thick ironbark, knocking it down beside their position in a shower of branches.

Jack cranked another anti-tank round into his rocket launcher and scanned for the jockeying tanks. He checked the burning engagement zone and caught the rear quarter of a tank in the smoke. He locked onto it, pressed the trigger. The round exploded, the white flames of the rocket arcing towards the tank. It connected with the rear, and the whine of an engine came as the turbine revved to its maximum. The tank exploded into a yellow ball, the twenty-tonne turret thrown clear of the position, tumbling through the air.

'Go! Let's go!' Jack sensed they had blunted their momentum and knew the only way back to safety was to move up the concealed rock path back to the Five Ways. As he climbed from the trench, a blast struck his side.

He felt a burning in his thigh, a hot skewer right through him. Ignoring it, he stood and ran.

The flames of the burning tanks lit the trees and the tracked carriers fired bursts that flew high into the tree line on the ridge. Constance pulled level with Jack and hooked her arm under his armpit. He reached for the source of the burning pain in his inner thigh. A long, thin shard of metal protruded from his leg, being jolted as he ran.

'My leg,' he said.

Constance pulled him behind a fallen tree and felt across his thigh. Jack screamed when she made contact with the metal shard.

She gasped. Jack reached for it.

'Leave it!' Constance blocked him. 'You'll bleed out.'

He pushed her arm away and grabbed the shard and

screamed as he yanked it clear of his leg, the serrations of the metal fragment sawing through his flesh.

Jack howled in pain.

The metal shard was a foot long, jagged and narrow, its edge like sharpened flint stone. A hot knife in his thigh.

'I said leave it.' Constance ripped his jeans open at the tear. The cut was no wider than an inch, but bright red blood streamed from it in bursts.

'Arterial bleed.' She pulled a field dressing off his pistol belt, opened it with her teeth and unravelled the khaki gauze. Jack was breathing hard and kicking the ground with his good leg.

'Grab me, as hard as you can.' She pulled his hand onto her muscled upper arm, then stuffed the strapping gauze into the open wound with her thumb. Jack screamed. Her thumb penetrated the full depth of the wound. Jack tried to pull her arm back as she stuffed his wound with cloth.

'I know,' she said. She pushed harder, and Jack went quiet. She looked at his eyes; they were unfocused. His grip on her shoulder relaxed.

He was out, unconscious.

'I told you to leave it,' she said. She strapped his thigh with a tourniquet.

More cannon rounds ripped the air above them and crashed into the trees over their position. She covered Jack's head with her body, then slapped his face with the back of her hand and jostled his collar. His head was lolling back. She pulled it up and shouted into his now-grey face.

'Move!' She yanked him to his knees and he came to, hopping on his good leg.

'Move. Faster.' Her bandolier of rounds had fallen down her waist, but she still had her grenade launcher slung over her side.

'Stop,' said Jack. 'Stop!'

'No!' she screamed.

He turned and hopped back through the rain to pick up an ammo case. The last two flechette rounds for the rocket launcher.

'Two hundred metres,' said Constance. 'Over the Hill, into the bunker.'

She pushed him. 'Harry's there.'

Jack was light-headed and stumbling. A missile cut the air beside him, the pink light and sparks dancing from the rocket. They could feel the terrain flattening out, they were on the cusp of the Five Ways saddle. That was the centre of the defensive position. They were still within range of the heavy armoured gun, still exposed.

She keyed her microphone 'Outrider and Constance approaching from the south. Need immediate medical for Jack. Priority one, femoral rupture, left thigh.'

'Get Harry,' Jack gasped.

Constance keyed the mike. 'Get Outrider Junior to the med bay.'

A gum tree shattered in blossoms of yellow sparks above her thanks to a blast of 30mm cannon. Shredded green leaves and sticks showered down with the hail. The rockets and cannon shells were so loud the sound physically thumped against her uniform. Clumps of burning phosphorous hissed on the ground, lighting their path.

Jack was slipping under her arm, and she was taking most of his weight. The infantry squads tonked away with grenade launchers, covering their movement, the whisper and cracks of the return fire whipping overhead.

Fifty metres to the command post.

'Stop,' she said.

She lay Jack on his side next to the root ball of a fallen iron-bark, the mass of rock and tree root were good cover. She knelt in the crater and pulled the rocket launcher open. She grabbed the flechette stump-nosed rounds and placed them on Jack's lap.

'Hit their depth units. A hundred metres,' gasped Jack.

She locked the round between her thighs then hefted the launcher and put the round in the breech. The rear would not slam home.

Jack spoke up in a slur. 'Rotate the round until it's flush.'

She turned it once and it slammed flush in the breech.

Before she could raise the launcher, a burst of 30mm rounds slammed into the root ball, sending rocks and shards flying across Constance. A rocket tore the air and slammed into a tree trunk only ten metres behind them. Constance gasped and wiped her face. She hauled the rocket up to her shoulder, stooped forward, and popped her head and shoulders around the side of the root ball. Jack held his breath, watching her in awe. Her silhouette was lit up by the machine gun bursts from the trenches and lightning from above.

The worse it gets, the harder she hits.

She braced her shoulders and fired level with the ground. The round exploded through a smoke pall and into the first row of assaulting troops. Its secondary charge fired, a thousand metal darts exploded among an assault section.

The firing slowed off, while the thrashing rain remained ever-present.

Constance stayed at the edge of the root ball and scanned the site she had just fired upon. A deranged howling came from depth position. A soldier yelled for his mother in Mandarin.

It could just as easily have been the other way around.

'Again.' Jack held the second round up to her with both hands.

Keep your boot on their throat.

Jack watched Constance as she knelt and set the second round between her legs, reloaded the rocket, and fired again.

The screams stopped.

Constance threw the launcher down. A Resistance fighter knelt at the lip and was waving them back towards the Hill.

Jack turned towards the open ground in the middle of the Five Ways.

Fifty metres left.

He tried to sit up, but couldn't. Constance rolled him onto his side, and he felt a bass rumble through the earth. He turned his head to the lip of the ridgeline beside the fallen tree. The broad, black underbelly of a T-90 shot over the rise into the early dawn.

The world fell silent.

There, perched at the cusp of the ridge, blacking out the dark clouds and the hail, sat sixty tonnes of armour. Jack could see the intricate angles of the hull and the gentle sway of a towing shackle at its nose. The tank collapsed to level ground, its tracks slamming into the earth.

Jack had wondered his whole life how he would die. In that moment, all the pieces came together.

The barrel of the T-90 tracked towards them, and Jack closed his eyes.

62

CONSTANCE THREW HERSELF ACROSS JACK AND COVERED HIS head.

'Sorry,' she said.

There was an eruption behind them, among the eucalypts. Splinters and branches showered down on them.

The tree began tipping on its axis towards the T-90, sheared through its base by cutting charges. It groaned as it fell towards the tank.

As the tree fell, the tank commander rotated its turret towards the trenches at the lip of the Five Ways. The tree scythed across the turret of the tank then rolled forward off the angled turret and onto the barrel. The turret popped off the top of the tank like a broken toy.

Constance pulled Jack to his knees and as they turned to flee the tank, a set of arms hooked her from the side.

'Down!' a voice from behind roared.

Cole appeared at the side of the root ball and fired a full magazine from his SCAR 150. He was covered in grime, red Hawaiian shirt under his armour, a cigar in the corner of his mouth and his rifle on his shoulder.

Jack wanted to cry. The man was a sight to behold.

Cole knelt beside Jack and put his broad hand on his chest. 'Hang on, big fella,' he said.

He sucked hard on his thick cigar, the red ember glowing in the dawn. In his hand was a mason jar with a rag tied to it. He pulled the soaked rag up to the cigar, shielded the ember from the rain, and pulled long drags. As smoke crept from his mouth and nose, he studied the tank.

He was in no hurry.

A soldier was pulling himself clear of the turret hole, jabbering in Mandarin. Cole watched him, unrattled.

Constance eyed him. 'Hurry,' she said.

The rag ignited with a whoomp and Cole watched the flame creep up the rag. He tipped the jar to its side, keeping one eye on the tank as he did. Finally, he wound his arm back and lobbed the jar into the turret of the tank.

The tank commander was climbing out of the turret hole when the jar and moonshine exploded inside the tank. He was enveloped in blue flames, but did not make a sound. A VMF man with a peaked cap climbed out after him, both his arms on fire, and Jack saw that most of the man's cheek was a mashed red mess.

Kayne Wilson's legs were on fire as he climbed from the tank. Disoriented, he ran towards the Resistance trenches, flapping his arms like a flightless bird.

From nowhere, a werewolf-sized dog hit Kayne at full speed, its teeth white as it vaulted the armoured ramp of the tank. Kayne collapsed under Zeus and the dog went for his neck, thrashing about as though possessed. Kayne howled.

Another Chinese officer burst out of the tank. He ran past the man being mauled by the Belgian shepherd and sprinted downhill.

'Zeus. Heel!' boomed a voice.

Jack was fading, but Dyson's voice roused him.

Unmistakable.

318

When a battle hung in the balance, that voice was the oxygen in the fire. They turned to see Dyson standing on the edge of the trench, firing a carbine from his shoulder at the fleeing tank officer. Cole appeared beside him with his rifle, gleaming brass rounds showering off its flank, his red Hawaiian shirt flapping as he fired. The tank commander collapsed, torn apart by a hail of bullets.

Upon Dyson's command, Zeus had released Kayne and raced back to Beetle and Sacha, who were covering Dyson and Cole.

Kayne rolled in the mud, blood oozing from the gashes in his neck. Satisfied that Zeus was out of the line of fire, Cole let it rip.

The heavy rounds struck Kayne from chin to groin, nearly cutting him in two.

Jimbo ran from the trench line down to the flaming turret opening and raised his carbine high. He fired a magazine down into the tank at full auto, taking out anyone else inside.

Beetle dragged Kayne's burning body into cover. As the flames died down, he ripped the dead soldier's shirt front open and pulled the tags off his neck. He thumbed the still-hot tags and called back to the others.

'Kayne Wilson.' He showed the tags to Cole.

'Cranbourne Boys just lost the boss,' said Cole.

Beetle cackled. He stripped Kayne's tomahawk and pistol from his belt and slipped them into his own waist belt.

Dyson walked down the line of the trench, carbine slung by his side. His claw grabbed Constance by the shoulder strap, and looked down at Jack.

'You were meant to keep *her* alive, Jack.'

Jack smiled. 'You know me. Is Harry alright?'

Dyson slapped his shoulder.

'He's good. Too good, actually.' He gave a wry smile. 'Let's go. More troops inbound.'

Dyson pulled Jack's arm over his shoulder and hauled him to his feet.

Jack looked down at his leg. One trouser leg had been blown to strips, exposing muscular calves that were streaked with tracks of blood.

Constance grabbed Jack from the other side and he swayed, faint. Blood oozed from one of his ears.

Dyson stood up at the trench edge with a long belt of ammunition hanging over his arm. He pointed back towards the Five Ways.

'Break contact!' He shouldered his weapon and loosed a full belt of rounds at the attacking force, flames reaching two feet from his barrel.

Constance staggered across the ridge, and the open bitumen junction of the Five Ways came into view. People stood up in the trenches all around the junction, waving her towards the command post. She had to get Jack there. Harry was there. The medical bay, too.

'Move,' she said as she helped him up the earth wall that lined the entrance to the bunker. He was leaning against the earthen bump, a grey pallor to his face. His eyes were sunken and dark and unfocused. His body conformed to the shape of the berm and he slid down like a sack as she dragged him in.

Constance looked over the parapet and saw the Four Horsemen, Dyson and another small-framed soldier bounding back through the fire tunnel towards the junction, returning fire as they went. Red tracers bounced off the trees, tumbling into the grey sky. Clumps of phosphorous were still burning.

Thirty metres short of the command post, Constance locked eyes on the small Resistance soldier firing off double taps at the enemy soldiers fleeing the ridgeline. The soldier sprinted back through the tunnel and hooked his arm through Jack's body armour strap. Constance grabbed the opposite strap and they turned and ran. She looked at the kid pumping his legs, hauling the man three times his weight.

It was Harry.

Harry, wide-eyed under a huge helmet, a shocked grin on his face, his carbine slung over his back.

Hauling his father.

Under fire.

Constance couldn't believe the bravery of this kid.

'What happened?' Harry said.

'He's okay,' Constance lied.

Jimbo and Beetle ran down the tunnel, Zeus bolting beside them.

Harry and Constance waved to them. They scooped Jack up and the four of them carried him to the medical bay.

Harry turned to Constance, his eyes earnest. 'Don't tell him. Please.'

63

THE FIELD DOCTOR WAS WASHING BLOOD OFF HIS APRON when they burst into the room and threw Jack on the stainless-steel gurney.

The room looked like it was half a medical bay and half an armoury. Littered between crates of medical supplies and rows of surgical equipment were weapons and ammo collected from fallen enemy soldiers on the battlefield, dumped here for Resistance runners to grab and take the gear to other areas of the front that needed a resupply. The prize of the loot sitting in the corner briefly caught Constance's eye – a mech exo-suit.

The doc and a medic stepped around on the muddy floor to get a closer look at the patient. He shifted the operating lights over Jack and then cut away what was left of his trousers and body armour. The medic rolled him onto his side as the doctor checked his back and chest for penetrating wounds.

The medic ran a hand scanner over the leg wound, and a 3D orange projection floated over Jack's body. His femoral artery was a hazy mess of red blood cells that tumbled down the artery as his heart pumped. A black tunnel penetrated his leg crossways.

A yellow annotation box popped up beside the wound and the doctor read it aloud.

'Triage: Femoral perforation. Subfascial hematoma. Priority one. Blood pressure 105/83. Pulse 100 BPM.' He ran his finger across the wound. 'One centimetre laceration of the anterior aspect of the femoral.'

'Is that bad?' Harry's voice was trembling.

The doctor pointed at the medic. 'Seal it up, then three units of O positive, please.'

Constance grabbed Harry's hand and put it on Jack's. He squeezed it while he watched the doctor work on his father.

The medic reached into a camping fridge and pulled out three bags of maroon blood, made an intravenous tap and hooked the line into Jack's wrist. Then he turned Jack on his side and splayed his thighs. He unfurled the packed, blood-soaked wound dressing, and from his kit he produced a device with a pistol grip and a metal nose cone, with an orange perspex shield attached. He keyed the trigger and shoved the nose cone into the leg wound. The device whined. A crackling noise came from the wound and a trail of smoke wisped out over Jack's leg. The stench of burning hair and flesh filled the tight quarters and the doctor screwed up his face as he focused.

The doctor produced a long syringe with a thick body, and took a long draw from a vial, then injected the wound site. He drew a second vial and injected that into the middle of Jack's thigh. The colour was coming back to his skin now, and his breathing was even.

Harry stood by the table holding his dad's hand, watching his hero come back from the dead. Constance put her hand over Harry's shoulder and as she did, he began shaking.

The doctor scanned his leg again, then turned to Constance.

'He's got adrenaline and antibiotics, and I've got a litre of O positive going into him now. He lost a lot of blood. The leg wound is cauterised. That leg will be out of action for a bit.'

'How long?' asked Constance.

'A normal person, a week. But knowing Jack . . . he'll be back on it as soon as he's upright.'

Jack grunted in approval.

The doctor smiled at her.

'The man survived a tactical bomb blast once. This is just a scratch.' The doctor reached over and grabbed Harry's shoulder. 'He's gonna live. Your dad's made from metal.'

The doctor eyed Constance as he pulled off his surgical gloves. 'There's gonna be more casualties. They've not even breached the trenches yet.'

Constance nodded. She had to get back on comms to see where the subs were at. The Resistance could fight, but there was more coming up that hill.

The radio on the signals desk came to life. 'Medic. Priority one, multiple gunshot wound, not breathing. South ridge trench. Send a litter.'

The medic grabbed his trauma bag and a collapsible stretcher and ran out the hessian door.

Constance sat in the tiny operating room. She held Jack's hand and put her arm around Harry. Tears ran down the boy's face.

'We're losing,' said Harry.

Jack thought about lying. He couldn't. 'Yes. Unless we get help.' He looked at Constance. Frowning, her lips moving, she was calculating something.

She pointed in the corner at an exosuit propped against the timber wall. It was in pieces, soot all over it and stained with blood. She eyed the armour spikes and hip actuators and the spinal column. The power pack was lit amber, at forty per cent.

When she looked back at Jack, he was propped up on his elbows, eyes shining, locked onto hers.

'You read my mind,' Jack said. 'Hook me up.'

64

CONSTANCE STRAPPED THE SUIT PARTS TO JACK'S LEGS. HIS face was losing its chalky pallor. He looked alive.

Heads ran through the hessian door, soaking, covered in mud. He held a waterproof satchel about the size of a notebook.

'Jack, I heard you were bad,' he said, looking puzzled.

Constance spoke up.

'We stopped at least a platoon, maybe two. The Horsemen killed Kayne. There will be at least another platoon coming. We don't know how many survived the tunnel fire.'

Heads nodded. 'Almost two-thirds of the force was destroyed in the tunnel. It was a bloodbath. The remainder of the main force diverted north around the Hill.'

'They'll lose time doing that,' said Constance.

'Agreed,' said Heads. 'We took a lot of pressure from four out of five sides on the Five Ways. Inverness Road was a close call.'

Heads held his hand up. 'Four minutes ago, we got a mobile intercept indicating that the Principal is leading a recon. That signal originated from the roundabout.'

'How about that,' said Jack. 'What approach did they not test?'

'The river,' Heads said.

Jack perked up. 'The river. From the roundabout, the most concealed approach is up the river to the Weeping Willow.'

Jack looked at Constance. 'Let's do it.'

Harry spoke up. 'That's where we washed Mum.'

Jack stood up. 'You'll be staying right here.'

Harry whined. 'Dad!'

'Stay here,' Jack told him firmly, 'or I'll take your weapon off you. You can walk around the position holding a stick.'

Harry humphed and frowned under his helmet.

Jack pointed at the ammo bundle. He opened his mouth to speak again when Jess Wilson stumbled into the med bay.

Jess collapsed onto an ammo trunk in the corner. There was a tourniquet on her arm, blood dripping from her gloves to the floor. Her black hair was plastered to her forehead and she was covered in leaves and muddy debris.

Heads spoke first. 'Quick trip. What happened?'

'My new ride. It's gone.'

Jack looked at Constance.

Is she a plant? Surely not, after the tunnel blast.

'What happened?' Jack repeated Heads' question.

'You could have warned me about the roundabout. My car got shot up. There were carriers and Chinese troops.' She pointed at her shoulder. 'I only just found my way up the river.'

'You're damn lucky,' said Heads.

She looked around the CP. 'You got a spare weapon?'

Jack looked at Constance. 'Come with us, I'll give you my M-79.'

He could see Jess weighing the situation up, before accepting her only option. To help.

'Sweet. Old timer's gun,' she said.

Jack frowned.

Jess went on. 'I'd wager you've got less than an hour until they come up the river.'

Jack eyed her, thinking. *If she's a plant, she's a bloody convincing one.*

Jack stood up off the bench and pulled the suit actuators up his body. The metal struts on his arms and the metal alloy shoring his spine up made him look even more solid.

'What if we can't hold them? Do you have another rally point?' asked Constance.

'There's nowhere else,' said Jack. 'We stay.'

'What about him?' She gestured to Harry.

Jack looked at Harry for moment. 'If we don't fight here, I guarantee we'll be dealing with an even bigger unit tomorrow. This buys us time.'

He locked his shoulders back and faced Constance.

'Tell them the main body is still transiting around the Hill.'

She stopped strapping him in and stared. 'The B-21s. They're missing.'

Jack stopped, stunned. He shook his head and rested his hand on her arm. 'I'm so sorry.'

She was caught out by his response. She'd expected fury. Instead, he showed concern.

'Well, looks like the *McRaven* it is,' he said.

Constance swallowed.

'I can't raise them. I'm still trying.'

Jack fitted the arm actuators on his body. The room fell silent. Just the clicking of the metal as Jack ratcheted the last parts of his suit to his limbs. A titanium pike slid into its retracted position along the suit's right arm. He slapped the actuators on his elbows and turned to Constance, locking his eyes on her.

'Huh. I risked my son and my ass to recover you, and all we've got in return is shit weather.' He gave her a wry smile. 'I want free beers for the rest of my life.'

Constance inclined her head. 'We need to plan on not getting the fires from them,' she said.

'I wouldn't worry.' Jack pursed his lips. 'We won't have any affairs to tidy up if that happens. We'll all be dead or on a train headed to the Yard.'

Constance hung her head and clamped her eyes shut. Failure was not in her vocabulary.

Jack turned to Heads. 'Can you watch Harry? Keep him with you.' Heads nodded, and Jack gestured to Jess. 'Grab a wheelbarrow. We're gonna need ammo.'

He picked up Harry and pulled his son into his chest. Harry wrapped his arms around him and hugged him tight. Heads, Jess and Constance cleared out of the room without making a sound.

Still holding Harry, Jack unclipped his son's helmet and put his hand on the back of his head.

'I love you. Forever and ever.'

'I love you.' He pulled away and looked his dad in the eyes. 'You have to come back.'

Jack nodded. 'Promise.'

I will.

Jack, Jess and Constance strode out of the CP and into the dawn light and the rain. Hail was coming down hard, piles of ice building up across the dirt like snow. Rivers of mud wove through the position and they sloshed through them, towards the Weeping Willow.

As they walked off the ridgeline and through the ferns into the river gully, Constance keyed her covert comms system. The cursor turned green when it made a secure link.

She said a prayer to herself as she pushed her earpiece in and set the device to transmit.

Something. Anything. Please.

'Dictate message: ground operations centre,' the AI recorded for her.

'Leopard Regiment is transiting from the Mullum Mullum Tunnel, northside of Mount Dandenong to alternate form-up point. Reserve forces are penetrating Hill defences. Request danger close strike on all assets.'

Anything.

65

THE RADIO MESSAGE FROM CONSTANCE BOOMED THROUGH the Trinity Airborne Relay Plane, through CIA headquarters at Langley, Virginia, and back to the Ted Sheean VC, Naval Communication Station in Fremantle. The ultra-low frequency station punched the message out with a single megawatt, 300 metres deep into the cold, black ocean off the coast of Tasmania, to the USS *Admiral McRaven*.

182 miles west of Tasmania

Captain Buck Jessup, commander of the Virginia class USS *Admiral McRaven*, read the urgent flash message on his terminal. He picked up the phone.

'Battle stations, battle stations.'

He read on.

'Strike package, Victoria: green light,' he said to himself, then turned to his weapons officer. 'Alter depth to launch depth, fifty metres. Prepare firing solutions for TLAM package.'

The WEPS triple-checked the firing solution while Jessup

stood behind him. They had both completed five tours on the same boat, but he still verified the solutions.

Luckily, these missiles had quantum guidance navigation. They worked independent of satellite and GPS. They were beautiful weapons, and the WEPS handled them with skill. The Block V submarine was an underwater missile boat.

The WEPS called, 'Firing solutions complete. Standing by.'

'Altering depth to firing depth, fifty metres,' said the dive officer.

The vessel climbed from the depths until its keel was fifty metres under the surface of the thrashing Indian Ocean. Cracks of sheet lightning bathed the shallows in a dull glow, but the massive submarine lurked beneath, in the pitch darkness of the ocean.

The three-inch-thick convex circular hatches opened whisper quiet on the missile carrier module. A UGM-109E Tomahawk Land Attack Missile in each module had the target coordinates and targeting options locked, their grey snub noses still protected from the water. Each was primed to be launched from the 140-metre submarine, track low over the ocean and then travel directly to the enemy off the flanks of the Hill.

The captain paused. 'Volley one: fire.'

'Aye, aye. Volley one: fire,' said the weapons officer. He flicked the cover off the weapons release button and pushed the button.

The submarine released each missile pair in five-second intervals. The missiles rose to the surface inside a perfectly formed air bubble, cleared the water, and engaged their missile boosters. A retrograde motor tipped the missile six metres on its belly, then once it hit 300 knots it deployed its fins, engaged the jet engine, and roared off towards the Hill.

The missiles shifted into a long diagonal trail as they crossed the limestone bays of Phillip Island, then dropped into the low valleys in a single chain, mapping the contours with terrain-mapping radar and whipping towards the raging battle on the Hill.

66

'MESSAGE SENT – LET'S JUST HOPE THEY RECEIVE IT,' SAID Constance. 'If we can hold them at the river, that might buy enough time to get rounds onto them.'

'Good. We'll need it. They get up here, and that's it.'

They descended the lip of the Five Ways and started down the gully to the river's edge. As they descended, the Weeping Willow came into view.

Jess trailed Constance and Jack, who led, pushing a wheel-barrow of rocket launchers, grenades and link ammunition. They stopped at the river's edge. It was running fast and thrashing away under the hail storm.

Jack picked up a Maximi machine gun and draped a belt of 200 rounds across his shoulder. He pulled a satchel of grenades over his other shoulder and then waded into the river. The cool water soothed his leg wound.

Constance and Jess pulled their weapons to their shoulders and started across. Jack reached the far bank and stayed behind the chest-high wall the river had carved into the mud and stone. He had walked the footpad along this river for years. He could see thirty metres to the closest bend in the track. It wasn't great, but it was a safe spot to fire from.

Jack turned back to Constance and Jess, who were halfway across the river, Constance holding her SCAR 150 over her head with both arms. The water was running around her neck.

Jack held his hand up, signalling for them to hurry. As he raised his hand, he heard a series of low thunks. He paused. There was a whipping over his head, then a series of concussions in the water around Jess and Constance. Geysers of water erupted around them, the white columns of superheated water reaching as high as the trees.

'Down!' Jack called. But it was too late; they had disappeared under the foaming water. The shock of the blast would have crushed their lungs. Someone had the drop on them.

Jack gasped. 'No. No. No.'

Adrenaline flooded his legs.

He hauled his Maximi up on the earth wall, opened the bipod legs and paused, finger hovering over the trigger. He didn't shoot.

He shouldered the weapon, then slid back into the river and walked along the river bank towards the enemy, weapon up.

He dared not look back for Constance or Jess.

'I got two!' screamed the VMF soldier from behind his six-barrelled grenade launcher. He clicked open the breech of the launcher and reloaded the weapon.

'Push up.' The Principal pointed at the river's edge. 'Look for the forward line. Once we spot them, you call in the fires.'

The VMF soldier nodded.

The Principal had closed the distance from the roundabout to the river's edge at a near sprint. He knew he would catch them reorganising after the failed armoured thrust up Inverness Road. His most aggressive moves were his best defence, and by closing the distance at speed, with only one other soldier, he had denied them the chance to reorganise.

The thermal splinter shield on his mech suit struggled in the intense downpour, and showed no heat signatures.

The Principal pointed across the river at a giant willow tree. Then he pointed to the VMF soldier. 'With me,' he said.

The VMF commander looked over the river, his long mullet of hair plastered to his neck.

'Righto,' he said, then stopped at the river's edge. 'I can't swim.'

The Principal hissed, 'Get in front. Go.' They slid down the reeds of the low river bank and into the fast running water, the VMF lackey patrolling ahead.

A half-submerged ironbark tree sat across the bank of the river, the current swirling past it, through the straining branches.

The Principal pointed at the tree and signalled across the river to the Weeping Willow.

They headed for the ironbark tree in the chest-deep water, then looked for the cross point over to the willow.

67

Jack stalked around the side of the river bank where the shooting had come from. A submerged ironbark came into view. He kept his Maximi up with one arm as he approached the tree, heading upstream. It was cover, but there was always the chance of a bigger raiding party further up the river line.

Jack whipped the hundred-round belt up with his left arm. He was five metres from the tree flank, in waist-deep water. He hit the safety with his thumb. As he closed to the stump, he pulled the weapon into his shoulder and stood from his crouch.

As he stood, the shocked face of a VMF soldier appeared a metre from the end of his barrel. He held a revolving grenade launcher that he was swinging towards Jack.

Jack pulled the trigger.

The man disappeared in the saw burst of the weapon. As he fell, the man's grenade launcher fired once, the huge round hitting Jack in his bicep. A bolt of white-hot pain shot up his arm, and his weapon dropped into the water.

The Principal was already submerged, cornering the tree to outflank him. Jack spotted him. The Principal levelled his rifle but Jack already had a hold of it. He caught the Principal's eye as they wrestled for the weapon. The Principal fired a long

336

burst from the AK-47, the flash and heat of the barrel shocking Jack as he wrenched it to the sky. He yanked on the weapon hard, hand on the foresight of the barrel, both their mech suits groaning from the force.

'C'mon!' Jack roared.

The AK-47 splintered in half, the barrel still in Jack's hand.

A titanium pike extended from the Principal's suit arm, and he swung it for Jack's head. Jack ducked and the pike missed his head by an inch.

He leapt backwards. He reached for his pistol, but it was gone. All he had was his tomahawk still on his waist, and his own pike on his suit arm. He dove into the water, submerged, and clawed his way towards the Weeping Willow.

He kicked and pushed his way through the dark water, the sound of clacking river rocks echoing in his ear. He heard the thumps of the Principal's mech suit behind him, chasing.

His lungs burned and his hands tingled as he clawed along the bottom of the river.

Gemma, help.

He planted his feet, turned back towards the Principal, and rose from the thrashing water. The river was a mess of hail strike and rain. The cold was gone from his limbs. He could not see the Principal, but he felt his presence.

Jack made his final choice.

Here, Gemma. This is where it ends.

Waist-deep in the river, he would use the rest of his life to protect his son, and avenge his wife's death.

68

THE PRINCIPAL ROSE FROM THE DEEPEST SECTION OF THE river, a dozen metres from Jack. The tall, strong man stepped and pushed into the current as he walked. He was heading to the river bank, taking long strides as he climbed the underwater gradient up to the shallows.

The Principal, risen from the depths.

The river water parted around his legs as he carved through it, scanning both banks, like a grizzly looking for salmon.

Jack stopped dead and watched him.

The Principal's titanium pike was extended, and as he walked, he reached to his belt sheath and drew a tomahawk, holding it by the neck of the blade.

The water thrashed around his feet and he stopped and held Jack's stare a moment, his dead eye like a fish belly in the dawn light.

'Mr Dunne.' He acknowledged his nemesis.

Jack said nothing, listening to the sounds that surrounded them. The hail smashing into the river. The gunfire rattling on the far banks. The willow swaying in the breeze. The rushing water.

The Principal levelled his titanium pike at Jack and slipped the tomahawk down in his hand so he gripped the handle.

Jack kept his eyes on the Principal.

The Principal circled around. Jack had only his own pike extended, the two-foot length of it. He found the knee-deep water and circled him in the opposite direction, closing the gap to striking distance.

The Principal thrust at him. He swept his pike at Jack's waist then slung the tomahawk in the other direction, scissoring the air to his front. Jack watched the arc of the pike returning for him as the Principal lunged again. Jack slipped the thrust, but it smashed into his shoulder strut.

The blow twanged off the metal like a cannonball.

Jack stumbled in the rocks, his hands going to ground. The Principal swept the tomahawk high and then chopped at Jack's foot. He yanked it out of the way as the blade crashed into the rocks. The Principal stood, a wry smile crossing his face.

He was playing for a wound.

There was method to his approach.

Every action was part of his design. The master sat at the chess board, moving parts of his life, the narrowing of all possible outcomes in his favour.

The Principal leapt forward again, thrusting his pike at Jack's sternum. Jack parried with his left forearm. He swung his own pike down as the Principal countered with his. The pikes collided at their midpoint, and the Principal's bent in the centre. He held up the bent titanium alloy and sneered, then bashed a button at his metal hip actuator. The pike fell away from his forearm and clattered into the shallows.

Jack dared not look away. He was afraid. His opponent was faster, stronger. Better drilled.

The Principal was in full control of his faculties, but Jack was beginning to shake from the cold and the adrenaline wearing off. His shoulder and his thigh ached. The dawn had turned a stunning orange and pink under the belting rain. He looked to the opposite bank. He just wanted to see Harry once more.

Spurred on by that thought, Jack sucked in a breath and moved into the waist-deep water. They stood ten metres apart in the hail, the river churning around their suits. The Principal watched Jack's movements, then stepped towards him, into the deeper water. His tomahawk blade glinted in the early dawn.

'Your family does not have a good track record against me.' He twirled his tomahawk, biding his time. 'Your wife got what she asked for. They came for me, so I killed her in self-defence.'

Jack's fear had evaporated.

He felt a vibration in the power bar on his forearm.

Zero per cent. Flashing red.

'I will wipe your bloodline clean,' the Principal said. 'I respect you, but I don't take chances.' The Principal swung his axe over in his hand.

'Your son. He won't suffer. I'll see to it myself.'

Jack looked back at the Weeping Willow. A woman in a white robe stood beneath it, her hair wet, her robe stuck to her body. She stood in the mud, palms held open, eyes locked onto Jack's.

Gemma.

Jack's suit beeped three times.

He hit the quick-release button and the suit slithered away from his body. He shrugged the struts off his arms, then stepped out of his armour and moved towards the Principal. Jack drew his tomahawk from his belt, and held it level with the water. Without the suit to support his weight, his thigh stabbed in agony, and his shoulder was covered in blood.

His lips moved in silent prayer for his wife.

See you soon.

He walked towards the Principal, axe in his hand. The Principal dropped into a crouch, his suit whirring as he stepped across the rocks. Jack could see the satisfaction writ on his face. Jack circled in the same direction as the Principal, meeting him at the shallow bank, like a boxer controlling the corners.

340

As Jack stepped onto the bank, he whipped his tomahawk around to gauge its reach. He wasn't cold anymore.

He took running steps towards the Principal and hissed as he swung high at his neck and then spun away. The Principal parried once and the metal on metal sparked and screeched in the hail. The Principal stepped forward and feinted with his spare arm. Anticipating the move, Jack swung his arm, back-handed, for a second strike at the man's hip.

The tip of Jack's axe connected with the Principal's hip bone. He gasped, and bared his teeth at the pain, but he did not take his eyes off Jack as he stepped inside his range and punched again, low into Jack's midsection. The blow connected with Jack's chest armour, knocking his breath from him. The same arm somehow struck him hard across the temple and a burst of white stars filled his vision. Jack tottered and stumbled into the river, both hands in the water. His tomahawk was gone.

From his rear, he thought he heard Constance. Maybe it was Gemma.

His head was swimming.

This must be it.

Jack went to stand but stumbled into the water. He looked up at the Principal. He was caught.

The Principal stepped forward, clocking the fear in Jack's eyes. He took the final few steps and hauled Jack up by the shoulder strap, raising him clear of the water. The straps of his body armour bit into his underarms. Jack scrambled at the Principal, trying to clinch his face, his neck. He missed. He clawed at the side buckle of his armour in an attempt to release the straps he dangled from, but his broken finger, a souvenir from the encounter at the roundabout all those days ago, could not force the latch open.

Only his feet were in the water.

Constance, again, behind him, screaming.

She's alive.

Jack held his hands up in a futile attempt to shield himself, expecting the tomahawk blow, but the Principal slammed him back down into the river, the blow knocking the air from his lungs.

There was the sound of muffled water running.

He felt the sharp bed of rocks at his back and the fists pinning him down. Jack reached for his belt.

The grenades.

But his belt was gone.

His lungs convulsed, and he pursed his lips. He gagged once, his diaphragm contracting.

The Principal yanked him clear of the water with a force that snapped his head backwards.

He slammed his fist into Jack's face and Jack heard the wishbone snap of his nose. Jack gurgled in pain.

The Principal pulled his face in close to his. He raised his tomahawk blade to Jack's strained neck.

The man's dead eye looked into his.

'The only reason you're breathing, is because I sent boys to do a man's job.' He studied Jack's face.

Jack felt a wooden handle thrust into his right hand, felt the wet leather of the grip, felt the familiar hand that passed the weapon to him through the rushing water. He locked his hand around it and summoned his last effort.

'Look at me,' the Principal said. He tapped Jack's neck once with the blade, testing his mark.

Jack kept his eyes on the Principal as he swung his axe at the Principal's thigh. There was a loud thwack of metal shearing through fascia and muscle down to the femur.

The Principal's eyes widened in shock. He let go of Jack's armour and reached for his leg.

The Principal turned to wade deeper into the river, but Jack pounced. He swung his tomahawk high in an arc at the Principal's head. The tomahawk sheared through the spinal brace of the suit and buried itself crossways in the Principal's neck. Jack's tomahawk severed his spine. The auto-balance mechanism in the suit kept him upright. He wobbled towards the river bank, gasping, his right arm swatting for the handle of the tomahawk.

He pivoted towards them, his eyes wide; they shone in wonder.

Jack launched at the Principal like a front rower, connected with his chest, and slammed him into the water. As they sank, Jack wove his arms through the struts and shields of the suit, searching for the man's neck. He gripped the chest power mount, found his feet and stood himself upright, then he shoved his fist into the suit lattice and latched onto the man's throat. He stood over the man, compressing his neck with all the force he could muster.

The Principal's arms flapped above his head, his eyes wide under the water. His arm swatted Jack's face and Jack howled with all the anger a father could muster. Smoke was now bubbling from the water, leaking from the exosuit. His hand reached for Jack's neck, the suit automation guiding the Principal's dead hand across his face. Gemma flashed through his mind, her broad smile. He screamed, cracking the cartilage of the Principal's throat. The suit thrashed and kicked, but it could not right his limp body.

Finally, it stopped dead. Jack held the Principal under, while he regained his breath.

He turned and yelled for Constance.

There was no answer.

Jack released his grip on the Principal, and the body rolled and tumbled along under the surface of the water.

Jack turned for the shore, but he couldn't walk. He couldn't see Constance anywhere. A shorter woman was running through the river water from the rebel side. Too short for Constance. She had a tourniquet on one arm, a broad gash across her bicep. Bloody rags of her shirt hanging from it. It was Jess.

'Gotcha,' Jess said to him. She slung his arm over her neck and wrapped her good arm around his waist.

'Constance?' he said.

Jess shook her head, her eyes stricken.

Jack surveyed the rough, sloshing water, desperately searching for Constance.

A sudden howling overhead and a shriek of missiles broke his focus. Jack saw the slow-moving missiles pass over them in packs of four, lit up by the morning sun, the bay doors at the waist of the missile opening and releasing their first payload.

Small tumbling canisters dropped across the countryside. The low rumble of cluster bombs built to a crescendo and lasted for a full minute. The missiles circled overhead, searching for targets. One by one, they started their descent into the main body of the enemy and the final reports crumped across the hills. Any enemy survivors would turn and run; the bombardment was devastating.

The *McRaven* had delivered. Constance had delivered.

'Constance,' Jack whispered.

He wanted to tell her he was proud. He scanned the river bank. Gemma was gone.

The rain stopped.

Jack limped across the river, leaning on Jess. He was bawling. He called out for his son.

The river had taken so much from him.

PART FIVE

THE BEGINNING

69

One day later

JACK STOOD AT THE RIVER'S EDGE AND WATCHED THE BURIAL team sing and hum as they washed the ankles of the body. Tears streamed down his face and he made no attempt to hide them. The sun was warm on his face. Streams of smoke still ascended off the Five Ways, the armoured hulks still burning. Three dozen fighting men, many on crutches, lined the path from the river up to the lookout.

Heads, Cole, Beetle and Jimbo hoisted the body to their shoulders and crossed the river rocks. Zeus walked beside them, whimpering and sniffing at the fallen fighter. Jimbo held his spare hand on his precious, shouldered cargo. Each one of the warriors cried openly.

The stretcher party crossed the Five Ways, towards the wooden pyre.

Jack limped, alone, at the rear of the burial party. His nose swollen and both eyes blackened.

They had presided over the first defeat of Chinese Forces in World War Three. A resurgent US had tasted victory. The Resistance, the entire country, the whole world was hearing about the Battle of Five Ways. A Chinese Regiment decimated, the Cranbourne Boys shattered, and enough armour to fill the MCG destroyed. It had bought them a victory, but more than that, it had bought them hope. For the first time in five years, the prospect of freedom filled their hearts. But the cost for Jack was high.

He stood at the Five Ways, with his arms folded.

The warriors stood in their tunnel, saluting with their weapons still slung. A thousand more people in the sun. The Four Horsemen placed the body on the pyre then stepped back and saluted. They turned and each one embraced Jack, who stood at the edge, expressionless.

Jack limped to the pyre, held his hand up and placed it on the body. He closed his eyes and prayed, then stepped back, opened his eyes and stared at the warrior he both knew and loved.

Dyson lay atop, dressed in his combat uniform.

His jaw sat strong and bold, even in death.

Sacha passed the burning sticks to Jack and motioned for Harry to join them. The bagpipes started their low hum and wailed into the morning air. A group of kids stood atop a smoking T-90, watching the cremation. The crowd, filthy, still in battle order, removed helmets and hats and bowed their heads.

Sacha sang as they leaned forward and touched the sticks to the pyre. It whumped into flames, the fire creeping up and spilling over Dyson's body.

They watched him burn.

A wedge-tailed eagle glided overhead and watched the fire, circling the Five Ways.

Jessica wasn't in the crowd. She was long gone. Headed west to free Australia.

Heads walked to Jack, shook his hand, and tried to pass him a small, thin box, but Jack waved him off. Heads gestured to the car waiting at the flank. It was a shining black HiLux, a twin to the one Jack had left behind at the border crossing checkpoint what felt like a lifetime ago. There was a fuel barrel tied down in the rear tray. Armoury pallet. Spare tyres. A toolbox full of gold and an esky full of moonshine, coffee and jerky.

Jack shook hands again with Heads, limped to the driver's side and climbed in. He inhaled the vinyl of the car and ran his hands over the leather-clad steering wheel. Harry climbed in next to him, and Heads passed him the box. The boy took it and opened it up. Inside was a gleaming, patterned silver medal. He smiled, then stared wide-eyed and in awe of his dad.

Jack pushed the electric start and the turbo diesel roared to life. The motor purred and rocked in its housing. He adjusted the rear-view mirror and caught Constance looking at him.

Images came to him from last night's battle.

Constance crawling out of the river on the shoreline, coughing and spluttering, followed by a desperate embrace from Jack – *I thought you were dead.*

Constance, puking over a board in the surf.

Staring down the scope of a heavy rifle, firing on an enemy checkpoint.

Hugging his son on the deck of a Blackhawk as it hurtled through the treetops.

Smiling at him, sharing a jar of moonshine on the road.

A lifetime of bonding, forged in just a few days.

Jack grinned at her reflection in the rear-view mirror.

'Let's go, soldier. You'll be late to work,' she said from the back seat.

Jack gave a weary smile. 'I'm retired.'

'About that,' Constance said.

'No. I'm headed to the beach.'

'Remember the B-21s that went missing?'

'No.'

'Yes, you do. We need to get a pilot . . .'

Jack put both hands against his ears.

'Just, no. Not until I've had a beer.'

'Okay. I think you've earned that.' Constance smiled.

He put the HiLux in gear and rolled off, windows down. He saluted the smoking pyre as they went.

The crowd parted along the tourist road and the car idled through them, crunching over the gravel. They stuck their arms out the windows and every person on the Hill ran forward to grab their hands as they passed. The barman thrust a bottle of whiskey – Macallan's '64 – through the window.

Constance took it, pulled the cork, and took a long pull.

'Love you all,' Jack told the crowd, hands slapping against the Hillsfolk. 'We'll be back.'

'You better be.' Jimbo slammed his fist on the bonnet and smiled at him.

Jack rolled the car off the Hill, picked up speed, and drove forward, into their future. Harry lifted the medal from the box. Its light whipped around the cab, clean and bright. Smelted silver from the Perth Mint, a surfboard embossed on the front, with a single word:

Outrider.

ACKNOWLEDGEMENTS

DEAR HARRY, I WROTE THIS STORY FOR YOU. IT'S A LOVE STORY about fathers and sons. It's also a warning. I have seen both versions of society – order and anarchy – and I know which one I prefer. I'll let you decide which one is worth fighting for. My father let me choose, and I always loved him for it. Read this back to me one day when I'm half-deaf and infirm. I love you with all my heart.

To my wife, Sam. For the second time, you watched me wrestle with a beast and encouraged me the whole way. This story is about our life in the Hills: the joys, the hardships and the community we love. Without your love, support and acceptance, this would never have come to life. I love you so much.

To the veterans that helped me write this, your insights I included are all hard-won through combat. Thanks for sharing them. Here are some of the contributsors to the book:

Sean 'Tiedown' Danowski, I'm sure people will be shocked to know you are a real pilot who instructed at Top Gun, flew F-16s in Afghanistan overhead when I was on the ground, slogging it out. You deserve your own character and I hope you like him.

James Kelly, as the only Submarine Engineer from the Royal Australian Navy to serve in the SAS, you should be proud and thanks for bringing the undersea world to life.

Miguel Gastellum, I needed a Nightstalker to show me the path on helicopter operations, I owe you a beer.

Josh Millgate, we came up with a Cessna AC-130 Gunship during the battles we fought on *Australian Survivor*. I kind of hope I see it for real one day.

Kayne Float, I told you I would turn you into a villain. Everyone knows you Cranbourne Boys are a bunch of pricks.

Doctor George Miller, Director of the Mad Max saga, I have stood in your Wasteland and I enjoyed it far more than I feared. Thanks for the inspiration. Fire, blood and guzzoline.

My publisher, Alex Lloyd, you have long suffered in the artistic torment of authors and you handle it with grace and good humour. I thank you for the hours of guidance and counselling. You took a bet on this one, and I hope Victoria in 2034 is the hellscape you wished for.

Thanks to the rest of the Pan Macmillan Australia team, including Rebecca Lay, Vanessa Lanaway, Candice Wyman and Tom Evans – a book always takes a team, and I had a damn good one.

Special shout-out to my agent Kylie Green, and Lisa Ryan for keeping me in line.

And give Louisa Maggio a medal for that cover.

Buzz, Robbo, Pete, Jazzy, Vando, Stano, Hastie, Beetle, Damage, Horse, Average Donno, VC Donno, Shep, Elvis and the rest of the Outriders: Who Dares Wins.

The Hill is a real place. You can find it on the eastern outskirts of Melbourne. If you go take a look, you'll find the Five Ways intersection, the roundabout and the Pig & Whistle. The Pig & Whistle is a family run pub, and Tim Roostan is the father, and the inspiration for the barman.

I'll see you there for a beer.

The Hill